MW00674494

AMIAYA ENTERTAINMENT LLC

Presents

THAT GANGSTA SH!T!
The Anthology

Featuring

Antoine "Inch" Thomas

Written by Antoine Thomas
Travis Stevens
Ralph Taylor
Vincent Warren
T.Benson Glover for Amiaya Entertainment LLC.

Published by Amiaya Entertainment LLC.
Cover Design by www.Apollopixel.com & Marion Designs
Cover Design by Antoine Thomas for Amiaya Entertainment LLC.

Printed in The United States of America

Edited by Antoine "Inch" Thomas

ISBN:0-9745075-3-9

[1. Urban-Fiction. 2. Drama-Fiction. 3. Bronx-Fiction]

Dedication

This book is dedicated to everyone who has
Kept it gangsta, one way or the other

Table Of Contents

Code of the Streets

Antoine "Inch" Thomas

CHAPTER ONE

E very summer for the past four years, former drug dealer turned community activity planner, Anthony Wheeler, also known as Tone, along with his partner Slick, put together a few events for the urban youth of New York City during Harlem Week. People from all over the place come together and hang out at one designated location. Today the event focused on Renown Charity Organizer, A.I.D.S. Awareness Fundraiser and Community Spokesperson, Flower Moore. Flower was a one-time resident of the Bronx who overcame her own adversities by forming social groups in her current hometown of Reading, Pennsylvania. Flower's priorities focused on domestic issues that were ongoing problems in society. The meetings became such an accomplishment for the twenty-two-year old, she was eventually nominated for two NAACP Awards for Outstanding Achievements of Black Culture two years in a row and was also recognized by Blackpeople Entertainment, Inc. as one of the most prominent figures in urban America. Because of her success, the government, with Flower's permission, adopted her format, created their own program based on her strategies and hired her as president of the organization, providing her with a six-figure salary. In Harlem, specifically 8th Avenue, stretching from 150th to 152nd streets with the blocks cornered off by police barricades, the neighborhood was experiencing an overwhelming sense of well being.

Street vendors were out with their fold out tables blanketed with bootleg merchandise to be sold at a fraction of a price, groups gathered to discuss business and everybody else mingled to their liking.

Tone and Slick had set up the "Flower Moore Rap Off," an event consisting of neighborhood rappers battling one another on a makeshift stage with a cash and prize give-a-way.

Third place winner was to receive $500 cash. Runner up would be taking home $1,000 cash, and the grand prize winner would be given free studio time in Tone's "T&T Entertainment" studio to put together a professional demo tape. Flower, accompanied by her husband Shawn, were among a group of community leaders discussing plans of support groups citywide that concentrated and focused on rape victims and victims of spousal abuse.

A crowd had formed around the stage where some aspiring rappers were about to give their best performances. Standing with his hands clasped behind his back anxiously scanning the rowdy crowd of spectators was *Nappy Black*, a local street rapper who hailed from 140th Street and Lenox Avenue in Harlem. The 5'7", 140 pound, dark complexioned kid dressed in a T-shirt and jeans with short nappy hair had a name that was self-explanatory.

His opponent, a 5'2", 125 pound, fifteen-year-old Puerto Rican kid dressed in oversized navy colored sweatpants, a dingy white T-shirt and a black Doo-Rag wave cap covering his one-week-old corn-rolled braids, called himself *G-Gotti*. G-Gotti's obsession with the late great mob boss, *John Gotti*, was what motivated him to adopt the name. He and Nappy Black went at it as the first two contestants of the Rap Off.

Black grabbed the microphone and confidently began rhyming over an instrumental of a current hip-hop song.

The enthusiastic crowd responded by clapping along with the music as the first of the two performers rapped while coasting up and down the stage like he owned it. *"Ayo_you claim you G-Gotti/a name that consists of cheese and_Fed time and mad dead bodies...You never owned a heater/you_never had whips, a crib, a bad bitch, a phone or a_beeper..."* The overzealous crowd chanted "oooh's" and "aaah's" as Nappy Black ripped into his opponent lyrically with line after line of disregard and lack of respect for his challenger. *"So how they gon fear it/when San Juan is_filled with thugs and big gunz, and you ain't even near_it...How you gon prove it/how you gon rep a block with no drugs, and how you gon move it..."* The crowd roared. A friend of Nappy Black climbed on stage almost falling to support his buddy by screaming and shouting how good a performer his friend was and how his adversary, G-Gotti, didn't have a chance.

The beat was reset to its beginning as G-Gotti nervously scanned the crowd and made his way to center stage. Without being given the cue, G-Gotti grabbed the microphone and started his rhyme. *"You claiming you a_gangsta, always caught with a chick/and you always making a_scene, that's cause you a snitch..."* G-Gotti's first couple of lines sent mixed signals to the crowd. His words were sharp and witty but his delivery wasn't articulate, and realizing his mistake, he became agitated but continued anyway. *"Bitch, you always talking 'bout taking it far/you_fake as the hood Jake and you stay getting robbed..."*

With the uneasiness filling the air, G-Gotti lost his self-esteem and ran off the stage.

"Ayo, you heard that bullshit son just kicked?" yelled one male onlooker.

"Word, son was some shit," screamed another youth who was dressed in jeans and a matching denim vest.

"I kind of liked him," I said with my 6'6", 200 pound, tan complexioned self. "I just think he got scared," I continued.

"Yeah, *whatever*. I still think homeboy was wack," said the one spectator who previously stated that the latter of the two performers didn't hold up well.

"Who's up next?" shouted Tone through a bullhorn. "I need my next two challengers up here *now*! We're ready to see somebody else get embarrassed up here on this stage." He continued causing laughter to explode from the exuberant crowd. "Okay, okay! Here we go!" shouted Tone, waving on the next two opponents who just climbed the stage.

Turning to my girlfriend I asked, "Who do you think is going to win this one, Charlene?"

"I'm going for the tall one, Larry," she responded, shortening my name because she said *Lawrence* sounded like a name that belonged to somebody's uncle.

"You're just saying that because you don't like short niggas," I continued.

"Whoever said I didn't like short guys?" Charlene asked, standing in her double-jointed, bowlegged stance, which is what attracted me to the 5'5", 125 pound chocolate beauty contestant in the first place.

"'Cause, I ain't never seen you around any short dudes," I uttered.

"That's because I'm always around *you*, sexy Larry. And you know I love me some Larry. Larry Luuv!" she shouted, screaming and old rap song from the 80s to compliment my name. "La La La, La La La, La La La La, Laarry Luv!"

"It's all good. I'm happy. And as soon as I make it to the pro's, everyone else will love me too," I said smiling.

Charlene and I had been dating for the past two years. We loved to hang out, so today we chose to focus our attention on the rappers that had been chosen to rhyme up on the stage.

Up next was an aspiring local rapper who called himself *"The Grim Reaper."* The short, heavyset teenager earned his name by lyrically killing all of the opponents he'd rapped against during his lunch periods at school. He, too, began rhyming over a hip hop instrumental.

"Ayo niggas wanna see if I'm right/that's why they ask they lil mans to come hear me, and see if I'm tight...In a minute I'm a be in the sight/of big Benzes and A&R's paying me a fee when I write...So if you niggaz think you real like me/let's go 16 for 16 and see if you appeal like me...if '98 was your meal like me/if you could zone out for Tone, and end up with a deal like me..." The Grim Reaper sang with a confidence level so high that it bordered arrogance. "Yeah, nigga!...What!" he shouted as he jogged around the stage.

"Hold up, hold up!" shouted Tone through his bullhorn. "Aye," he continued. "I like how you slid my name up in your rhyme during your last couple of bars. That was slick, but being *slick* ain't gonna get you anywhere. No pun intended," said Tone looking over at his friend Slick and laughing. "Shorty," shouted Tone looking at the next rapper up for battle, "you gon have to come better than your man right here," said Tone passing *"All*

That" the microphone and signaling to the DJ to start the music.

"All That," an average heighted teen with a muscular physique and a tattoo on both of his biceps, walked toward the front of the stage then circled back in his brand new white cotton tank top T-shirt, black jeans and white Air Force One sneakers. "All That" gripped the microphone with the smoothness of a winner.

After Rayshawn's mother purchased him a quarter carat diamond stud earring, he told everyone to call him "All That" because he said Rayshawn wasn't a rap name. Also, all the young ladies that he'd recently been courting due to his newly acquired jewelry, led him to believe that the name suited his personality perfectly. The kids in his neighborhood, on the other hand, respected his moniker because his rap style appeared to be more advanced and unique than the other young street rappers in his neighborhood.

As "All That" took to the stage, his eyes told the crowd that he commanded his position, and the words that came out of his mouth confirmed this truth.

"Ayo check how I'm strong on the bricks, dog of the click/my second win and never got along with a snitch...I'm often the kid, in the cut chump, offing that clip/take it to your wake and toss it in that coffin you in...You assed out like a thong on a chick, mourn if you would/it's bodies in the Jects like a morgue in the hood...Boss of the streets, kid wit my name in the biz/my neck so cold, I gotta keep my chain in the fridge...Flop never, a Champion, I stay wit a gig/And Rock Fellas like I'm Jay-Z or Damon and Biggs, Holla..."

The crowd went into a frenzy as *"All That"* gave the spectators punch line after punch line of true raw talent.

"Fifty! That's the next fucking 50 Cent!" screamed Tone as he made his way from the side of the stage back to where the microphone stand was set up. "Holla at me son! Word up. Holla at me, you heard!" continued Tone as everyone dispersed into their own private little groups commenting on the talented young aspiring rap artists.

"Charlene, walk me to the Chinese restaurant. I'm fiending for some Chicken and Broccoli," I said, walking toward 153rd Street and 8th Avenue where a nearby Asian restaurant had a section of it carved out for customers who like to sit down and eat.

Charlene twisted up her lip and gave me a stink look to indicate that she noticed how self-assured I was about myself. She fixed her face and asked me to slow down as she trotted to catch up to me. She grabbed my hand, looked at the side of my face and asked, "Do you love me, Larry?" Her teeth had grown in evenly making her smile something to look at. Charlene was always persistent with her line of questioning, and she showed it as we waited for our orders. "Larry!" she quietly shouted. "Do you love me?"

Familiar with her persistence, I answered, "Yes, damn! What's gotten into you? You act like you don't know how I feel or something. Come on, Ma, you know I love your ass to death," I said grabbing, hugging and kissing her on her lips and forehead.

Outside, a black conversion van with tinted windows pulled up right in front of *"Mr. Lee's Chinese Takeout."* In front and behind the van were four Ford Explorer's with tinted windows. All five vehicles were outside of the 153rd Street eatery as Charlene and I stood inside enjoying our conversation. We waited on our food, totally oblivious to the convoy that sat right outside. All 16 doors of the vehicles swung open as several plain clothes officers ran inside the restaurant and aimed their heavy artillery at my face and at Charlene.

"Get down! Get on the fucking floor now!" screamed the lieutenant in charge.

Everyone in the store including Charlene and myself immediately dropped to the floor and placed our hands on the back of our heads.

"Is this him?" asked the lieutenant talking into his two-way radio as he kept his A.T. 9MM rifle pointed at my head. I knew the make and model of the gun because a friend of mine had one just like it.

"Stand him up and face him toward our direction," said the voice over the walkie talkie.

"Get up!" said the lieutenant, keeping his gun pointed at me. Charlene was on the ground beside me crying and shaking.

When I stood up, the lieutenant grabbed me and brought my hands down behind my back. He led me near the large restaurant window that provided potential customers with an eyeful of what was on Mr. Lee's gourmet menu and told me to face outside. Holding me firmly as I faced the street, the lieutenant spoke into his radio. "Is this the suspect, sir, yes or no?"

"Hold on," said the voice over the radio.

The silence that filled the air made it seem like one could hear a mouse piss on cotton. The few seconds it took for confirmation felt like a lifetime.

"10-4," said the voice, then the walkie talkie went dead.

"Cuff him! Cuff his ass!" yelled the lieutenant to his assisting officers.

"Yo, what the fuck are y'all taking me for?" I screamed as I struggled with the small army of officers.

"Get off of him!" muffled Charlene who, as she tried her best to help me, was quickly subdued by two female officers.

"Leave it alone, young lady! Leave it alone! ... Now!" screamed one of the female officers who had Charlene in a chokehold.

"Just call my moms. Call my ...," I yelled as I was dragged and thrown into the backseat of a waiting patrol car.

The officers kept their guns drawn as they slowly exited the oriental takeout. As quickly as they came, we were gone.

Charlene struggled to open up her purse and retrieve her cellular phone as the tears from her eyes temporarily blurred her vision. Dialing my home number, the telephone was answered on the third ring.

Ring...Ring...Ring!

"Hello, Mrs. Robinson speaking," answered my mom sounding very proper ever since talent scouts had begun calling our home showing an interest in my performance on the court.

"Ma, Larry got locked up!" shouted Charlene into the phone over her tears.

"Noooo!" screamed Mrs. Robinson.

CHAPTER TWO!

In another section of the city, the sun illuminated the sky as Curtis Martin and his mother, Danielle, prepared to leave their home.

"Curtis," said Mrs. Martin, calling her son in a cordial, relaxed manner. She looked in her purse to reassure herself that she had everything she needed. She made sure her keys, her money and the coupons she spent all week cutting from the newspapers were tucked into her small pocketbook. Closing her handbag, she looked toward the staircase that led to the second floor of her Queens home and called out to her son once again. "Curtis."

"Yes, Mom," replied Curtis in a respectful manner.

"Are you ready to take me shopping?" she kindly asked, looking up the steps.

"One second, Mom. I'll be right down," he said, keeping his tone leveled at a respectable note.

Curtis was a twenty-three-year-old drug dealer who lived with his mother in their Queens home. At 5'9", he had an average build weighing about 175 pounds. His chestnut complexion is what attracted most women to him, and his flawless skin is what locked them in. He had almond shaped eyes with thick eyebrows and a thin mustache.

Mrs. Martin was still young and looked even younger. She was sixteen when she birthed Curtis. After his father left for the war, she never bore another child because her husband never returned. Derrick Martin was considered missing in action two months after his arrival in the country of Afghanistan. When a year had passed and still no word from the Middle East, Derrick was considered a Casualty of War. His wife was presented with his medal of honor. A sergeant from the United States Marines knocked on Mrs. Martin's door one morning when Curtis was just four months old and awarded her his Purple Heart for Bravery. She framed it and let it hang in her living room next to her father's photo. He, too, died fighting a war that to everyone else who wasn't a soldier of the United States seemed senseless, worthless and very expensive.

After stuffing ten thousand dollars in each one of his front pants pockets, Curtis put on one of his oversized button up Polo shirts. The three sizes too big allowed him the ability to easily conceal the bulges that jutted out from his trousers. Looking in his full-length mirror, Curtis turned his body from side to side making sure his attire looked normal and presentable. The half smile and popping of his collar was physical affirmation that he was set to go.

Carefully trotting down the stairs, Curtis hit the automatic start on his brand new Ford Expedition, then affectionately yelled to his mother, "I'm ready, Mom."

Closing her bible, Mrs. Martin placed the Good Book back on their dining room table, slid herself to the edge of the sofa and stood up while simultaneously saying, "About time." She grabbed her purse and walked toward their front door where Curtis kindly held both the wooden and screen doors for her.

She walked past him, nodded her head and said, "Thank you, sweety." She eased her way down the porch steps using the handrail as a reinforcement.

Curtis locked both the sturdy wooden and frail screen doors of their home and quickly ran to the passenger side of the SUV to assist his mother entering the large vehicle.

"I'm okay, Curtis baby. Just bring your butt on in so we can get going," she said in the sweetest voice. Mrs. Martin practically lived for Jesus Christ, so everything she did or said, she tried to do it in the name of her Lord and be as warm and sincere as possible about it.

Curtis turned on the passenger side overhead television and pulled down the visor exposing a 6"x6" color television monitor. Looking over at his mom, he asked, "Do you want to watch *Big Momma's House*?" Curtis was referring to an urban comedy starring acclaimed comedian *Martin Lawrence*.

Looking like she could pass for his sister or girlfriend, Mrs. Martin replied by saying, "I'm okay. I'll enjoy the scenery as we coast down the boulevard."

"Okay," he replied. He flipped the visor back up and the two of them peacefully rolled down Queens Boulevard listening to the sweet sounds of *Luther Vandross*.

After driving for a few minutes, Curtis noticed the signal he'd been looking for. Two blocks up on the right, a man held up a homemade sign that read, "Car Wash $10.00."

"Mom," said Curtis softly, "I'm going to pull over here for one second."

"Boy, I know you're not going to wash this truck again. You just washed it yesterday," said Mrs. Martin observing the guy holding the sign. Normally, she would've overlooked the stunt as just another black man trying to get his hustle on legitimately, but the diamonds that glistened on the guy's wristwear caused her to analyze the scene more carefully.

"I'm not washing this truck again. I forgot to grab some air fresheners," said Curtis looking over at his mom. Once they caught eye contact, he turned his attention to his rear view mirror on which he then placed his hand indicating that it was lacking its usual fragrance ornament.

His mother looked at him and a feeling of relief took over her body causing her to smile and say, "Just hurry up back. Mommy wants to get to Pathmark before it gets crowded."

With that, Curtis exited the jeep and walked over to his waiting associate.

"What up, son," said the young black guy holding out his hand requesting their usual ghetto handshake as a friendly gesture.

"If he's the guy, shake his hand, then give him a hug. And I thought you said he operates alone. It seems he brought along his girlfriend," said an undercover Alcohol, Tobacco and Firearms agent looking through the lenses of his high-powered binoculars. Hearing the agent speak through a mini microphone which transmitted his voice to a small earbud in his ear, Curtis' associate was able to act out everything that he was told. The agents had set up a sting operation to get Curtis on a buy and bust sale, but since Curtis was now accompanied by someone, what was supposed to be a simple sale, had now become a conspiracy.

Looking around observing everything normal and suspicious, Curtis' preoccupation blurred his view and he didn't notice the cable company van parked directly across the street.

His sixth sense was preprogrammed by the law enforcement television shows he saw everyday on T.V., so all he was prepared for was zeroing in on dark colored Crown Victorias or Chevrolet Caprices. "What are you all happy about, son. You're all touchy feely and shit today for some reason." Curtis sensed something wasn't right, but the irresistible smile his contact had sprawled across his face made him dismiss any foul play.

"Give me a hug, my nigga!" said his associate.

Curtis hugged the guy establishing himself as the target.

"You got the dough?" asked the guy, referring to the buy money as they separated from their embracement.

"Yeah, when do you want it? Not here in the open," said Curtis looking around.

Sighing, the guy said, "Nah, dog. Of course not out here. Just act like you're looking inside this van right here," said the contact pointing to a multicolored conversion van. "The coke is sitting on the front seat. Just exchange it with the money and I'll holla at you later. Cool?" asked the connect nervously. Before he allowed Curtis to answer, he added, "Oh yeah, you gave me $200 extra last time and since your money is always rubber banned up, instead of removing it from what you just brought me, I left the two bills sitting next to the work."

"Yeah, yeah. Okay," said Curtis walking over to the van.

The van was equipped with a camera that was placed into the face of the radio. As most men would do when entering a vehicle, Curtis entered the van through the passenger side which wasn't facing any traffic, looked at the package of cocaine, then looked at the stereo in the van where his face was being recorded.

"As he's driving off, throw your right hand in the air and

wave goodbye to your friend. That will be our signal to move and you better not pull no fast one on us or our deal won't be worth diddly," said the agent.

Curtis exited the van, gave the guy another handshake and headed to his vehicle. He hopped back in his truck, wrapped the air fresheners around the rear view mirror and said, "Mom, do you need this?" he asked holding up two one-hundred dollar bills.

"Curtis, where'd you get that?" asked Mrs. Martin with a concerned look on her face. She looked at her son and squinted her eyes in tight slits and said, "I told you about getting money from those guys."

"Mom, I told you they still owed me from a long time ago. I'm not in the streets anymore. I told you, I'm finished." Curtis didn't know the latter part of his sentence was true—*he was finished.*

Mrs. Martin grabbed the money from her son's hand, but his words had fallen on deaf ears. Mrs. Martin was fed up with her son's lying. She was unaware of the transaction, but in a few moments, everything would all come to light.

Pulling off, Curtis heard his friend yell, "Ahight, yo!"

Curtis put his hand out the window forming a peace sign with his pointer and middle fingers causing his associate to react by raising his own hand giving the officers their cue to handle their business.

Mel Drake's side of the deal was done. Mel had been arrested the night before for driving while intoxicated. The DWI summons led to an impound of his vehicle. When his Mercedes Benz entered the police impound lot, the skillfully trained canines immediately descended upon the trunk of his $80,000 car signifying that drugs were present. A subsequent search ended with the police retrieving two 9mm semiautomatic handguns, 200 rounds of ammunition and a half pound of marijuana. Mel was so afraid of going to prison that he spilled the beans on his marijuana connections and his cocaine dealings. The authorities asked him what would he be willing to do or give them in exchange for his freedom. Without hesitation, he said *Curtis Martin*.

As Curtis drove off, a multitude of squad cars descended upon his automobile with guns raised in the air.

"Don't fucking move, Curtis Martin!" yelled an officer approaching the car with his gun raised. "And tell your lady friend to do the same. Tell her to stop moving, now!" he screamed.

Mrs. Martin was nervous, so she began shaking uncontrollably. She had never seen a gun in real life, only on television.

"Grab her and retrieve whatever it was that Curtis handed to her," said the officer motioning with his weapon to a female officer standing nearby.

The female cop walked over to the side of the vehicle, opened the door and dragged Mrs. Martin to the ground. As she pleaded for help, three more officers went to the aid of their coworker and helped restrain the woman. Pulling the two one-hundred dollar bills from Mrs. Martin's purse, the female officer yelled, "I got it!"

"Is it marked?" said a voice over her radio.

Flipping it over, the lady cop recognized two red lines that were strategically placed at the left hand corners of the bills. She pressed the side button of her radio, brought it to her face and gleefully said, "It's marked."

"10-4," the other voice responded. She placed her walkie talkie back on her belt, lifted Mrs. Martin from the ground, aggressively brought her hands down behind her back, cuffed her and said, "Take her too."

The officers led Curtis to an awaiting squad car and violently shoved him into the back seat.

By this time, Mrs. Martin had gotten a hold of herself and stopped hollering. She figured this was all a mistake and possibly racial profiling, and as soon as they reached the precinct, everything would be figured out.

Curtis peered out the back window of the police cruiser and caught eye contact with his mother who was in another cruiser twenty feet away. With tears forming in the corners of his eyes, Curtis moved his lips mouthing the words, *I love you, Mom. I'm sorry."*

Mrs. Danielle Martin, who never saw her son in such a desperate state of anguish, took on a worrisome and fearful look herself. Her eyes were wide and the tears never stopped falling. When one of the officers hit the sound button on his squad car, the lights flashed and the siren began screaming, bringing the reality of what just transpired to an even more elevated level. Mrs. Martin jumped in her seat and focused her eyes on the officers who now entered the vehicle that she occupied. The assisting officer turned around, looked at Mrs. Martin like if he cared and said, "What a shame." He turned back around, took off his hat, placed it on the dashboard and pulled the built in computer closer to him. As he began typing digits into the small keyboard, Mrs. Martin glanced back over to her son who was now being driven away. The car she was in jerked as the senior officer brought the vehicle out of *"Park"* and placed it in the

"*Drive*" position.

As if everything were rehearsed, all the patrol cars raced down Queens Boulevard in unison, one behind the other, all headed to police headquarters.

What began as a beautiful, lovely summer afternoon now seemed like an ugly, repulsive nautical day. And it was just the beginning.

CHAPTER THREE!

As I sat in an empty room of the 51st precinct located on 147th Street and Edgecomb Avenue, I could hear telephones ringing, typewriters popping non-stop and the occasional sound of static coming from the speakers of police radios. My wrist began to hurt from the position that my arm was in because I was handcuffed to a metal bar that sat two feet higher than the bench that I took refuge in. I guess you could call it a holding cell because it was damp, cold, and it possessed your customary toilet/sink combination.

It didn't have the traditional bars like the jail cells you would see on television. Instead, it had a steel door with a small window located at the center of it. My bladder was full and my stomach ached from emptiness. I should've been thinking about why I was being held, but the only thing that came to my mind, however, was the order of chicken and broccoli that I was waiting on when I got arrested.

After being held in that room for *I don't know how long*, the turning of the lock let me know that the games were about to begin.

As the door opened, I could see a figure being led down a nearby hallway with some type of cloth covering his or her head.

I didn't know whether the individual had anything to do with me or not, but I did watch enough television shows that dealt with law enforcement to understand that the possibility existed that I was allowed to *see* what I *saw* for a reason. A white officer that seemed as cordial as one of the guys at my church undid my handcuffs and led me to another room which was set up like the interrogation rooms I'd seen on shows like *"NYPD Blue"* and *"Law & Order."* I didn't feel guilty of anything because I knew I hadn't done anything, but my natural instincts caused me to recollect on things that I may have done in the past. My palms were sweaty and my knees were weak because I was nervous, but as a child, I used to lie to my parents sometimes to get things that I wanted which enabled me to maintain a look that made me appear calm on the surface.

In came the *"peanut gallery"* dressed in their designer cotton trousers and loosened up ties giving me the notion that we were going to be there for a while. Two detectives sat right across from me whipping out their ballpoint pens and yellow legal notepads while two uniformed officers stood in the corners of the room that I couldn't see, because my back was facing them.

"Good afternoon, Mr. Robinson, I'm Homicide Detective Tom Morano," said the 5'9", 180 pound detective. Folding his hands on the table, the detective continued. "And this is my partner, Richard Burns," he said, introducing his partner who resembled Detective Morano except his partner had a receding hairline.

I kept quiet because I knew my rights and I knew I didn't have to say anything if I didn't want to.

"Mr. Robinson, as you know, you're not under arrest," said

Morano straightening up in his seat. "Just cooperate with us and we'll make everything go as smoothly as possible." He brought his hands together and rested them on the table in front of him.

I remained quiet. I just sat there staring at the detective like if I was trying to read his mind. I guess he got uncomfortable because he kept squirming in his seat until he figured we wasted enough time.

"Mr. Robinson, a little over a month ago, the fourth of July to be exact, could you by any chance recall where you were, from let's say 6 p.m. till around midnight?" asked the detective, tapping his pen and looking me in my eyes. I guess he was looking for signs indicating that I was lying or about to lie, but as I learned in my childhood years, if I stay calm, I'll be ahight.

I raised up from my slouched position and looked the detective in his face noticing a small bruise between his nose and upper lip. I figured he received it shaving his mustache earlier that day, but since it wasn't my concern, I simply said, "None of your business. And I ain't saying shit else unless my attorney is present."

I presumed the detective knew my tough guy attitude was all a bluff because he came running around the table like a mad man and put his hands all up in my face. "Larry, you listen here, young man!" he yelled. "Now I'm not playing around. You're in *my* damn precinct and I'll do whatever the hell I want to without being questioned. You piece of shit! You play this innocent college basketball crap but I ain't buying into it! I've seen your kind before." He continued yelling at me becoming more furious. Standing with only about an inch of distance between us, I never blinked. "You act like you're this good kid. You carry a basketball in one hand and a pistol in your waistband. Now tell me, Larry, where the hell were you on the night of July 4th?"

It was clear that he was pissed off because at this point, he had the majority of my shirt balled up in his hands. I couldn't take the humiliation. Plus, I figured, if I just tell this pig the truth, which is what I thought he wanted to hear, maybe we could get all of this over with as soon as possible. So I complied.

"I was at a motel getting some pussy. There! You happy?" I think my answering him eased him a bit because he let go of my shirt. He drilled me after that.

"With who?" he asked, making his way back around the table and finding his seat.

"You don't know her. She don't fuck with white boys," I said sarcastically.

Then Officer Burns cut in. He'd been quiet the entire time. But as a team, Burns knew it was his time to shine.

"What motel?" asked Detective Burns, leaning toward me as he rested his palms on the table.

"This lil hole in the wall joint on 145th Street," I said referring to a privately owned tenement building that illegally operated as a $20 per hour love haven.

"With who?" asked Detective Morano. They were trying to confuse me going back and forth.

"One of my shorties," I said, not wanting to divulge any names so as to avoid involving anyone else.

"Her name. Give me her name!" screamed Burns.

"Joanne," I said.

"Joanne what?" asked Morano.

"Joanne gives-some-good-ass-head, that's what," I said surprising myself with the joke and sarcasm.

The detectives leaned in toward me indicating that they meant business and weren't there to play any games.

"I don't know her last name," I said as I turned my head. By this time, I was beginning to feel uncomfortable.

"You sleeping with a woman that you don't even know?" asked Morano.

"Nah, I know her, I just don't know her last name. Her last name ain't an issue with me. Her lips are," I said smiling.

"Who signed for the room?" asked Detective Burns.

"You don't have to sign for any rooms at that spot. You just give the dude in charge a 20 spot, get the key, and go and handle your business. Simple as that," I said, looking at Burns who was now sitting on the table.

"So no one signed for the room?" asked Morano.

"No. I just told you *no*, right?" I said becoming frustrated myself.

"So no one can verify your whereabouts for the 4th of July?" asked Burns.

"Yeah," I said, "*I* can!"

"Well, you said this guy charges $20 an hour. What hour time frame did you guys occupy the room?"

"I copped the joint for the whole night," I said, meaning I rented the room for the entire evening. I continued. "Homie gave me a deal because I know him."

"Oh, *now* you know him? What do you do, sell him crack?" asked Detective Burns trying my nerves.

"I don't sell drugs, homie. I play ball and fuck bitches."

I guess I struck a nerve in the detective because Morano leaned back into my face closer than he had the first time and said, "Listen, boy! I'm not your homie or one of your little street thug friends. There was a shooting at a party on 149th Street and Seventh Avenue and we have a witness who placed you at the scene. This witness also said he saw you shoot this kid several times near the side of the building. Now you mean to tell me that you was laid up in some illegal motel with some girl named Joanne that you don't even know, for the entire night, for $20, and you have no way to prove it?" Backing off and rolling up his sleeves, he continued. "I believe your girlfriend is in the lobby of our precinct and according to our records," said the detective flipping through his pocket notepad, "her name is Charlene Portis, not Joanne. Can you explain that, Larry?"

"Yeah, I can explain that," I said, leaning toward the detective. "I wasn't hitting wifey that night. I was sliding up in my lil down low shorty," I said explaining to the detective in street slang that I was cheating on my girlfriend.

"Really?" he asked.

"Yes, *really*," I kindly answered.

"Well, do you know anything about a kid getting shot that night?" he continued picking.

The streets talk so I heard about what allegedly happened that evening. I felt it would be no big deal to say some of what I knew because I really *didn't* know exactly what happened, but I *did* know who pulled the trigger. Everyone in the hood did as well. I knew the incident took place and I had heard details about how and why it went down. So I said, "I heard about it."

"What did you hear, Larry?" asked Morano, rubbing his chin as he paced the room.

I began to believe that every time the detective thought he had something, he would refer to me by name. So now I figured dude thought he had a crack in his already loose case.

"I heard some Spanish kid from the Bronx somewhere was at a party in my neighborhood and was acting up," I said crossing my arms. I had this awkward feeling that sort of felt good knowing that even though I wasn't directly involved in any of the gritty street antics that took place in my neighborhood, there were people who made sure our neighborhood wasn't violated by anyone.

"What do you mean, '*acting up?*'" asked Detective Burns knowing exactly what I meant.

"I heard he was fronting. Telling dudes they couldn't enter the premises because they were black."

"Well what happened after that?" continued Detective Burns.

"I really don't know," I said, trying to illustrate in my head what might've happened. "I guess dudes wasn't trying to hear that bullshit. They said the kid came downstairs still on that racist shit and started walking around with his gun out like he owned our hood."

"So he had a gun on him?" asked Detective Morano looking at my hands.

"Yeah, he had his heat on him," I said with confidence. "But they said he must've forgot that he wasn't wearing a vest because all that fronting got him sent back to the essence."

"So, his behavior wasn't tolerated by your crew so you guys killed him," said Morano staring at me looking for something.

Mrs. Robinson didn't raise no dummy. I was already prepared for his tricky questioning and reversed psychology.

"From what I hear, his behavior *wasn't* tolerated. And *no*, I *don't* have a crew and I *didn't* kill anybody, if that answers your question," I said.

"Who shot him with the 22 caliber, Larry?" he immediately shot his question at me.

I heard the kid from the neighborhood who shot the guy used a forty-five semiautomatic, so now I was sure that these toy cops didn't know what they were talking about. Now it's my time to start busting people's bubble. So I thought.

"He didn't get shot with a 22. He got hit up with a four pound. 4.5 baby. Blew his fucking melon back."

The detective gave me that look of confidence again and my name was the first thing that came out of his mouth. "Larry, no one knew what kind of gun this kid Louis Gonzalez was killed with except our coroner and our forensics office. That's a vital piece of information, Larry," said Morano matter-of-factly.

"Especially if you weren't present at the time of the shooting," said Burns looking at me with his hands in his pockets.

Bursting through the door like a S.W.A.T. team making a raid, a heavyset black guy dressed in a dark suit to camouflage his 240 pound frame entered the room and made his presence immediately known. Peering down on me with his beedy, dark brown eyes, small Afro, thick connecting eyebrows and Richard Pryor mustache, Sergeant Dennis Sherman delivered the terrifying, unfortunate news I had been hoping to avoid all day.

"Morano, Burns," he looked at the detectives. "I just got a call from Judge Burich at 100 Centre Street two minutes ago. Our witness testified before a Grand Jury and the people returned an indictment," said the sergeant, holding a sheet of paper that he pulled from his fax machine just moments ago. He looked over at me and shook his head in disbelief, then turned back to his subordinates and began reading from his paper. My heart dropped before the first word left his mouth and I just knew I was going to vomit at that very moment. The lack of food prevented me from throwing up, but the sergeant's next words almost caused me to move my bowels right there where I sat. "Under indictment #1536-02, Mr. Lawrence Robinson, you will hereby be formally charged with the murder of Louis Gonzalez on July 4, 2002 on the following counts."

I heard the first count, but I must've went into a deep shock because count one was the only count I thought I had until I went in front of the judge for arraignment. When the sergeant read the counts to me, had I been conscious and not on cloud nine, I probably would've heard him say, "*Count one*, 125.25 Murder in the second degree; *Intentional Murder. Count two*, 125.20 Murder in the second degree; *Depraved Indifference. Count three*, 120.20 *Manslaughter in the first degree. Count four*, 120.15, *Manslaughter in the second degree. Count five*, 230.40 *Possession of a weapon in the first degree. Count six*, 230.35 *Possession of a weapon in the second degree* and *Count seven*, 310.80 *Reckless Endangerment in the first degree.*"

I realized I was still in the interrogation room when Detective Burns pulled me out of the chair to go and finger-print me. "I can't believe this shit is happening to me," I thought. "*Murder? Not the kid. Not Larbury.*" They had to fingerprint me over and over at least three times because I had no feeling in my hands or feet. I'm surprised I stood up long enough for them to get anything out of me.

I was eventually read my rights and placed in an official holding cell with prison bars. My arraignment was set for 9 o'clock that evening and I was finally given something to eat. Two sandwiches, a milk and an old rotten apple. One of the sandwiches had only cheese in between its slices. The other sandwich had two slices of mystery meat in between its slices. I think I ate everything all at once because my mind went blank after that.

I can imagine how I looked all alone in that cold cell that evening, like a homeless man in his homemade cardboard Condo.

CHAPTER FOUR!

Resting in a police precinct in the Kew Garden section of Queens, the couple sat uncomfortably in separate interrogation rooms. Curtis sat perched with his back slightly slumped and his arms crossed. His lips were contorted as if he were expressing his disbelief of what happened, but his eyes told another story. His eyes said to anyone who looked that this young man was scared.

Staring at nothing in particular on the table in front of him, Curtis' eyes never seemed to have blinked. The skin between his eyes was puckered and wrinkled from the agitated look that seemed to sit easily on his face.

Mrs. Danielle Martin, on the other hand, sobbed uncontrollably. The desperate feeling of not knowing is what affected her most. She would look toward the door whenever she heard the noise of someone walking by and her eyes would search the room when the commotion got louder. Paranoia was nothing, Mrs. Martin was terrified. The events that lay ahead would only determine how strong Mrs. Martin and her son really were.

Entering Curtis' room were four men. Their grand entrance snapped Curtis out of his momentary trance and back into reality. He observed each man carefully as if his visual analysis could determine what each man was thinking. It wasn't surprising that one of the four officers was black either. The way Curtis perceived it, they needed someone who could possibly get him to talk. The same strategy they pulled with Mel Drake. However, they way the authorities looked at it, Curtis was going to talk regardless.

The quartet sat on the opposite side of the table and as Curtis suspected, the black man spoke first.

Looking down at the defendant's paperwork, the 6'2", 220 pound, baldheaded detective read over the charges to himself, and in the rear of his mind he thought, *Another one of my brothers chasing a lost cause.*" He placed the papers back on the table and began to speak. Their eyes never connected with one another, but both men could see how the other one felt. "Mr. Martin, do you understand the seriousness and severity of the charges brought against you?" he asked, only glancing at the defendant.

Curtis straightened his arched back, stopped fidgeting with his fingers, peered at the detective and softly replied, "Can I call my lawyer?"

Prepared that the young man would say that, the black officer pulled himself closer to the table, tilted his head slightly sideways and calmly spoke. "You can call an attorney, if you can get to a telephone. But from what I see," said the detective holding his hands out on the table signifying that his palms were empty, while simultaneously looking around the room, "there aren't any phones here." Returning back to his relaxed position, the large black cop continued to talk. "Listen, Curtis, I know you're a smart kid. And smart kids make wise decisions. What you need to decide now is if you're willing to let your mother suffer for your misbehavior." After giving it a thorough check, it was confirmed that Mrs. Danielle Martin was indeed Curtis' mother and not one of his female associates as the cops had assumed. "You involved your mother in this. It wasn't us." Once again leaning closer and lowering his voice, the detective continued. "Make the decision right now, and you and your mom walk. Right now, right this moment, and I can make all of this disappear," said the detective explaining everything with his hands. "It's up to you, Curtis. The ball is in your court. Tell us who buys the coke from you, we investigate your lead, you make the confirmation and we make the arrest."

With a smirk on his face, Curtis quickly shot back. "So basically all I have to do is tell you guys who I deal with. You know, help you guys set him up like Mel set me up," said Curtis smiling now, "testify against him in a court of law if he decides to take it to trial, and my mother and I can walk free?" He raised his brow to indicate that he wanted an answer.

"You guys walk right out that door," said the officer pointing toward the door with confidence.

"Well, here's what I'm willing to give you," said Curtis preying on the man's hunger and feeding his famine ego a bunch of crap. "I'm willing to give your Uncle Tom ass the finger," said Curtis counting on his fingers beginning with his middle, "and another opportunity to allow me to contact my lawyer. Now one thing is for sure and that is, Mrs. Martin's son ain't no fucking rat. So leave me alone with that snitching bullshit." Then Curtis returned to his slouched sitting position.

Fed up at the conclusion that Curtis wasn't going to work with them, the detective slid his chair backward, stood up and walked toward the door. Once he reached the door with his three stooges in tow, he turned back toward Curtis and said, "You're a young kid, Curtis, don't wait until it's too late."

The officers exited the room and left Curtis drowning in the words that were last spoken. He leaned his head back, looked toward the ceiling and thought to himself, *"I'll take the rap for this. A lil ten years ain't shit. There's light at the end of that tunnel. And hopefully, my mom will forgive me one day for this mess."*

A female officer exited the room that Mrs. Martin was being held in as the foursome headed her way. With an exhausted look on her face, Officer Carla Jiminez stood with her back to the door and crossed her arms as the small group of men approached her area. She began to speak as Detective Steve Todd braced himself for the unacceptable news.

"Todd, I don't think she knows anything," said Officer Jiminez shrugging her shoulders.

"Well, what's her story?" asked Detective Todd crossing his huge arms.

"She maintains her story that she was simply on her way grocery shopping. I...I mean, she still has the coupons she cut out and they all matched the items she wrote down on her grocery list." Dropping her arms and sighing, she sympathetically asked, "What do we do with her? I think she's innocent."

The detective looked at Officer Jiminez and said, "It's simple." He brushed past her, opened the door of the room where Mrs. Martin sat crying and walked over to her. Towering over the poor lady, Detective Steve Todd exhaled and thought to himself, *"I hate this job."* He then proceeded to read Mrs. Danielle Martin her rights. "Mrs. Danielle Martin, you are under arrest for conspiracy with intent to sell 1,000 grams of powder cocaine. You have the right to remain silent." He continued as Mrs. Martin buried her head in her hands and began weeping uncontrollably. She jerked every time the words, *"You have the right to,"* slipped from the detective's mouth. "You have the right to an attorney. If you cannot afford one, one will be appointed to you." The words slid out of the detective's mouth with an echoing effect. Detective Todd peered down at Mrs. Martin like if he were about to answer her cries for help, and before he could let her childlike aura take a toll on him, he knelt down near her ear and whispered, "I'll do whatever I can to convince your son to make the right decision. Hopefully, you'll be able to help me out. I'm sorry, Mrs. Martin," said the detective patting her softly on her shoulder. He stood up, turned and left the room.

CHAPTER FIVE!

"**W**hen I call your name, give me your I.D. number and address." Ms. Jackson, a short broad with a super fat ass and a long weave ponytail was admitting us from court into the *"Receiving and Departure"* area of the *"Beacon"* on Riker's Island. We arrived around 11 o'clock that evening, but due to an incident in one of the housing units, myself and the other two inmates that were also being admitted had to wait patiently on the prison bus in the parking lot until a little after midnight.

Ms. Jackson, with her ghetto pretty self proceeded with the names, "Colon!"

"Ayo!" yelled the other guy that was with us. The Spanish kid, Colon, was knocked out and I guess homeboy that was with us had a little less patience than the Colon cat and I.

Colon jumped up out of his sleep with his hands cuffed in front of him and said, "Yo!" Had I not known any better, I would've thought this Colon guy was a crackhead by the way his eyes protruded from his head. But then again, he just woke up.

"Your I.D. number and address?" You could tell that Ms. Jackson had done this many times before because it was no sweat off her brow that the Spanish kid was wasting time.

"Que?" he said.

"Your fuckin' name, nigga!" said our third passenger. "That's why I hate y'all *German* ass niggaz. Ma'fuckas can sell us all that coke, but you can't speaky no English." Then the guy looked at Ms. Jackson and said, "Tell him you want some *pedico* and I bet you he'll answer your ass in English then." He looked over at Colon.

Ms. Jackson had to be tough to be a C.O. on Riker's Island. But like anybody, when something funny is said, someone's going to laugh. Ms. Jackson chuckled at *Mr._"Antsy's"* remarks but remained patient.

I figured it was time for me to step in because I was starving, tired and I really wanted to lay my ass down. So I interjected, "Como se llamo?" Everybody looked at me like I was crazy. But I turned right to *Mr. "Rude Ass"* and said, "School nigga! I took up Spanish my sophomore and junior years. Ever heard of it?" I asked homeboy with a touch of sarcasm. *Shit, I was on the Island, a nigga had to be hard_to survive on the Rock.*

"Ever heard of what, nigga?" Dude was all in my face, but I knew wasn't anything going down. We were all still handcuffed.

"School, ma'fucka!"

"What!" He was even closer in my face than before. And Ms. Jackson's ass still hadn't intervened.

"Tranquilo, tranquilo!" Colon was telling us to chill out. "Eight-nine-fiye-cero-wong-sis-wong-wong. I lib in 1878, Crotona Abenue."

Fake ass Mike Tyson looked at me like he wanted to say, "*I told your stupid ass this nigga speaks English.*" At that point, Colon got his handcuffs removed and walked over to an open cell where one of the R&D orderlies had a warm plate of rice and beans waiting for us.

"I know you're happy as shit now. *Bean and rice eating ma'fucka*," yelled the guy. Colon just turned around and continued stuffing his face.

"Jackson!"

"*I wonder if we're related?*" Mr. Jackson, who I came to know as CJ, was flirting with the attractive corrections officer.

Ms. Jackson didn't smile or anything. She switched her weight to her other leg, popped the gum she was chewing two quick times and rolled her eyes.

CJ got the picture. "Six-nine-nine-0-four-double-0-seven. 1331 Jefferson Avenue. *Brooklyn, ya heard!*" He ended his address with a smirk on his face. Ms. Jackson undid his cuffs and sent him on his way.

"Robinson!"

I already told y'all I was starving and sleepy. *A nigga like me didn't waste no time.* "895-zero-sixteen-twenty-seven. 1611 West 150th Street." As soon as I grabbed my plate, I was spooning shit into my mouth before I found me a seat on an empty bench. Shit, blacks are some bean and rice eating ma'fucka's too. Don't get it twisted. Just 'cause down south they be stuffing their faces with Hog Mog and shit don't mean we don't eat beans. We all the same anyway. Puerto Ricans, Dominicans and Cubans are just as black as we are. The only difference between a black and a Hispanic, in *my* opinion, *for most of us*, is the texture of our hair. Let me put it simpler, put us in a police line up and watch both of our asses get picked.

After we finished eating, things got quiet. Colon went back to sleep, on the floor of the holding pen this time, CJ was standing at the gate with his arms through the bars like he had done this many times before, and I was sitting there looking worried, thinking about my moms and my girlfriend, Charlene.

CJ turned to face me, extended his fist and said, "Niggas call me CJ."

I looked up at him and said to myself, "*Niggas should call you asshole*," but instead I returned the gesture and kindly said, "Larry, but niggas in my hood call me 'L'." After my fist touched his, I guess he got tired of flirting with "*Big Butt*" because the *clown* took a seat next to me.

"Are your people's coming to get you out?" he asked as he kept his eyes glued to Ms. Jackson's rear end jiggling, as she walked by.

Again I wanted to say something to irk his ass like, "*Is the monkey that abandoned you coming to get your funny_looking ass?*" but I remained cool about the *twenty-one_questions* and as I looked over at Ms. Jackson who was now bending over I said, "I might not be getting out any time soon."

He looked at me, "Why not?"

I sighed and said, "I got a body", then my voice trailed off as Ms. Jackson walked by us again, "but I ain't do it though," I added.

"Me either," he said.

"I guess that makes two of us." I looked over at Colon and caught him scratching his butt through his filthy ass jeans.

"Did they find a weapon?"

I looked CJ in his face to see if he was genuinely concerned or just being nosy. I settled with him being concerned and I told him, "I don't know. I told you I ain't do it."

"Yo, lookie here, lil brah," I figured CJ to be about 40 years old or very close to it. Son was about 6'2" and about 200 pounds. "Them bodies ain't no joke. But at the same time, they're also easy to beat." He smiled, "A dead man can't tell no tales."

"But faggot ass, lying ass snitches, who probably want to get out of their own situations will." I relaxed my head against the wall, looked up in the air and sighed with a hint of frustration.

"Let me ask you something, young'n." CJ put on his big brother routine, so I played my position.

"*Shoot*," I told him.

He looked at me.

"Nah, not like that. I mean, kick it." I was beginning to relax now.

"How old are you?" he asked.

"Eighteen."

"You still go to school?"

"Just graduated."

"You got a girlfriend?"

"Several."

"Do you have one you can *trust*?" He sat a little more erect after he asked me that.

I noticed it so I looked at him, "My boo, Charlene, why?"

He relaxed himself, "Don't lose her."

"I'm not." I sat back against the wall.

"Don't push her away either. You said you got a homicide, right?"

I nodded my head. I was definitely trying to see what his point was in all of this.

"Well, you're going to be here at least two years fighting this thing. I just beat a body last year."

"*Go figure*," I thought.

"I laid up like thirty-two months before I beat them on a technicality. I lost my wife being hot headed though. She told me she wanted to go out to the club with her girlfriends one night. I was only in jail for like a month at that time, so I wasn't really trying to hear that ole girl wanted to party while I was pressing my rack. But I told her to go ahead and do her, and to be slick, I told her to go and find a nigga that'll tolerate that club hopping bullshit. The bitch called my bluff like a ma'fucka. I tried calling her the next day to apologize but I didn't get an answer. I kept calling for like a month straight, still the same fuckin' thing. Guess how I found out that she was done with me?"

"I know, the dude got knocked and y'all ended up in the same unit." *This nigga must think I'm new to this broad shit.*

"Nah, when that nigga was digging her guts out one afternoon, I guess she was trying to turn the ringer off and must've accidentally knocked the phone on the floor and off the hook. I heard this bitch telling some nigga his dick is like money, *guaranteed to keep her cumming.*"

I didn't want to laugh because dude looked hurt, but when he turned and looked at me I could tell he wanted to laugh too so I set if off. Ole boy joined me and that broke the ice, *so to speak.*

He was into his zone so he continued, "Don't fuck up like I did, young'n. Keep your broad. You're gonna need her. This shit is rough doing a bid by yourself. Ain't nothing like a lil visit here and there, some mail, a few flicts from those who love you. Mind you, I said those who love you, not those who *you* got love for. There's a difference."

"No doubt."

"Got any kids?"

"Nah," I said.

"I thought that all you young niggas had babies all over the place."

"*Wrong young nigga*. I'm trying to play ball. I'm trying to get this scholarship to North Carolina. I need this break."

CJ looked at me. This time he stared as if he were studying me. "*I hope this nigga ain't gay*," I thought.

"I believe you, son."

He used the word "*son*" more like a father figure would as opposed to a homie, so I took it that way and asked him, "You believe what?"

"I believe you ain't kill nobody."

I didn't need his opinion. "I told you that already," I said.

"Do you know who did it?"

"Yeah, but I ain't telling."

"Why not?"

Fuck he mean why not? I ain't no snitch. "Fuck you mean why not?"

"Why not? Why won't you tell on the person who really committed the crime you're charged with? That sounds crazy to take the weight for someone when your life is at stake here."

"'Cause," I was beginning to feel uncomfortable now.

"Because what? Give me your reason. Convince me because I'm missing something here and I know it."

"Because it's the *code of the streets*! That's why!" I was on my feet now.

CJ thought to himself, "*I guess some people still abide by the code.*" With that he got up, motioned for Ms. Jackson and when Ms. Jackson opened up the cell and just let him walk out, that shit bugged me out. But what happened next is something I'll never forget. CJ walked out of the cell, kissed Ms. Jackson square on the mouth, then looked back at me.

The nigga pulled his badge from his pocket, placed it around his neck, called Ms. Jackson *"Honey"* and told her that he'd see her in the morning. Before he left in the unmarked patrol car that sat outside waiting in the cut for him to return, he turned, looked at me again and said, "If you won't tell us who killed Louis Gonzalez, I hope you're attorney can convince a jury the way you convinced me." With that said, Detective Corey Jackson shook his head and exited the building.

CHAPTER SIX!

Officer Carla Jiminez entered the interrogation room where Curtis had been questioned almost two hours earlier. He sat leaned over, with his arms crossed, resting on his knees and his head resting on his arms. People had been in and out of the room the last past couple of hours so Curtis didn't budge when the female officer entered.

Ms. Jiminez sat down opposite of Curtis, placed her hands quietly on the table that separated the two and cleared her throat.

Curtis looked up. Officer Jiminez stared at him intently, trying to read whatever it was that was on Curtis' mind. But it was going to be hard trying to figure this young man out, especially by looking at him. Curtis Martin had his poker face on and had the two of them been gambling against one another, Carla would have been scared to make her move.

When the officer didn't say anything, Curtis placed his head back into his lap.

"So what's it gonna be?" she asked. She gently bit down on her lip.

Curtis kept his head in his lap. "Is my lawyer here yet?"

"Apparently your attorney couldn't make it. He said he was attending a trial and wouldn't be here until after night court was over. It's 7 o'clock now so that gives you at least three more hours with us." She was looking at her watch that always read military time.

Curtis sighed and said, "Well, just let me know when he gets here."

Ms. Jiminez tried another approach. "Do you think that your mother could forgive you after causing her to spend ten years of her precious life in prison because of you?"

This caught his attention. Curtis looked up and said, "My moms ain't going to jail. Y'all only got me. Y'all know the drugs were mine and that she ain't have *shit* to do with it, so save that bullshit for the birds."

Carla Jiminez slid the arrest report over to Curtis so that he could examine the document for himself. He read where it said that his mom was charged as his codefendant for conspiracy. He also knew that a conspiracy was an automatic *ten years*. "Call your boss in here," he said.

Officer Jiminez jumped up and raced out the door. After a few moments she returned with Detective Steve Todd.

Steve sat in the seat that his subordinate had previously occupied. He looked over at Curtis and said, "Your mother shouldn't have been put through *this* much."

Curtis got right down to business. "Check this out. I'll give y'all my buyers, but they won't just deal with *anybody* and they know not to talk crazy over the phone. We're gonna have to set up like a buy and bust. Like how y'all did with me and Mel." Officer Jiminez stole a glance at Curtis and caught the devilish grin he had on his face. "But they don't give me any money up front. I fronts them, and they hit me with my cheddar when I bring them the next pack. It's been going on for a while like that so the operation runs smoothly now."

"How many of them are there?" The detective was smiling, but he wouldn't let it show on his face.

"It's three of them. They're like one little crew."

Steve Todd grabbed his pen and pad and positioned his hand to start writing. "What's their names? Give me their names?" He looked down at his paper.

"Slow down player. I don't know their *real* names. You know we all go by our *street* names."

"Well, what are their street names? And by the way, we never caught your street name."

"You'll soon find out," Curtis said to himself, but out loud he said, "Their names are 'H', 'K' and Dee."

"What the hell," the detective chuckled, "you running an alphabet crew?" He laughed harder.

"You won't be laughing for long," Curtis again thought to himself.

"How do you contact them?" asked the detective.

"It's funny you asked. Y'all fucked up my plans for meeting up with them earlier. What I usually do is cop from Mel, do whatever it is that I have to do, then go and meet them."

Carla stepped up. "So they're still waiting on you now?" This time Ms. Jiminez couldn't maintain her anxiety. She had to speak up. She was trying to get promoted and this collar would surely help out.

Curtis looked at her wondering where she all of a sudden retrieved her voice from. He said, "Yup," then he smiled at her.

"Let's set it up then. Give us the location and we'll have our people set everything up like if it's you that's making the drop. But we'll surprise their asses, won't we?" said Carla looking over at her boss.

He nodded.

"I'll have to page them and put in my code to let them know that I'm on my way. They usually hit me right back on my pager telling me it's okay to come through. So if they hit me back, y'all can roll. If they don't, it'll be a waste of time to set up *y'all's* operation."

"Jiminez, go get his cell phone." Curtis could hear the smile in the detective's voice.

When Ms. Jiminez came back, she passed Curtis his phone and let him do his thing. Curtis punched in seven digits and waited for a second. The room was quiet so everyone heard when the three loud beeps sounded off after the single ring.

Ring...Beep...beep...beep!

Curtis entered his code, "*1-007-5-0-225-60-30.*" He pressed the pound button to insure the message got to his people as soon as possible.

Across the city in the borough that birthed Hip Hop, *Homicide, Killer* and *Danger* sat parked on their Yamaha Banshee 4-wheelers in the park of their housing development.

"Ayo, I love this project," said the 5'8" lanky fifteen-year-old. *Homicide's* name was self-explanatory. Aside from selling drugs all day long, Homicide *murdered* people for a living.

"Ain't no other project on this planet like Edenwald," retorted *Killer*. He, too, was a lanky, 5'8", fifteen-year-old. He was a little darker than *Homicide* was, and every time Homicide *murdered* somebody, Killer would be right beside him emptying his gun into the victim as well.

"*Yeah, the BX, nicknamed Cook Coke Shit. It should've been called Homicide Bronx, The Killer Bx or the Dangerous*

Boogie Down," Danger chimed in with a little more enthusiasm than his two buddies. Everyone thought the trio were brothers due to them hanging around one another all day, every day. It was also their exact same height and close facial resemblances that caused others to think that way. As far as *Danger* and *his* reputation, everyone knew that *he* had committed just as many killings as his two friends had done.

Homicide's pager sounded but Killer had it in his possession because earlier that day, the threesome were being pursued by the police and to confuse the authorities, the trio switched coats to camouflage their identities. *Sort of like a mix-up thing.*

Killer looked at the device and got quiet.

"What's up, homie? What's popping?" Homicide was referring to the page on his beeper.

"Yo, who the fuck is code #1?"

Homicide tried to snatch his pager away, but Killer pulled it from his reach.

"Gimme my shit, son!" Homicide yelled.

"Who is it, yo!?" Killer retorted once again.

"That's my cousin, nigga. *C-Murder.*"

"Yo, it's some more shit on here, son."

"What else do it say?"

"It says 1, *dash*, 007." Killer looked at Homicide for an explanation to the rest of the code.

"Yeah, that's cuzo, the double 0 seven means *beef*, go head," he told his homie to continue reading the message to him.

"Five *dash* 0," he looked at his homie again.

"That's the police, *nigga.*" Danger stopped in mid-pull of his marijuana cigarette. *It was time to be alert.*

"225."

"That's us, that's here. Two twenty-fifth, nigga, *our* block."
Homicide had a look on his face like, *"Damn, nigga,_you act
like you ain't know."*

"Six 0."

"Sixty minutes, son. One hour is his E.T.A."

Danger looked at Homicide because he wanted his buddy
to explain to him what the abbreviation meant.

"Expected time of arrival," said Homicide. He then looked
back at Killer.

"Three, zero."

"Huh," Homicide and Danger said, *"Huh"* at the same time.
Then Homicide mumbled to himself, *"Three, zero. What the...?"*

"Turn it upside down, Killer." *Danger* made this request. He
knew what the code meant because he was the one who made
it up.

Killer complied and said, "O, E?"

"That ain't an O, y'all. That's a D. *D, E.* He means pull out
the Desert Eagles.

With that, the trio's faces lit up like Christmas lights.
Homicide pulled out his cellular phone and paged his cousin
back.

Back at the precinct, Ms. Carla Jiminez shouted, "They just
returned our call. It says 10-4. I guess that means they're ready
and waiting." She was looking at her boss and smiling through
her eyes.

Back in the *Edenwald Projects*, Homicide started the engine
on his bike first. Killer followed his homie's lead and Danger
did the same.

Homicide revved his engine by pushing his thumb throt-
tle, waited for the motor to simmer, grabbed the clutch, put the

ATV in first gear and then pulled off. *Itchy and Scratchy* were right behind him. They all hit second gear at the same time, gave it some more gas, placed their right foot near the back brake lever and put the quad's in the air. *Moe, Larry and Curly* each had one of their knees in the seat while their other foot stayed near the back brake as they wheely'd through the projects on their way to the stash house where they kept an arsenal of artillery.

One Hour later ...

Creeping through the 225th Street drive at 5 m.p.h., Curtis' Ford Expedition rolled through with only its fog lights lit. That was a sign that he wasn't in the vehicle. Curtis hated using his fog lights, but warned his lil homies that if they ever saw his truck come through with the fog lights illuminated, that meant someone was scheming and to send his SUV to *Kingdom Come.*

Inside the large vehicle sat Detective Steve Todd, Officer Carla Jiminez and narcotics officers John Santos and Ernie Williams.

The quartet fought to see through the dark tint that blanketed Curtis' windows. The area where the drop was to take place seemed unusually clear for that time of day during the summer season.

A few leaves blew across the ground. It also didn't help ease the tension that hovered in the truck that some of the lights in the neighborhood seemed to be out as well.

But whenever *Homicide, Killer and Danger* rode through the projects on their four wheelers, the tenants *knew* something was up and they always made it inside of their apartments as fast as they could.

"You ready, lil homie?" Homicide was talking to the passenger on his bike.

"No doubt, big homie," replied Lil Hahmo. *Lil Hahmo* was twelve years old. Since the day he turned ten, Homicide had him under his wing.

"Are you ready, young'n?" Killer was talking to his sidekick.

"No doubt, Killer *The Cap Peeler*," replied Lil K.I. *Lil K.I.* was trained just like Lil Hahmo was. They were the two oldest of the triplets.

"B.G., *Baby Gangsta*, you good?" Danger was talking to the third and smallest triplet.

"If it ain't rough, it ain't right. Let's get it popping, big homie," said B.G.

The Ford Expedition came to a halt when the nails that were strategically placed in the street pierced all four tires of the heavy vehicle.

"*What the fuck?*" Steve Todd felt the tires deflate and knew that something was terribly wrong. Then he heard what sounded like a lawn mower come to life.

Homicide and Lil Hahmo came flying from behind one of the buildings closest to the driveway on their two side wheels. When the bike leveled off, the duo pulled up right beside the driver's side window.

Killer and Lil K.I. came from the other side of the street and positioned themselves on the opposite side of the SUV, but in an area where they wouldn't be in the line of fire of their compadres.

"*Say hello to my little friend!*" It was cliché, but Homicide didn't care. Them lil young niggas were from the hood so anything they said sounded gangsta. As soon as Homicide made the statement, he leaned over to the side and gave Lil Hahmo all the elbow room that he needed. Lil Hahmo opened up his Mosberg pump shot gun like an umbrella and emptied his entire 17 shot drum clip into the driver's side front and rear windows and gave whatever else he could to the weak ass windshield. The bullets ejected from Hahmo's rifle like he was shooting a semiautomatic handgun. Glass and brain matter were everywhere.

Killer sat on his bike with two Desert Eagles making the passenger side of the jeep *strip itself.* As the large handguns turned the once luxurious car into recycled metal, K.I.'s lil crazy ass was off the bike walking towards the vehicle firing his two cannons singing, "*I'm from the Bronx, New York, things happen.*"

After the fireworks stopped, Danger and B.G. rode up with two containers of gasoline. The duo ran around the $40,000 heap of twisted metal and emptied the gas in and around the vehicle. B.G. jumped back onto the back of the bike where Danger patiently waited for him, looked at all of his homies who were ready to roll and yelled, "*Bttaatt! Bttaatt!*"

Danger lit his blunt, took a pull and tossed the match into the sport utility vehicle. The truck went up in flames and the *Dream Team* took off like *the fast and the furious.*

Back at the precinct in Queens, the police were beating the *dog shit* out of Curtis. Before going unconscious, Curtis looked up at the big brawny officers who were reenacting the Rodney King incident and mumbled, "*Code of the Streets, nigga,*" then he fell out.

THE END!

Eight months after Larry was arrested, the murder case against him was dismissed due to the apprehension of the real perp.

Curtis died two days later at an area hospital. The press released a report that said he died of a heart attack. But a female nurse sent the original hospital report to Curtis' mom. The document showed that her son died as a result of the beating he took at the precinct. Ms. Martin took the report to Internal Affairs and an investigation has been underway ever since.

Elm City

Travis "Unique" Stevens

CHAPTER ONE

"**W**hat's popping," Stutter asked as he entered his apartment building with his wife Donnicia.

"Just cooling, getting this money as usual," replied Prince. Prince led Stutter and Donnicia through the apartment door. Once inside, Stutter and Prince proceeded toward the rear of the domicile and entered the bathroom. Stutter secured the lock and gave Prince a boost. When Prince grabbed the stack of money from the ceiling, Stutter let him jump down from his cupped hands. "This is what I made today, $8,500," said Prince.

Stutter grabbed the stack of money and was startled by a knock on the door. The taps on the door were a code letting them know that it was one of their own and not a stranger. Hearing this, Stutter became calm again and expected to see Boo Boo on the other side of the door.

Boo Boo was the infamous neighborhood crack runner. Everyone, dealers and users alike knew him. He also worked for Stutter and Prince.

"Who is it?" asked Stutter. As a sign of caution, he placed the money back into the ceiling and walked towards the door. With the chain in place, Stutter cracked open the door. Before he could close it back, the door came crashing in followed by approximately ten masked gunmen.

The assailants were dressed down in camouflage fatigue suits and black military boots. With his gun raised in the air, one of the stick up kids yelled, "Y'all know what it is! Everybody lay on the fuckin' floor!"

A big dude about 6'3", 220 pounds, grabbed Stutter by the nape of his neck and swung his pistol around striking Stutter in the face. "Where the fuck is the stash?" he yelled. While he handled Stutter, the rest of the team went to work searching the apartment.

Prince and Donnicia lay with their heads facing the floor while two of the masked men stood over them with guns pointed at their heads. One of the guys kicked Prince in his side and said, "Nigga, where is the shit?"

"I don't know what you're talking about," he replied nervously. He reached over and tried to comfort Donnicia with a hug, but the guy kicked him again.

"Aaahh!" he screamed.

Donnicia couldn't bear the sight so she sobbed uncontrollably.

"Please don't kill us." Prince was begging for his life.

"Let the girl go. We don't have anything," Stutter chimed in from his position in the living room. He wiped a portion of the blood from his face and decided to make a move that would perhaps ease the tension in the apartment. He dug into his shirt and pulled out his diamond flooded necklace. "This is all I have," he pleaded.

The leader of "*The Midnight Miradas*" put his Glock 40 semiautomatic handgun up to Stutter's head and said, "If your stupid ass tries anything funny, you and your people will be dead in a heartbeat, 'cause I ain't got no problem scattering a nigga's brains all over this here living room."

"We have him with us now," said one of the masked men into one of the mini walkie talkies. "Everything is going as planned," he added.

Hoping to save him and his friends' lives, Stutter decided to show the gunmen where they kept their stash. He motioned for the guy who was holding him to follow him to the bathroom. He looked toward the ceiling and said, "It's up there."

The gunman smacked him with his gun and said, "Well get it, and you better not try anything funny."

Stutter stepped on the toilet, then the sink, slid a portion of the drop ceiling over and grabbed the bundle of money. Nervously he said, "That's everything we have, I swear. You have my shines, you got my dough, please, let the girl go," he begged.

"Show us where the back door to this place is," the stick up kid in charge of Stutter stated. When Stutter complied with the man's request, the rest of the posse was right behind them.

Stutter guided whom he'd come to know as "*The most feared gang in the city*" to the rear exit. He silently prayed along the way that he and his friends would make it out of there alive.

"It's dark back here, so watch your step," said Stutter. "*The drama is almost over,*" he thought.

The small crowd followed Stutter down a narrow staircase in a single file. They held the tails of one another's garments so as not to lose each other as they crept through the dark exit way. The only light the group had was from the beams on their infrared scopes. The crew successfully made it to the exit. Once they were outside, Stutter looked at his shirt in an effort to wipe off any dust that may have accumulated while they traveled through the stairway. What he noticed next, he had only seen in a movie once. Several tiny red dots covered his white T-shirt. *"I'm about to be a dead man."* thought Stutter.

"Where's everyone?" one of the gunmen screamed through his two-way radio.

"Everyone is out, send the other two through now," the leader replied.

"10-4," was all that was said. A moment later, they heard two gunshots. In the background, what could be heard as a muffled scream crept through the passageway.

"Let's get the fuck outta here!" yelled the leader. He waved his gang on as they all ran and jumped into their getaway car. A lone masked man sat nervously behind the wheel of a dark grey fifteen-passenger club van.

Stutter and one of the gunmen stood in silence as *Clint Eastwood* waited for the last *Midnight Mirada* to make his appearance. "I should body your ass right here," said the masked man. He raised his gun to Stutter's head and demanded that he turn around.

"If you're going to kill me, you got to kill me face to face." Stutter knew the man was serious, but he had to take a chance.

When the last gunman exited the building, he grabbed his comrade and said, "Come on, nigga, fuck him, he good," he trotted along, stopped after a few steps and looked to see if his compadre acknowledged him. When he got his confirmation, he continued on and hopped up into the van with his crew.

Stutter snapped out of his trance because when the last gunman spoke, his voice seemed very familiar. The man sounded like a guy named John John that lived over on Truman Street. Stutter knew his voice because every week that same voice would ask him for his weekly supply of five ounces of crack cocaine. Stutter thought to himself, *"This nigga just saved my life, if it's him. But why?"*

"You're a lucky ma'fucka. I should've blown your wig back when I had the chance," yelled the gunman. He gave Stutter one more long ugly stare, then dashed off and met the other masked men inside the van. The over-sized vehicle sped off and disappeared down the street.

Stutter heard cries from inside the apartment. He raced back toward the building and as he got closer, the moans got louder. He ran up the steps and made it back to his crack spot. When he opened the door, he yelled inside, "Prince! Donnicia! Are you guys okay?"

"We're in here," screamed Donnicia. She ran into the kitchen and met up with Stutter. She assured him that the remaining gunmen were gone, that they left out the front door and jumped into an awaiting car.

"Where's Prince?" he asked nervously.

Donnicia looked over toward the living room. Stutter brushed past her and almost passed out when he spotted his cousin balled up on the floor in the fetal position. Blood was leaking from his chest as he tried to breathe.

Prince looked up at his cousin and in a low tone said, "They shot me in the chest. I tried to make a run for it, but I wasn't fast enough."

"Hang in there, kid, you'll be ahight," said Stutter. He handed Donnicia the telephone so she could call 911. The trio waited patiently until the paramedics arrived. Once on the scene, the medical technicians did all they could as they placed Prince inside the ambulance. The crew worked feverishly as they tried to save the dying kid's life on their way to Yale Medical Center.

At the hospital, Stutter paced up and down wondering if his cousin would make it. Over and over again he said to himself, *"Boo Boo had to set this shit up."*

When the doctors at the hospital told Stutter that it would be a while before anyone knew anything, Stutter decided to go home and wait until he heard something further. Stutter was extremely emotional. "They shot my cousin, and he might not make it," he yelled. Stutter marched over to the kitchen sink, knelt down and reached under it. He pulled out a shoebox that contained a stack of one hundred dollar bills and a rusty 38 revolver.

Curious, Donnicia looked at Stutter as he examined the old weapon. "What are you going to do with that gun, Stutter?" she asked.

"I think I have an idea who could've done something like this to us," he said matter of factly. Stutter loaded the weapon, tucked it into his waistband and waited for the hospital to call.

When Stutter's cell phone rang, Donnicia answered it and was delivered the disturbing news that Prince didn't make it. Immediately she burst into tears. "Noooo!" she screamed, then dropped the phone.

When Stutter retrieved the phone from the floor, the caller had already hung up. Donnicia was hurting so Stutter waited for her to calm down so she could brief him with the details. After about two minutes, she told him what the doctor told her. "Those bastards shot Prince in the chest. The bullet penetrated his heart." She was crying again. "We lost him, Stutter." Stutter stood there helpless, with tears in his eyes and revenge in his heart.

Stutter looked up toward the sky and said in a low tone, "I'll get whoever did this to you, cousin, no matter what it takes."

Stutter lowered his head and with his fingers made the sign of the cross on his face and chest. At the end of the motion, he kissed his index and middle fingers and said to himself, "I love you, kid."

CHAPTER TWO

Stutter and Prince were first cousins. Their mothers were sisters with Prince's mom being the younger of the two. Both families grew up in a small city in Connecticut called New Haven. Though Prince's mom was younger than Stutter's, Prince was four years Stutter's senior.

As the two teens got older, they decided they wanted to live together. Being jobless forced them to the slums of Elm City, Truman Street.

The apartment was in Prince's name, his mom cosigned and the duo spent eight months fixing up the place making it comfortable and livable. During the time they spent there, Prince and Stutter met and became friends with a few people on the block. A few female acquaintances came by every so often and spent whatever time they were allowed with the two youngsters.

Stutter and Prince made their living selling drugs via cell phone. Then one day Stutter happened upon a guy named Boo Boo. Boo Boo used to be a big time heroine dealer throughout the 90s, but started to decline once he started getting high on his own supply. Afterward, he turned into being the neighborhood crack runner. To support his habit, Boo Boo would run customers to another neighborhood crack dealer by the name of John John. That was until a little guy named Scotty that he found sitting on his right shoulder one morning told him to *beam up to the mothership*. When Boo Boo asked *how*, Little Scotty told him to *put the pipe to his mouth, flick his lighter and inhale*. Later on, he came to his senses in a hail of punches by John John and his crew. After he recovered, Stutter became his new boss.

Stutter and Prince agreed to run a crack house with Boo Boo as their #1 runner. The trio made up a particular knock for their door, to assure one another that it was one of them knocking and not the police or stick up kids.

Little did they know that John John was still the man in charge of Truman Street. He felt if a nickel bag was sold on the block, he wanted in on it. John John was in control of a young crew of thugs who were eager to rob, steal, hustle drugs and even kill if they had to. The team called themselves *"The Midnight Miradas."* They were known for flooding the city with guns and drugs, and they had a reputation for leaving dead bodies wherever they wanted to. They also had a trademark to let you know it was them; infrared beams attached to all of their weapons. They were also known to travel in groups in a large dark grey club van. During the day, people were safe because the Midnight Miradas only hunted their victims after dark.

No one dared to go through Truman Street if they didn't know anyone. The street was six city blocks long with one way in and only one way out. The area was known for its abundance of drugs, drug users and drug dealers, and it also had the highest unsolved murder rate throughout the entire city. Statistically, Truman Street averaged fifteen homicides a year.

After four months of flooding the streets with crack and heroine, Stutter and Prince's business began increasing. Then one day John John decided he'd had enough.

"They're stopping too much money around here," John John stated to the other members of his gang.

"We should get with the kids from Adeline Projects," one of the members of his crew suggested. John John reluctantly agreed and the two proceeded to the six-story housing development in search of a guy named *Tiny Tim*.

Tiny Tim was a big, husky dude about 6'3", 200 pounds, and about twenty-six years of age. Tim controlled all of the money that came through the Adeline Projects.

When they met up in the front of one of Tiny Tim's spots, the three of them discussed the issue of Stutter and Prince and how the duo was stopping money from flowing. When the trio came up with their plan, they agreed that it would be ten men to enter the premises, while five men waited outside. Their force of entry wouldn't be forced at all. They would simply use their former pal, Boo Boo.

"But we'll still need an inside source to know when Prince and Stutter would be in the apartment together," said John John, as his fist rested on the bottom of his chin.

"We'll do it *Midnight Mirada* style. Masks and fatigues, so no one can identify us," said Tiny Tim with a smirk on his face.

"Let's find Boo Boo," Blitz said in an anxious tone.

The small group proceeded to look for Boo Boo. They searched every crack building in the area. They went to every down low crack spot in the neighborhood as well and no one had seen him.

Then Tim began to recollect. His marijuana use caused him short-term memory loss and when they really needed him, his mind decided to work in their favor. "Yo, I think I seen that nigga on the boulevard last night, over Paula's crib," he said in an excited tone of voice.

Everyone looked at him like, *"You knew where the nigga might be all this time, stupid?"* Then John John said, "Oh, the skinny chick that got the mole on her forehead, right?"

When Tim nodded his head in agreement, he ran around to the front door of his silver Lexus 430 and unlocked the passenger doors. The men hopped in and sped off in the direction of Paula's crib.

When they approached Paula's neighborhood, Blitz spotted Boo Boo first. "There goes that clown right there," he shouted. Blitz pointed in Boo Boo's direction and when John John spotted their target, he told Tim to pull up to the corner store and blow the horn.

Beep!...Beep!

Boo Boo acknowledged them. "What's going on, my main man John John?" Boo Boo seemed surprised to see his former boss.

"Get in the car!" yelled Tim. Tim exited the car, ran around to the passenger side of the vehicle and opened the door for their mark. Boo Boo hesitated at first. He smelled trouble. When Tim showed him the butt of his gun that sat in his waistline, Boo Boo reluctantly got in the back of the luxury sedan.

"What did I do?" Boo Boo screamed. "I thought my debt was clear with you, John John." John John ignored him and let Blitz handle the situation. Blitz pulled out a 9mm and placed the barrel of the gun in Boo Boo's mouth.

"Yo, be easy kid. We're on the road. We don't need any blue and whites catching feelings, now do we?" John John rearranged his statement in the form of a question so it didn't seem like he was trying to belittle his partner. John John was turned around facing Blitz and Boo Boo.

Tim turned down Truman Street and when he reached the building, he backed the large sedan around the back of the complex.

"What's going on, man?" cried Boo Boo. "I thought we were done," he added.

The men exited the car and John John led them into the apartment building.

"You ahight, kid, I'm not going to harm you. I just need some vital information about some niggas in building 25. Stutter and Prince." As he let his statement sink in, he opened the door to one of his crack houses and led everyone inside.

"I can't do that to them. Them niggas are good people. Them cats only did good things for me when I was down and out. When y'all niggas dissed me, Stutter and Prince held me down," explained Boo Boo. He realized that he had probably crossed the line by praising Prince and Stutter, so he glanced at the trio's faces to see how they felt about his feelings toward his homeboys.

"You don't have a choice, *nigga*. You're either gonna tell me what I want to hear, or you're gonna catch a slug to your melon," said John John in a harsh tone. He threw Blitz a $20 sack of Purple Haze, weed, and let Blitz do his thing on the roll up tip.

As Blitz administered his artwork with the rolling of the blunt, he shared what was on his mind. "Let me scatter this ma'fucka's brains all over the wall, homie."

Boo Boo knew Blitz was serious. If he didn't tell John John and them what was up with Prince and Stutter, he knew he'd end up with his toe tagged. Reluctantly, he agreed.

"I'll help y'all, but y'all have to keep this shit on the hush hush tip. Y'all can't let anyone now that y'all got this information from me."

"Don't worry, we got you." John John smiled his famous smirk.

Boo Boo went on and on telling the trio the in's and out's to Stutter and Prince's business and every day affairs. He told them how much money they brought in on a daily basis and he went as far as telling them about the customary knock.

When Boo Boo seemed like he was done spilling the beans, John John treated him like he was supposed to be treated. "Get the fuck up outta here and go run me some sales or something, you fucking fiend," John John yelled at him and tried to kick him in his back as he exited the apartment.

Once Boo Boo was off the premises, John John grabbed the blunt of Purple Haze from his buddy, took one long pull, and passed the joint to Tiny Tim.

"Yo, we got 'em now. We just need an inside source to let us know when them niggas are going to be inside the spot together," said John John as he blew smoke through his nose.

"That's going to be hard. You know them niggas don't fuck with nobody from the 'Hill.' They only fuck with niggas from the 'Ville,'" said Tim. He grabbed the blunt and took a few drags.

When he offered it to Blitz, Blitz declined and said, "What's popping with Pretty?"

Pretty was a distant member of the "Midnight Mirada" crew. Pretty was a drug dealer who only sold his product in large amounts from a housing development called *"The Jungle."* "The Jungle" is an eight-building complex known for breeding the flyest of dudes. Pretty was the one member of the crew that slept with almost every female around town. He drove a black on black 500SL Mercedes Benz and he also owned a black on black Ducatti motorcycle.

"He's supposed to have this exclusive party jumping off tonight," said John John as he accepted the blunt from Tim. After taking a pull, he proceeded to call Pretty.

Ring... Ring...

"Speak to me," Pretty answered his phone on the second ring. He was pulled over on his motorcycle already speaking with someone when John John buzzed in.

"I'm downtown. Where are you?" Pretty asked in a curious tone. Before John John could answer, Pretty said, "As a matter of fact, meet me at the Omni Hotel. I got a room up there."

"I'll be through there in a minute. Be outside by the red carpet," John John stated. John John and his crew jumped into the Lexus and headed for the Omni Hotel.

When they arrived at the hotel, Blitz noticed Pretty as soon as they pulled up.

Pretty was standing beside his bike with a printed helmet and a Prada motorcycle jacket to match. "Pull over here and park," Pretty said, directing the trio with his hands.

"What's the deal?" John John asked as he hopped out of the car and gave Pretty their customary handshake that ended with two snaps of their fingers.

"I'm cooling, trying to get this party in order," Pretty replied. He told his associates to hold on, then answered his cell phone. "What's up, baby girl? Let me call you back in a half hour."

"Okay, Beau," the female on the other end replied.

"Damn kid, who was that?" Blitz yelled. He walked over to where John John and Pretty stood.

"Oh, that was this 'jumpoff' that I met last week in Manhattan, in 'The Village,' I was down there shopping."

"Does she have any friends?" Blitz asked.

"Nizz-aw, as a matter of fact, she from New Haven, and she got some herb nigga for a husband. She said he hustles somewhere around here for Prince and Stutter. Something like that." Pretty wasn't sure, but he remembered her telling him something like that.

"That's Prince and Stutter from the 'hood, building 25." Tiny Tim shouted in a gleeful state of shock.

"What's her name?" John John asked as he placed his hand on Pretty's shoulder.

"Donnicia," Pretty said.

"Donnicia!" Blitz said. He looked at John John with a smile on his face.

"What's popping?" Pretty asked.

"Yo, them herb niggas you talking about are getting a little money. And they in our hood," John John said with anger in his voice.

"Yeah, we gave them a pass and they started cutting our throat. So now we have to get rid of them niggas, or scare them up or something. I don't think they're built like that anyway," Blitz said. He reached for the handlebars on Pretty's bike.

"Well, I'm supposed to be getting up with her and her friend tonight. I'll see what's popping with her. You know, if she loves the nigga or not," said Pretty.

"My man, like fifty grand," John John stated.

"So, John John, I'll see if her friend wants to holla at you. I'll let you know after the party," Pretty assured him. Pretty placed his helmet halfway on his head and jumped on his motorcycle.

"One love," shouted Tim. The threesome then entered their vehicle and continued discussing the issue concerning Prince and Stutter.

Hours had passed and the big party that Pretty had thrown was over. Pretty jumped into his spacious 500SL and picked up his mobile phone. He called Donnicia to see what was up for the night.

Ring...

"Hello?" It was Donnicia.

"What's good, baby girl? I'm cooling, I had a nice time tonight at the party, but I would have had an even better time if I could've gotten up with you and your girlfriend. I have my man with me and we're looking forward to having some fun," Pretty said as his frame was tucked low in the driver's seat of his Benz.

"Sure, why not? My husband ain't around and that nigga don't be giving me shit anyways. He don't run nothing," Donnicia stated in her drunken state.

"So yo, come to the Omni Hotel, room 64, 5th floor. Me and my man will be here waiting for y'all," Pretty replied. He hung up with Donnicia and called John John. Once he got in touch with his man, he told him what went down and told him to meet him at the hotel.

"What room, nigga?" John John asked. You could tell by his voice that he was excited.

By 3 a.m., every one had made it to the room. The sight of the suite fascinated the two women and John John was eager to find out what he needed to know about Prince and Stutter. When John John and Pretty felt that they had the women under their control, the duo decided it was time to break the news to Donnicia about what they had in store for her boyfriend and his cousin.

"I mean, we ain't trying to hurt them niggas. We just want to scare them niggas off. We really think it's in their best interest anyway. Some dude is already talking about killing them niggas," John John said convincingly.

"Shit, I could care less. The nigga don't be blessing me like that anyway. As long as y'all don't kill them cats, I'll let you know what's up," Donnicia said. She took a hit of the marijuana cigarette and passed it to her friend.

"Don't worry, sweetheart, I'll make sure they don't get hurt. You just play your part like if you're a victim yourself," John John stated.

The plan was in motion, so all the "Midnight Miradas" had to do was wait.

CHAPTER THREE

Stutter had rage in his heart. He and Donnicia ran down the stairs and jumped into his candy apple red Lincoln Navigator. They raced down the one-way street and headed for Stutter's two-bedroom condominium in West Haven. West haven was about fifteen minutes away from the city. They arrived at his parking lot. During the entire fifteen minute ride, the duo sat in total silence.

Donnicia broke the silence by saying, "I'm sorry about what happened tonight. Prince tried to make a run for it toward the rear of the apartment, but one of the guys let off two shots. Prince wasn't fast enough."

"I'm sorry, but we have to move on. We have to plan for the future," said Sutter.

"Why don't you come in so I can run you a nice tub of hot bath water," said Donnicia.

"Nah, I'll be ahight. I have a lot of thinking to do. Besides, I have to explain to my aunt what happened." Stutter's response was low, and he seemed very sad about the fate of his cousin. He clutched Donnicia's hand and gave her a kiss on her forehead.

"Don't be out all night. I might start worrying," said Donnicia as she stepped away from the big SUV. Stutter waited until he saw Donnicia walk into the six-story complex, then he drove off.

When Donnicia entered the elevator, she quickly reached into her Salvatore Ferragamo pocketbook and pulled out her cellular phone. She scanned through the list of names she had programmed into her Nextel and stopped at the initials "*P.Y.*" She pressed the "*send*" button and waited for it to ring.

Ring... Pretty picked up.

"Hello!" Donnicia screamed into the telephone.

"Speak to me," Pretty said as calm as he could ever be.

"What the fuck did y'all ma'fuckas do tonight?" she yelled. She pressed "6" and rode the elevator to the sixth floor.

"What are you talking about?" Pretty asked, sounding confused. He got up from his sofa and grabbed the remote control to his plasma T.V. and added, "What happened?"

"What happened? John John killed Prince, that's what happened. I thought you ma'fuckas promised me that nobody was gonna get hurt," she said, pissed off. When the elevator reached her floor, Donnicia exited the conveyor, walked down the hall and entered into her apartment. She placed her keys along with her purse on the counter in her kitchen and took off her knee high boots to relax her feet.

"I'll find out what popped off. I didn't participate in that bullshit. I don't have any beef with your peoples. That's John John and them," said Pretty.

"Well, this nigga is about to do something crazy. They killed his cousin. So be careful," Donnicia said. Then she pressed the "*end*" button.

She thought to herself, "*What have I done? I should have never trusted them grimy ma'fuckas in the first place.*"

Meanwhile in New Haven ...

Stutter roamed the streets in search of Boo Boo. He went building to building looking for the scared crackhead. He was about to pay Paula a visit to see if she had seen or heard from Boo Boo. On his route to Paula's crib, he spotted Boo Boo walking from the direction of Paula's house. He pulled his Lincoln Navigator over and jumped out. Boo Boo tried to run, but because the drugs tore into his once athletic body, it was to no avail. Stutter quickly caught up to him.

"What's popping, nigga. Why you running?" Stutter asked while catching his own breath. He looked around, and when he noticed that the coast was clear, he pulled out the 38 revolver he had snatched up earlier. He pointed it at Boo Boo's head.

"Please, don't kill me. Please, please," Boo Boo begged.

"You had my cousin killed. Tell me who was involved with this bullshit," Stutter yelled. He then put the gun in Boo Boo's mouth.

"It was John John and Blitz. They threatened to kill me if I didn't tell them what they wanted to know," Boo Boo stated. He gagged on the barrel of the revolver. "I didn't mean for it to go down this way, man. Please, forgive me," he continued.

"Ask God for forgiveness ma'fucka!" Stutter replied. He held his hand steady and pulled the trigger.

Boo Boo's eyes closed, and a moment later, the back of his head was blown all over the concrete. Stutter ran back to his truck, jumped in and pulled off. His heart raced 100 miles a second. He trembled as he held the steering wheel steady. He began wiping blood from his T-shirt. Paranoid from what just transpired, he pulled into a dark alley to calm down.

Back at Pretty's Place ...

Pretty paced back and forth as he waited for John John to answer his cellular phone.

"What's hood," John John answered. He put his index finger up to his lips to indicate to Blitz and Tiny Tim to quiet down.

"What's going on? Shorty called me bugging out. She said something went wrong and ma'fuckas got killed." He lit a cigarette and waited for a response from John John.

"I tried to make shit clean, but one of my little homies shot the nigga. He said the nigga tried to rush him," John John explained.

"His man is out there looking for niggas right now. That nigga, Stutter. And shorty said he was strapped, so stay low," Pretty said in a concerned tone of voice.

"I'm good. I'm about to get some sleep. I got things to take care of in the morning," John John replied. He wasn't even concerned about the information that Pretty just gave him. He ended the call and went on to tell the other members of the "Midnight Miradas" to stay low and stay alert.

In the dark alley, Stutter sat in shock. He couldn't believe what he had just done. He thought, *"Who could've known that I would have gone to pick up money at that hour. I didn't tell anyone except Prince."* Police sirens startled him. He snapped out of his thought, put the SUV in *"drive"* and crept out of the alley. He looked in both directions, scanning the boulevard. He was looking to see where the police went when he noticed a traffic jam with police and an ambulance present. Stutter cruised by in the slow moving traffic. He passed the scene of the crime and almost threw up on himself when he noticed all the blood around

Boo Boo's mangled body. He glanced at the detectives and noticed that they were New Haven's Homicide. Stutter made the first turn, picked up his mobile phone and called his aunt, Prince's mother. He had to explain to her the tragic news about her son.

As he pressed the numbers on his cell, he thought about Prince and how and why they decided to hustle on Truman Street in the first place.

When his aunt picked up the phone, he briefed her about the situation.

"No, no, no!" she cried. She screamed into the phone, "Please don't tell me they killed my baby. That's my only son. What did I do to deserve this?" she questioned herself as well as her nephew.

Stutter tried to comfort his aunt. "It wasn't your fault. Some jealous dudes on Truman Street did this. I'll get them if it's the last thing that I do." He pulled over, put his hazard lights on and lit an already rolled blunt of Purple Haze weed. "I'll talk to you tomorrow," he added, then placed the phone back on the stand.

Stutter took long, slow drags from his blunt. He put his truck back in "*drive*" and proceeded to go and find John John. He rolled through the Adeline Street housing project, but no one was out there except for a few crack fiends. He passed back through Truman Street, pulled over and parked. Stutter leaned his seat all the way back and killed the engine. He grabbed the 38 and placed it under the seat, and with his heavily tinted windows, he relaxed in the softness of his sofa-like seats.

A moment later, he zoomed in on a lady that was walking by. He cracked open his door and waved her over to his vehicle.

She acknowledged him and that's when he noticed it was Sheila, an old heroine addict.

Sheila was in her mid 30s and if you didn't know she was an addict, you couldn't tell simply by looking at her. She had a honey brown complexion and stood 5'4". She also weighed about 130 pounds. Her measurements were 36D-28-40.

"Yo, let me get at you for a minute," Stutter stated. He stepped out from his truck to show her who he was.

"What you got for me, Stutter baby?" Sheila asked with her scratchy voice. She tugged at the zipper of Stutter's pants.

Stutter jumped back and said, "No, no. I'm trying to find John John and them. Have you seen any of them around?"

"I seen them in building 17 about two hours ago," Sheila answered. She was getting frustrated because Stutter wouldn't let her suck him off for a fix. He walked back over to his Lincoln, opened the door, and just before he entered his Navi, undercover officers came closing in on him from all angles.

"Freeze, don't move! If you move, I'll blow your fuckin' head off!" one of the detectives shouted. He had his gun pointed at Stutter as he walked toward him. The officer pulled Stutter from his sport utility vehicle and searched the jeep. Two other officers searched Stutter, cuffed him, turned him around to face them and began asking him a slew of questions.

"Why are you out here at this time of night?" one of the officers asked.

"I live in building 25. We had a tragedy in my family tonight. My cousin was killed. I was just coming to make sure the apartment was locked," Stutter replied.

His eyes stretched wide when one of the detectives produced the revolver he had tucked underneath the seat. The officer held the weapon up in the air, looked at Stutter and said, "What do we have here? What were you doing with this in your possession? There's been a shooting in the area and this could be the murder weapon." The officer pulled out a plastic bag, placed the rusty gun inside of it, looked at his fellow officers and chuckled, "Malcolm X wouldn't like this one bit. We have another one killing their own brother."

"I didn't kill anyone. I'm clean. I live over here. The lady that y'all let go is the one who left that gun in my truck," Stutter tried to explain with tears streaming down his face. "Please, call my wife."

"Tell it to a judge," The lead detective stated in a calm manner. They forced Stutter into the back of the tinted Nissan Altima, drove him to Whalley Avenue Precinct and placed him in a holding cell.

Once inside, Stutter thought to himself, *"This can't be happening. First my cousin, then I go and do some stupid shit like this. I should've stayed my ass home when Donnicia told me to. Now I'm looking at twenty-five to life."* A small, clean-cut white man with glasses popped open the steel cell door and told Stutter to follow him. Behind Stutter was a uniformed officer with bags under his eyes. The duo proceeded to fingerprint Stutter, and after he was finished, he was taken before a judge, arraigned and denied bond.

After his court appearance, Stutter was brought back to the precinct for interrogation.

"Look, son, you can help yourself," suggested Sergeant Robinson. He looked into Stutter's eyes, leaned back into his office chair and folded his arms.

"What do you mean I can help myself?" Stutter asked confused.

Sergeant Robinson lit a Marlboro cigarette, blew smoke in Stutter's face, grinned and said, "I know you know who killed your cousin tonight. So if you help us, we can help you explain to Judge Nevas why you were parked on Truman Street with a gun in your possession that was just used in a homicide."

"I wish I could tell you who killed my cousin, I would be glad to," Stutter said. He asked the officer for a drag off of his cigarette. The officer waved him off.

"So you wanna play hardball? When you go in front of the judge tomorrow, maybe you'll come to your senses," Sergeant Robinson retorted. He got up and signaled for his fellow officers to take Stutter back to the cold holding cell. One of the officers gave Stutter a roll of blankets, some sheets, a plastic bag that contained a bar of soap, a tube of toothpaste and a toothbrush.

"Where is my one phone call? I need to call my attorney!" Stutter yelled through the slot of the steel door. When he saw that the officers weren't going to give him his one phone call, he unwrapped the blankets and sheets, then made himself a bed on the cold, hard floor.

CHAPTER FOUR

Back on Truman Street ...

John John was preparing to rob old man Slick. Old man Slick was a black dude in his late 40s. He ran a boot legging house that operated after hours. Slick was leery about putting his money in banks, so he kept all of his earnings in a safe in his bedroom.

John John and Blitz used to play numbers at Slick's spot. They watched Slick for weeks and realized if they pulled their heist during the early morning hours, no one would suspect that the Midnight Miradas were behind it.

John John stumbled over to the couch where Blitz was asleep. He yelled, "Yo, it's 6:30 in the morning. Get up. We have to go and meet Nut on Howard Avenue." John John tugged on Blitz's arm until his eyes popped open.

In a sleepish tone, Blitz responded, "I'm up already." He slowly regained his composure, stretched, got up and went to use the bathroom. The duo got dressed in their usual attire consisting of Army fatigue suits and boots, and hopped up into their club van. They headed for Howard Avenue to meet Nut, the one who pulled the trigger on that fateful night, killing Prince. Nut was in position where he was to meet Blitz and John John with a few ski masks and three semiautomatic handguns. Little did they know they were being trailed by two undercover detectives in an unmarked Ford Taurus. At the meeting place, Nut was patiently waiting with a black Nike duffle bag. When John John and Blitz pulled up, Nut jumped into the van with his two homeboys.

"What's popping? Do you have everything?" Blitz asked anxiously. Nut nodded and Blitz reached over and grabbed the huge bag hoping to get first dibs on the artillery. John John slapped Blitz's hand and told him to wait until they reached old man Slick's crib.

Before the trio could proceed with their plan and pull off, a small army of undercover task force agents descended upon the large vehicle. The agents pulled right up to the driver's side door, blocking John John from trying to escape. Nut and Blitz made a run for it, but one of them was unsuccessful. One of the task force officers chased Blitz down and caught him a half a block away. Nut got away but had to leave the duffle bag with the loaded weapons behind.

The officers pulled John John from the van and proceeded to search him. They handcuffed both him and Blitz, shoved them into the unmarked squad cars and headed for the Whalley Avenue county jail. There, they were booked, fingerprinted and taken to a small room. John John was interrogated first.

A tall, thin, Spanish detective grabbed the arms of John John's chair, leaned into him and said in a nasty, raspy voice, "The word around town is, you guys belong to some kind of gang from off of Truman Street. That's my area, and a whole lot of dead bodies have been turning up on my tour. Please, tell me you're not responsible for any of those killings."

John John looked on, relaxed. He tried to see if the detective really knew anything. He cleared his throat and said, "I'm not from Truman Street, and I don't belong to any gang. I was just giving some friends a ride home."

"We've been watching you for four months, John John. Our surveillance team has gathered up enough evidence to put you away for a long time. Now that we have you, you better act smart and save yourself," Detective Gomez stated. He circled John John, stopped, looked him up and down, reached into his shirt pocket and pulled out an old pack of Newports. He tapped the base of the pack, pulled out a loosy, lit it and reluctantly offered a smoke to John John.

John John declined with a simple wave of his hand and said, "You may as well take me back to that holding cell so that the judge can see me, because I don't know anything and I'm not talking to anyone until I see my lawyer."

"Fine, tough guy. We'll see how tough you are when you realize that you might not be seeing your family as a free man ever again." The detective laughed. He signaled for one of the uniformed officers to take John John back to the holding cell, and for them to also bring in Blitz.

For two hours, the questioning went on. Neither John John nor Blitz violated the code of silence. Afterward, the duo was brought before a judge and arraigned on a charge of 924C, possession of a firearm while already a felon. The case was federal. For hours, Blitz and John John thought of ways to come up with the hefty bond of $250,000 while they sat in the holding cell.

"I wonder if Nut got away?" questioned Blitz. He laid back and gazed off at the wall in front of him.

"Let's give him a couple of hours and then we'll call him

over at Rita's house," John John replied. He sat beside Blitz and began fumbling with his hands.

"No, wait!" Blitz yelled excitedly. Like a kid in a candy store, he jumped to his feet and said, "Pretty. Let's holla at Pretty. I know he got the money."

The duo heard keys, then the steel door popped open. It was a correctional officer. He asked the guys if they wanted lunch, and if they had anyone they wanted to call. They both agreed to lunch and the phone call.

Stutter was awakened when he heard voices coming from the outside of his cell door. When his door popped open, an attractive black lady in a C.O.'s outfit cordially said, "Mr. Troy Best, get ready for court. I'll be back in a moment."

"What time is it?" Stutter asked. He got up and grabbed his small cosmetic bag.

"It's 7:30 a.m.," she said before closing the door behind her.

Stutter freshened up the best way he could and waited for the officer to return. As he sat, he thought to himself, *"How can I get myself out of this jam? Maybe they don't know about Boo Boo's murder?"*

The female officer returned and told Stutter to stand up and turn around. He did so and after the woman handcuffed him, she led him to a nearby staircase. They walked up to the eighth floor and proceeded to Judge Nevas' courtroom. Stutter went to see if he would be granted bond, and once again, his request was denied. Stutter was also appointed an attorney and was immediately given time with his new esquire to discuss his case.

Stutter was escorted to a nearby booth where his lawyer

was anxiously waiting. "Hello, Mr. Best, I'm Mr. Hall, your attorney." The two of them shook hands. Mr. Hall continued. "You can still hire yourself a private attorney if you choose to, but if you can't afford one, I'll gladly put forth my best effort in defending you." He smiled a fake smile. Mr. Hall adjusted his glasses with his middle finger, then added, "Mr. Best, you've been charged with murder in the first degree. Also possession of a firearm. This doesn't look too good so far," he said while shuffling through his paperwork.

"I know, but I didn't have that gun that they're charging me with. I mean, I didn't own the gun. Someone left it in my truck." No matter how guilty he was, Stutter was adamant about sticking to his story. He looked toward the ceiling, then back at his attorney and asked, "Can I please make my phone call? I would like to call my wife because she's the one who can verify my whereabouts when this incident allegedly took place. She'll vouch for me," he said.

Mr. Hall signaled for the court officer, then added, "I can help you get a deal if you'd like. The prosecutor says if you help them, they'll pull some strings to help you get out of this mess."

When the marshal arrived, Mr. Hall explained that Stutter was never given his phone call and that he would appreciate it if he could take Stutter down to booking so that his client could use the telephone.

"Sure, why not? I'll confirm it with the judge and the prosecutor, and we'll take him right down afterward," insisted the marshal.

Mr. Hall looked at Stutter, raised his brow, sighed and said, "I hope you understand what kind of trouble you're in, young man. Whatever happens, I would love to see you do the right thing. I know if the shoe was on their foot, and they had a chance to tell on you, they most certainly would. I'm sure of it."

Two burly marshals along with Mr. Hall marched Stutter down to the first floor. There he waited an hour before he was cleared to use the telephone. One of the court marshals asked Stutter to give them the number that he was trying to reach. He slowly began reciting the numbers out loud. "1-203- um, 1-203-931-5555." He grabbed the phone and waited for Donnicia to answer.

Ring ... Ring!

"Hello," Donnicia answered. She was worried.

"Yo, what up?"

"Where are you, baby?" she asked sounding concerned.

"I'm in fucking jail, for a murder. The only thing I need for you to do is confirm my whereabouts. Let these people here know that I was with you when this crime took place," Stutter explained as he glared at the marshals who were talking with his attorney.

Donnicia cried as the news she was just delivered placed her into a state of shock. "No, no, no. Please tell me that you didn't go and do anything stupid." She wiped tears from her eyes and continued, "I'll be there in a minute." Then she hung up the phone.

"She's coming down here to tell you guys where I was when this crime took place," Stutter said calmly. He sat back in the office chair and massaged his shoulders while he waited for his girlfriend to arrive.

CHAPTER FIVE

Blitz and John John ate their cheese sandwiches, then John John went to make his phone call. He called Pretty to see if his partner would post the ten percent of the hefty $250,000 bond.

The phone rang. Ring... Ring!

"Speak to me," Pretty said in his usual bossy drawl. He stood in front of his eight housing unit complex.

"Yo, it's me, John John. The police got me and Blitz down here on Whalley Avenue. They pulled us over and found some heaters. The toasts were clean, but they gave us a $250,000 bond," John John whispered.

"Two hundred fifty thousand! Damn kid, I got a little something, but I won't be able to come and scoop the both of y'all. I'm only holding like fifteen thousand right now," Pretty said. He immediately made a U-turn in his Benz and headed for his stash house.

"Yo, family, that's good enough. I'll add what I have to that, and once I touch down, I'll come back and get Blitz myself," John John stated. He was a little bit more relaxed now that he had spoken to his man Pretty.

John John hung up the phone and the uniformed officer placed him back into the holding cell. He then motioned for

Blitz to come and make his phone call. Blitz called Nut over at Rita's house. Rita was the mother of Nut's son's. On the third ring, she answered.

Ring... Ring... Ring!

"Hello" said Rita.

"Rita, this is Blitz. Have you seen Nut?" Blitz asked. He spoke softly into the receiver. He looked around to see if any of the marshals were watching him, then he continued. "This nigga got away, but me and John John weren't so lucky. Po Po snatched us up on some bullshit and now we need a little money to get outta here. So when you speak to him, tell him to make sure that he hollers at Pretty for me. Tell him that Pretty will explain everything to him when they kick it."

"Alright, but I hope y'all don't put me up in y'all's mess," Rita replied in a motherly tone.

The marshal came to see if Blitz was finished and once confirmed, he took Blitz back to the cold holding cell where John John sat quietly.

Two court officers bent the corner with Sutter in tow. Stutter and Blitz caught eye contact and immediately recognized one another. The officer lead Blitz into the cell and shut the steel door while Stutter was rushed into an adjacent cell.

Confused, Stutter asked, "Excuse me, C.O., what is that guy doing in here? The guy I just passed. And *please*, get my lawyer for me again. I need to see him, now."

"I don't know what those guys are in here for, but we'll go and get your attorney for you in a second," said the marshal. The court officer and his partner walked over to where the other correctional officers stood and began casual conversation.

In the meantime, Stutter thought to himself, "*What the*

fuck_is Blitz doing up in here? I wonder what they locked him up for?_It can't be for Prince." Stutter didn't know that John John was also locked up. When the marshal said guys instead of just guy, Stutter wasn't paying it much attention so it never dawned on him that someone else was arrested with Blitz.

In the other cell, Blitz stood around in a state of shock. He said to his partner in crime, "Yo, that kid Stutter was with two officers just now. They were putting him, like two cells over."

John John thought about it for a second and said, "You must be losing your mind, kid. That couldn't be that ma'fucka."

Blitz sat beside John John and with one eyebrow raised said, "For real man. That was that nigga Stutter. That nigga looked like he was being charged with something."

"Okay, okay. Say it is him. He don't know that we're over here, or at least he don't know we were the one's who pulled the heist." John John tried to give Blitz some comfort. He continued, "Just be easy. Pretty is on his way and once he scoops me, I'll be right back to grab you up."

Pretty called Donnicia ...

Ring... Ring!

The letters P.Y. appeared on Donnicia's Nextel screen and she quickly answered her phone. "What up, Beau."

"Baby, Blitz and John John got locked up. I don't know what for, but it could be for what happened on Truman Street," Pretty said.

Donnicia cut his words short and tried to explain. "Stutter is locked up for murder and he wants me to go and talk with some agents, for me to tell them that we were together the entire night."

"Murder?" Pretty was shocked. "Something is going on and I don't know what it is, but I'm not getting in the middle of it. And I suggest you don't involve yourself in it either."

"We'll talk some more later," Donnicia said. She hung up the phone and began pacing back and forth wondering what her next move should be.

Back at the Whalley Avenue jail, Stutter waited for his attorney to tell him that the charges against him were being dropped down to simply a gun possession. Hours had passed before Stutter heard keys at the cell door. One of the officers opened it and told Stutter that his attorney wanted to talk with him. Stutter accompanied the officers to a room where his lawyer was waiting for him. He spoke to one of the officers that placed Blitz into the other holding cell. "What did that guy get arrested for? The one you put in the other cell about two hours ago?"

The officer shrugged his shoulders indicating that he had no idea to whom Stutter was referring. He opened the door to where Mr. Hall waited and led Stutter into the room.

"What's new?" Stutter questioned his attorney. He felt a little relieved after being in that cold cell for so many hours.

"Well, here's the situation. Your girlfriend never showed up or called us back, and you are from the Truman Street area, right?" Stutter nodded. "There are two individuals from that same area being held here at the jail. The authorities need some help. Maybe you can give these people some information that might be valuable to them, *and* helpful for you." Mr. Hall raised his brow again, crossed his legs and placed one of his hands on the toe of his shoe.

"*She never called?*" Stutter asked. He looked at Mr. Hall to see if he was serous about Donnicia not coming through for him. When his attorney didn't budge, he realized that he wasn't lying and added, "If I give you some information on those guys, what kind of time will I be looking at?" He gazed at the photos of John John and Blitz that his attorney had sprawled out on the table. Without even waiting for his lawyer to answer, Stutter began telling his attorney and everyone present in the room about the robbery and murder of his cousin, Prince, and about other criminal activities with which Blitz and John John were connected that he knew about.

When he was done, his lawyer said, "Good, Mr. Best, you did the right thing. I'll work out a deal with the prosecutor. He's a friend of mine." Mr. Hall smiled, placed his hand on Stutter's shoulder, motioned for the officers to take Stutter back to his cell and said, "Have faith in me, kid."

Six months later ...

Stutter was the key witness in the Midnight Miradas' federal trial. John John and Blitz were both sentenced to life without the possibility of parole. Stutter was released from custody after the trial but was later killed by Nut. Nut became the new leader of the remaining Midnight Miradas. Pretty and Donnicia continued seeing each other. They conceived a child and later moved down south.

Travis 'Unique' Stevens is an up and coming exciting new writer. He is currently working on his full-length novel, *I Ain't Mad at_Ya*. Unique's creative writing style will impact this new genre in black novels for years to come.

Gem City

R. Kevin Taylor

(A Polo Novel)

CHAPTER ONE

"Yo, Nell, them New York niggas got to get the fuck up out of here, dog. I ain't been able to sell shit since they started hustlin' in these projects!" Champ stated as they were standing out on the back side of Edgewood Projects.

"Yeah, Champ, they do have shit on lockdown out this piece. You ain't the first nigga I heard saying they tired of their shit, dog."

"Tell you like this, Nell, why don't we get our crew along with anybody else who wanna ride against them and send their asses back to the big apple, hopefully in body bags."

"That shit sounds good, dog, let's see if we can get it poppin' off like that with everybody else first. But even if the crew ain't with it, I'm with it, dog."

"One more thing, Nell, watch who all you mention this shit to cause you got some of these niggas around here who be riding on them New York niggas' dicks 'cause they selling their work for the low."

"I'm already thinking like that, Champ, when shit hit the fan, we'll just set fire on the dick lickers' asses also. Yo, I'm about to roll this blunt of Dro I just bought from my white boy out on the East End, you trying to smoke or what, dog?"

"What you waiting on, Nell? Roll that shit up."

Champ and Nell were at one time two of the biggest drug dealers in Edgewood Courts. Both men were still sitting on decent bankrolls at the present time, but at the rate things were going, they both would be leaking in the pockets in a matter of months. Champ was tall and light skinned with braids. Both his arms were heavily tattooed, most of it jailhouse work done while he was serving three years for drug trafficking. Nell was shorter than Champ with the same light complexion and natural wavy hair. Even though Nell had the appearance of a pretty boy, he had a rep all through Dayton, Ohio about his work. Legend had it that a few unsolved murders in the city had come from his hands.

• • •

"Yo, son, when we go back home this time, I'm gonna buy three bricks myself, kid. That's a helluva comeup from where I started, son!" Mutt exclaimed.

"Mutt, just keep flipping your loot like you've been doing. Before you know it, you'll be sitting on a few hundred gees. I told you this town was a money magnet and these niggas is loving us," Jazz answered back.

"Jazz, we got this whole project on lock. Everybody spending their dough with us. You even got Cincinnati and Columbus niggas stepping through to buy weight. I think it's about time we brought some more homeys from the hood up here to show our real power."

"Mutt, if we bring them niggas down here, they gonna fuck our whole operation up. You know they gonna terrorize this town if we do that. I ain't bringing nobody down here, kid. You lucky I brought you, nigga. For real."

"Jazz, you know you couldn't leave me in New York, son,

ain't no way you wasn't gonna bring me here to hold you down. For all you knew, that little chick, Drea, you met in Atlanta could've been fronting when she told you how much money was in this town."

"Mutt, if it wasn't for Drea, we'd still be in New York trying to eat off of one punk ass brick for the whole block. Now look at us, brand new Navigators, bricks out the ass and a fat stash. I love that bitch, Drea, son. They said it's something jumping at the K-9 Club tonight. You with it?" Jazz said as he and Mutt were cruisin' in his brand new Navi.

"Hell, yeah, nigga, that's hoodrat heaven, son, and you now me, Jazz."

Both of them yelled in unison, "We love the rats," and started laughing hysterically.

Jazz and Mutt, two childhood friends from South Jamaica, Queens, had finally found their niche in life. Jazz, the older of the twosome by one year, was a hustler since as long as he could remember. All of his family was in the game when he was growing up and anytime his older brother left some work laying around, he would steal it, then go on the block and sell it along with his boys. Nobody would fuck with Jazz because of the rep his brother had in the hood.

Curt, God bless the dead, had the hood on lock. When he was alive, his gun would bust with the best of them. Curt was getting crazy cake also, but his life was cut short by a stray bullet outside of the Tunnel Night Club on his twenty-third birthday. Two crews were beefing outside and Curt and his crew came out just before the melee turned into gunplay. The bad thing about the incident was that Curt was the only one killed that evening. No one else was hit. That night changed Jazz' life forever because Curt had spoiled Jazz unconditionally. He kept his little brother fly and when Jazz got old enough to get a license, Curt bought him a used Acura Legend. Jazz idolized Curt and when his older sibling died, a part of Jazz also died with him.

Up until then, Jazz was a laid-back type of individual. You could almost say soft, but after the death of his brother, it was like Jazz turned into a new and improved Curt. Whereas Curt was the type of nigga who stayed in flip mode, Jazz had to be provoked to go bananas on you, but once you crossed that line, you best be assured that you had problems coming.

After Curt's death, Jazz scurried up all of Curt's money that he could find and kept the block afloat. But without a solid connect, Jazz was making peanuts compared to how his big brother was moving. Then Jazz went to the freak-nic in Atlanta on a whim and met his new sweetheart, Andrea, in the lobby of the Marriott Marquis downtown. After Andrea kept pressing him to come visit her, he finally relented and stumbled upon the goldmine, The Gem City (Dayton, Ohio). After seeing how work was moving in Drea's projects, Jazz went back to New York and got his main man, Mutt, and left the Apple for good.

Jazz was a light brown skinned cat of medium height and a slim build. He had a tattoo on his neck that said, R.I.P. Curt in large letters.

Mutt, Jazz' best friend since childhood, went along with anything his man said to do. Jazz was the first person to ever put money in Mutt's pockets and made sure he was alright. Both of Mutt's parents were dope fiends and they never gave a fuck about him or anything for that matter except that next spike and where it was gonna come from. Mutt got his nickname from

Jazz the first week he moved to the hood. Jazz and a few other guys were fighting pits in an alley and Mutt, intrigued by the dog fights, went and found himself a stray dog, a pit bull and chow chow mix, and brought him to the fight. His dog held its own with the other dogs for a few days until he got overmatched and slaughtered before the fellas could break them up. Mutt cried like a baby when his dog went down, and ever since that day, Jazz started calling him Mutt, after his warrior dog.

Mutt was slightly taller than Jazz with shiny black skin. He wore his hair in braids and had a scar on the side of his eye, the result of a brick he took when he got jumped some years back.

CHAPTER TWO

"Yo, Jazz, this parking lot is on full, son. I know I'm gonna have a ball in this piece." Mutt was scanning the parking lot as Jazz hunted for an empty place to park.

"Yeah, son, shit do look mad packed. I wonder if we gonna be able to get in the club with our gats. Ya heard."

"Yo, I got the doorman wrapped up. For a few extra dollars, he'll let us straight in, Jazz. I always get up in the club with my shit."

"There it is then. Here, Mutt, give Duke this C-note for us, that should definitely hold him, son."

"Keep your loot, Jazz. I got shit covered. Remember you ain't the only one doing it real big anymore. I got a little bankroll too, kid."

"Okay, big timer, my fault. I ain't got no problem with letting you spend some of your newfound wealth, son. You can buy all the drinks too if you want."

"Nigga, just chill, I got you. Are you trying to leave up out of here with some pussy or what?"

"Mutt, I ain't just trying to fuck anything, but if I see something bad, I'm gonna do me." Jazz was looking at his homey.

"Well, I'm gonna find me something for tonight. I ain't had no ass in a couple of days, so somebody's gonna get hit tonight, son."

"Come on, Mutt, you doing too much talking. Let's get up in here and see what's really happening." The duo hopped out of their vehicle and proceeded into the club.

• • •

"Yo, Champ, look who just came up in here, dog," Nell said, as he was guiding Champ's eyes in Jazz and Mutt's direction, who were now making their way towards the bar and speaking to a couple of people they knew. Nell, who was feeling the full effect of the trees he'd been smoking all day, was itching for some shit to jump off, but at the same time, he was fully aware that this was not the place to confront the New Yorkers about bouncing from his projects. Everybody whoever got into some gunplay out in Jefferson Township where the K-9 Club was located ended up getting jammed up in the process.

"Nells, you see what I'm talking 'bout? Look how these sissy ass niggas be sweating them boys. When shit do jump off and we take back over, them bitches can't buy shit from me."

"Nah, fuck that, Champ, we just gonna rob their bitch asses. Let them try and buy some shit from me, I'm gonna bag their asses and sell them some flour mixed with sheetrock. Know what I'm saying. Ah, shit, I can't take too much more of this. Look at my so-called man, Marty, all in them cat's faces." Nell was full of venom this particular time because Marty at one time was a partner of his when he first got started selling dope. Now, the sight of Marty hugged up with his new enemies sickened him. Any respect he had for Marty before that moment was voided. Marty was definitely gonna pay for shitting on him. Nell turned to the waitress and ordered a triple Hennessy.

* * * * * *

"What's up, Marty, you alright, son? I ain't seen you in about a week."

"Jazz, everything's all good. I just been out of town moving my shit. I be going down to Indiana, dog. You think Dayton is sweet, I make three times more in Indy. A twenty cent piece here sells for fifty down there, and it's all crackers buying the shit. I ain't ever seen so many of them strung out in my life. And them white bitches, they love sucking on some big black dick. I'm gonna stay here in Dayton for a few days before I go back down there. You and your man are welcome to come if you want. It's enough money down there for all of us players."

"No, thanks, son, I ain't trying to leave this spot right now, just having you spend that paper this way is enough, feel me?" Jazz answered back.

"Well, alright then, Jazz. If you change your mind, you know my numbers, dog. I'll need one of them bricks from you before I bounce, too."

"Alright, son, no problem. Just holla at me then." The gentlemen concluded their conversation unaware of the venomous look on Nell's face who was at a boiling point with Marty. *"I got something for your bitch ass, Marty,"* Nell thought to himself. Mutt walked up on Jazz who was now sitting at the bar by his lonesome.

"Yo, Jazz, why you over here chillin' by yourself with all these shorties running around here trying to catch."

"I was just talking to the kid, Marty, about some business. I ain't really had enough time to scope the scene for real. I'm alright though. I'm gonna go stay over Drea's apartment when we bounce. Do you though, homey, I'm cool. I got this short bottle of Mo to keep me company for now."

"Let me see if that shorty over there with the fat ass I was dancing with is trying to bounce with me. If so, you can drop me off in the projects at my truck. But I'm telling you, Jazz, if shorty ain't with it, we ain't leaving till I find me a piece of ass."

"Nigga, I told you go ahead and do you. I ain't in no rush. I got a dime piece laying in the bed waiting for me right now, probably butt naked, son." Jazz watched his man take off in the direction of the shorty he pointed to just before that, and peeped his man say a few words to her. He watched Mutt grab her by the hand and start walking back towards him. *"Guess my man came up,"* he thought to himself. He turned his bottle of Moet over and guzzled the shit down before his man made it over to him.

"Let's bounce, Jazz. Me and shorty getting up out of here. Talaya, this my man, Jazz. Jazz, this is Talaya."

"Nice meeting you, Talaya." Jazz looked her up and down.

"Same here, Jazz," Talaya answered seductively. For the first time, Jazz really paid attention to shorty. He liked what he saw. Mutt wasn't lying when he said shorty had a fat ass. From what Jazz could see, shorty was the complete package. He thought that Mutt needed to see what this shorty really was all about. Then they headed out the door together with Nell's eyes burning holes through the back of all their heads.

● ● ●

"Marty, what's up, dog? I wanted to say something to you earlier, but I saw you kicking it with your man from New York."

"Dude alright, Nell, you could've came over and kicked it with us. I would've introduced you to dude."

"Maybe next time then, Marty. But yo, dog, what you getting ready to get into?"

"I'm gonna chill here for a minute then I'll probably hit one of them after hour spots, why, what's up?"

"Shit, dog. I wasn't doing nothing. Matter of fact, I was about to go in, but if it's cool with you, let's roll together for old time sake."

"You know I'm cool with it, Nell, as soon as I'm ready to bounce, I'll let you know then."

"Alright then, Marty, I'm gonna go and let Champ know I'm chilling with you for the rest of the evening."

• • •

"Yo, Champ, I just talked to Marty. We're gonna chill out together, hit a couple of bootleg spots and shit, so I'll catch up with you tomorrow, dog."

"Nell, what's up. I know you got something on your mind, you got that look."

"Nah, you know Marty's my man from way back. We just gonna kick it on some other shit. Just call me on my cell phone sometime tomorrow afternoon, dog. We'll get together then."

"Alright then. I'm gonna get ready to go. I'm tired of looking at these same tired ass bitches, that's why I don't like going out no more."

"Just make sure you get with me tomorrow, ahight?"

"I got you, Nells, tomorrow then." The two friends gave one another a handshake, then departed.

CHAPTER THREE

"Jazz, is that you?" Drea popped her head up from the pillow.

"Yeah, Drea, I was trying not to wake you up, boo," Jazz replied as he closed the door quietly behind him.

"That's okay. I wasn't asleep. I just laid my butt down. I was watching one of them bootleg DVDs you brought back from New York. That thing was super clear too. You can't even tell the difference between them."

"I tried telling you, Boo, but you ain't wanna listen. That's why I ain't wanna take you to see those movies 'cause we already had them here. But you thought I was making an excuse not to spend time with you." Jazz sat on the bed and began playing with Drea's hair.

"Alright, Jazz, you made your point, but you still gonna take me somewhere tomorrow. I don't care where it is either. I just wanna get out of this doggone condo. I've been staying home everyday for the last two weeks and I'm about to go crazy. Maybe if I was still staying with my family in the projects, I wouldn't feel like this at all.

Drea was frustrated. She wasn't used to being locked down by a man like that.

"Drea, you know why I moved you out of them projects.

Anyone in this town that knows about us, they know that you're the only person in this town that I care about. And I think that anybody who's gonna try me, will try to get at you, to get me. I love you too much to see that happen. So please, bear with me, crazy mama." Jazz leaned over and kissed Drea on her neck.

"Jazz, you know how to pick me up whenever I'm down, that's just another reason why I love you so much," Drea said smiling.

Jazz laid beside his girl and started kissing her passionately. Drea slid from under the covers revealing her sexy lingerie that Jazz picked out for her at the Victoria Secrets store in the mall. The fabric clung to her five foot, thick ass frame and revealed all of her curves. Drea's red boned skin and long silky hair made Jazz' eyes light up when she raised up off of the bed to start undressing him. Jazz wasted no time sliding Drea's lingerie off of her. He hesitated a few seconds to admire her ripe breasts and bulging pubic mound. Every time Jazz stared at this woman's body it excited him and made the loving that much better. Jazz started by rubbing his hands in circular motions on Drea's breasts, as she moaned at the touch of her man's hands. Jazz then started working his tongue on her nipples. He slowly started working his way to her mound. Once there, she clutched her man's head tightly as he was flicking his tongue on her swollen clit. After a while, he knew it was time to give Drea the piece of meat that she kept begging him for.

Jazz slid his snake into Drea's love nest causing her eyes to roll back into her head. Every time he entered her, he had that effect on her. Jazz started pumping her relentlessly and she was loving all of it. Drea screamed when she climaxed and a few hard strokes later, Jazz did the same. Jazz laid limp on Drea's body and afterward they fell asleep.

•　•　•

"Damn, Nell, I'm surprised you ain't try to fuck one of them ho's that was up in the club. Back in the day, I know for a fact you would've hit something," Marty said while he was driving his Acura Legend to his favorite after hour spot.

"Nah, homey, you know how it is, you outgrow shit and change for the better, or sometimes the worse." Nell adjusted himself in the passenger seat.

"I just wish we could get the old days back, remember all that money we were getting back then, Nell?" He looked at his friend.

"Yeah, dog, shit was sweet for real. Actually it was still sweet until them New York niggas came and started taking over!" Nell said with venom in his voice. He returned his homeboy's glance.

Marty refocused on the road. "Nell, why you say it like that? I know them dudes ain't stopping your flow."

Nell heard Marty's last statement and that was all he could take from his bitch ass. Nell reached in his waistband and pulled out his nickel-plated Berretta 9mm. "Pull this car over, bitch ass nigga. Matter of fact, turn down this street and turn into the alley on the corner." Nell motioned with his head while he pointed his gun at Marty.

"Nell, what the fuck are you doing, dog? What the fuck did I do for you to flip on me like this?" Marty was nervous. He began to swerve.

Smack Nell busted Marty upside the head with the Berretta which opened a gash on the side of his head. Marty was leaking profusely. "Shut your bitch ass up and pull this car over. You make one wrong move and your wig will be all over this bitch. I seen you all up in the club on them niggas' dicks. You done said fuck your homeys. You don't give a fuck if we live or not." Nell had the gun at Marty's temple again.

Marty straightened the car out and began to slow down. "You bugging, dog. I ain't down with them like that. I just spend my money with 'em." Marty pulled into the alley as directed and parked. Nell searched him for a weapon. There was no way he was going to let a nigga like Marty catch him slipping. The alcohol and weed had Nell feeling no pain. He was definitely gonna get rid of his old partner in crime without having any regrets at all. This was his silent message to anyone who wanted to deal with the New York cats. Eventually, they would all get the same treatment.

Nell made Marty get out of the car as he followed behind him. Nell squeezed three shots in Marty's dome like it was nothing. Marty's head exploded, then his body crumpled. Nell quickly hopped in Marty's whip and sped off in the direction of the projects. His car was there in one of its parking lots. He figured he could ditch Marty's car a few blocks away, then jog to his car and go off to one of his bitch's crib. That way he would have a nice alibi if five-o ever tried to fuck with him.

CHAPTER FOUR

Ring… Ring… "Hello," Andrea answered her telephone. "Hey, Drea, this is Mutt. Is my man awake yet?" Mutt questioned.

"He's in the shower right now. Want me to give him a message?"

Mutt looked at his watch. "Drea, tell him to come to the phone, it's important."

"I'm gonna take him the cordless, give me a second."

Mutt sighed. "Thanks, Drea."

Jazz grabbed the phone and gave Drea a squeeze on her butt. "Mutt, what's up, son? What's really going on?" Drea smiled and walked off.

"Yo, Jazz, I was just watching the morning news and I seen your man Marty's picture. Son is deader than ma' fucka, yo!"

"You sure, Mutt. We were just in the club with the nigga last night. I think you bugging, yo." Jazz started flicking channels with his remote.

"Believe what you want, kid, that was son, I'm telling you. The news said that he was shot execution style in an alley over in Dayton View multiple times in the head. Somebody split his fuckin' wig yo." Mutt wiped his forehead.

Jazz walked over to his window and peeked through his

mini blinds. "Yo, Mutt, where are you now? Come and pick me up. I'm gonna let Drea hold my truck today because her car is in the shop."

"I'm in the parking lot at the Waffle House on my cell phone. Let me drop shorty off after we eat then I'll be over there. I figure it shouldn't be no longer than an hour." Mutt glanced at the clock in his vehicle.

"Aiight then, son, I'll see you when you get here. Oh yeah, did you blow shorty back out or what, nigga?" Jazz was beaming.

"Jazz, I'm in love like a ma' fucka. Shorty ain't no joke." Mutt looked over at his companion and smiled.

• • •

"Mack, what the fuck is going on around here? Five-O been through these projects creeping all morning. Niggas can't get no money like that. Know what I'm saying, dog?" Ron was looking around, wondering what was going on.

"Yeah, Ron, I think we need to call Jazz and tell him we gonna close down business until this heat dies down. I ain't trying to get knocked off. Ya heard, son?" Mack counted his money for the fourth time, folded his wad and placed it back into his pocket.

"Yo, what's up with that son shit, Mack? You starting to talk like Jazz and Mutt now. You fake ass New York nigga," Ron said while laughing at the same time.

Mack and Ron were Jazz' people who ran the projects for him. Mack and Jazz' girl, Drea, were first cousins. When Jazz came to visit Drea for the first time, she introduced them, and after talking for a while, they found out that they both were into the same life, selling drugs. Mack showed Jazz Edgewood housing projects, and how much money was coming through there. The rest was, as they say, history. Jazz spent every dollar he could muster on cocaine and sent Mutt via Greyhound to Dayton, Ohio. That was six months ago. Now, Jazz was going back home to buy no less than ten bricks at a time. Mack was the real reason Jazz had come up beyond his wildest dreams. He knew everyone in the city who was getting any kind of money and he also had an impeccable reputation for doing good business. So when Jazz started coming through with the coke, Mack had no problem moving it.

• • •

"Yo, Mutt, turn your system down, my cellie is vibrating. I won't be able to hear with that music blasting." Jazz was reaching for his cell phone.

"Hurry up, nigga, you know I ain't trying to pause my *Reasonable Doubt* CD too long." Mutt was feeling *Jay Z's* album, but he lowered the volume for his friend.

"Hello, who dis?"

"Yo, what's up, Mack, everything alright?" Jazz looked over at Mutt.

"Yeah, Jazz, we ahight. I was just calling to tell you we chilling today. Shit hot as fish grease around here. Five-Os is all through this bitch. I don't know what they up to, but I feel it's better to be safe than to be sorry. So I had Ron take the work to the stash."

"It's all good. Walk around the projects and see if anybody knows what's going on. Hit me back as soon as you find something out, ahight, son?"

"I got you, cuz. Talk to you later," Mack said.

"Oh, yeah, I almost forgot. You heard about Marty, right?"

"Nah, dog, what's up?" Mack's antennas went up.

"Mutt told me he got murked last night. Somebody put his brains all over an alley in Dayton View, kid."

Mack couldn't believe it. "You bullshittin', dog. Marty wouldn't bust a grape in a fruit fight. All that nigga wanted to do was get a little dough so he could trick a little something. You know that nigga's people still live in the projects here. Damn, let me go over there and see what I can find out. I'll definitely be calling you back real soon, Jazz. Keep your phone on."

• • •

Bang, bang, bang... Nell thought he was dreaming when he heard banging on his front door. When he gained some of his senses, he reached over on his night stand, grabbed his pistol and headed for the door to see who the fuck was banging on his front door like they were crazy. He immediately ruled out the police because they would've kicked the door in already. Looking out the peephole, he saw his main man, Champ, and all his adrenaline quickly eased. Nell welcomed Champ into his crib and Champ let him have it.

"Are you fucking crazy or what, Nell? I saw the fucking news this morning. That nigga Marty's face is plastered all over it every five fucking minutes, dog. I know you did that dumb shit, nigga." Champ's eyes were wide open.

Nell motioned with his hands. "Lower your fuckin' voice. My neighbors might hear you."

"Fuck your neighbors. What if somebody seen you and Marty leaving the K-9 together, then what? I'll tell you. Five-O gonna lock your stupid ass up and try and stick a needle in your ass for capital murder". Champ had his finger in Nell's chest, emphasizing his point.

Nell walked off. "Champ, don't act like you didn't know that I was gonna douse that bitch ass nigga. He was down with them New York niggas so he got what he had coming, feel me." He turned around. "I told you yesterday, and I ain't playing no games. Those ma' fuckas getting their asses out of Edgewood. As a matter of fact, they getting their shit out of this city."

Champ walked up on Nell and said, "Nell, listen carefully, dog. I want them cats gone just as bad as you do, but we got to do shit right. All that gung-ho shit will do is get us fucked up. I talked to Bo and Kai and they're with us also. I say we need maybe two more niggas, then we all get strapped up and take our beef straight to them cowards." Champ took a breather.

"Champ, you forgot my cousins, the twins, dog. They gonna roll at the snap of my fingers. All I got to say is I got beef and roll those lunatics a couple of fat blunts. They'll be ready for whatever." Nell gave a smirk.

Champs eyes lit up. "I don't know how I forgot about them, Nell. So there it is, we're straight. Just lay low a while and see what's up with this Marty shit first. If you're straight, we'll run them niggas out of this city in no time. Aiight, dog?"

Nell embraced his friend. "Say no more, Champ. Get ready to bust your guns."

CHAPTER FIVE

"Yo, Mutt, we gonna get up out of here for a while and go back up top for a couple of weeks, son. I just talked to Mack again and he said the police found Marty's car a couple of blocks away from the projects and they thinking that's maybe where the suspect fled to. We ain't getting caught up in no shit like that, son." Jazz wasn't trying to get locked up for no bullshit.

"That's peace with me. I'm trying to go back around the way shining anyway, show all them niggas how I came up down here. Plus, you know I'm trying to buy them three bricks I was telling you about." Mutt was feeling himself at the moment, despite all the drama.

"I'm gonna take Drea down with me this time. She's been sweating me about spending some time with her anyway, so it'll be perfect," said Jazz.

"I see Drea really got your ass open now. What are you going to do about your shorties you got up top? You know when they hear you in town, they're gonna be riding past your mom's crib to see you. Specially the few you have that live *in* the hood."

"Mutt, fuck them bitches, son, Drea's the one who helped a nigga take his game to the next level. Ain't none of them bitches bringing shit to the table but a piece of ass. Ya heard, son?" Jazz was counting his money and rubber banding it up.

"I'm with you, Jazz. I just hope no crazy shit jump off at your mom's crib. I can see her flipping now. That will be some funny ass shit." Mutt smiled.

"Oh, yeah, I'm gonna go meet this kid named Chook from over there by 107 and Guy R. Brewer. Rhondu called me and said that the nigga and his crew are doing it real big. They supposedly have whatever it is a nigga need for cheaper than what everyone is paying uptown." Jazz gave his buddy a slight nod.

Mutt waved Jazz off. "Yeah, right, Jazz, you know it ain't no niggas getting it like that on the south side. You need to smack the shit out of Rhondu for even saying some shit like that."

Jazz looked at Mutt. "He put that shit on his daughter, Mutt, you know that nigga ain't bullshitting when he put Shay Shay on it, yo." Jazz rubber banned another bundle.

"We got to meet this Chook nigga, Jazz. Hurry up and pack your shit so we can go home."

• • •

"Drea, I'm glad you're here. Pack your bags. We're gonna go up to New York for a couple of weeks. I know it's sudden, but something came up and I got to go handle it." Jazz looked at Drea for a reaction.

"Give me a few to get my things together, baby. Do you want me to pack your bags also?" She looked at her man seductively.

"Yeah, that will be perfect. That way I can call a couple of my mans in New York and tell them I'm on my way. Thank you, Boo." Jazz walked over to Drea and kissed her on her lips.

• • •

"Hello, yo, what's up, Du? This is Jazz. I was just calling to let you know me and Mutt will be home tomorrow. So let your man Chook know so we can meet."

"I already told money, he's waiting to meet you, kid. Wait till you meet this nigga. He's real as shit. Nigga helped my pump our block back up again."

"See you soon then, Du. I'm out." Jazz hung up and got ready.

• • •

"Damn, cuz, you keep the bomb ass Dro; every time we get together, I get high as a kite," said Larry, pulling on the freshly rolled blunt.

"That shit cost four fifty an ounce and you two smoked out ass niggas be smoking my shit up like it's free," Nell shot back.

"If you gonna cry, Nell, you shouldn't tell us to help ourselves to your shit," said Gary, the other half of Nell's twin cousins.

Larry and Gary, Nell's twin cousins, were known all throughout the city of Dayton. They were notorious stick-up kids from the DeSota Bass Housing Projects. All they'd do is smoke marijuana, then go out and rob niggas. They were so gangster with it that they would rob a nigga early in the day, then go out to a club later that night and give their victims dap and a hug like they were the best of friends. Nell and everybody else close to them wondered why the twins weren't six feet under already. They guessed the twins just knew how to pick 'em.

The twins were real short. The only difference between them was that Larry wore dreadlocks and Gary wore his hair in braids. Nell was the only human being alive who could control them, but that was only to a certain extent. Nell at one point tried to get the twins to quit the robbery shit by putting them down with his operation, but that went south when Nell sent them on a drop-off and the twins took it upon themselves to rob the customers for their loot. Nell was so furious with them that it took every ounce of control in his body *not* to rock his cousins to sleep himself. He only recently started back fucking with the twins. And even in the present, the twins were still leery about being around Nell.

"Cuz, the reason I called y'all over here is because I got a problem and I need you two to help me take care of it. It's these two cats from New York doing it real big over there in Edgewood, and I'm getting ready to step to them. Y'all with me or what?" Nell looked at his fam.

Larry spoke for the twins. "I heard about them niggas. It's a couple of little homeys from the Bass that be spending money with them. I tried to get them to help me set them up, but they wasn't going for it. To answer your question though, just let us know when it's going down, we'll be there."

"It's gonna be real soon, dog, in the next couple of days I'm sure, so don't go and get off into no stupid shit because I'm really counting on y'all for this." Nell kept his expression serious.

Gary interjected, "You know we gonna take whatever we can get off of them cats when shit jumps off. It ain't gonna make no sense if we don't do that, Nell."

"Whatever you get, y'all can keep. All I want is to get them faggots out of the projects. So just be on point when I'm ready to do this."

Gary gave Nell some dap. "We got you, cuz. Just call us and we'll be there. We about to bounce, cuz, let us get some of that icky sticky to ride with, dog."

"Ahight, but I don't want you all smoked out when we go

do this." Gary and Nell separated, then Nell gave Larry a hand-shake and hug.

"Nigga, we do our best work when we're blitzed, you'll see. We out, dog," said Larry.

CHAPTER SIX

"Yo, Jazz, ain't it some crazy shit to come across this George Washington Bridge and not see the Twin Towers when you look over at the skyline? Every time I see that shit, I think about how bad them terrorists fucked our city up, son." Mutt was looking in the direction of where the World Trade Center used to be.

"Yeah, Mutt, that was some crazy shit. I'm just glad we back home though, kid. Ain't nothing like N.Y., yo. And we coming back sitting on crazy loot, nigga. New York is definitely the place to be when you got bank," Jazz said while he was driving his Navigator across the G.W.B. Drea was sitting in the passenger seat asleep. Jazz was about to wake her up because he knew how much she enjoyed seeing the city from the highway. This was only her second time to New York and on her first trip, she didn't get to do any sightseeing. This time though, Jazz made it a priority of his to show his woman what his town really had to offer. He nudged her. She leaned up, looked around, spotted New York, then smiled.

"Yo, Jazz, drop me off over my mom's crib. I'm gonna stay in for the rest of the night with my fam. I'll get with you first thing in the morning," said Mutt, praying his moms wouldn't be doped up. She had been trying to get herself back together.

"That's alright, kid. Did Denise drop your son off over there yet?" asked Jazz.

"My moms said he been there all day. I can't wait to see him, yo. My lil man is the spitting image of me. I hate it that me and Denise had to split, but that bitch was too crazy for me. That little episode where she pulled my pistol out on me while I was asleep, 'cause she thought I was fucking her friend, was enough, son." Mutt looked in the rearview mirror and caught Jazz' eye.

"Mutt, you still love shorty, don't front on me, son. I got y'all getting back together before it's all over, yo!" Jazz focused back on the road.

When they arrived, Mutt said, "Let me out this truck, Jazz. I'll see you tomorrow, son. Make sure you call Rhondu so we can see what his man is talking bout. I need to know how much loot I can jack off while I'm up here."

They shook hands, then Mutt walked into his mom's crib.

• • •

"Champ, I'm telling you, dog, them New York niggas bounced up out of here yesterday. I heard Mack telling his man last night when we were shooting craps in the projects. He told the dude that if they needed some weight they had to see him 'cause he didn't know when his peoples were coming back," said Kai.

"Kai, are you sure about this, dog? 'Cause if you are, this shit is gonna be easier than I thought. All we gotta do now is just run Mack and Ron's bitch ass out of the projects, then when them New York niggas get back, we'll tear they ass up if they come through."

"Yeah, dog, that sounds like it'll work. You know Mack

ain't going down without a fight. He's been getting money in Edgewood forever yo, probably longer than all of us," Kai responded.

"Fuck Mack, when I make that nigga suck on this pistol like it's a dick, he better get as far away from the projects as he can, and never bring his bitch ass around no more. I'm getting ready to go and see Nell in a few and tell him that the shit is about to go down."

"Aiight then, Champ, you now where to find me when you're ready."

• • •

"Damn, Du, I've been calling your ass all morning, nigga. Where've you been?" Jazz asked.

"Jazz, I went out last night, yo. They had an album release party for this kid around the way at Jimmy's uptown. It was crazy shorties up that piece too, son. Do you remember little Rico? He always used to come through rapping and shit." Rhondu was trying to get Jazz to remember.

"Yeah, I remember, duke. You used to mess with his sister. I see he trying to make it out the hood, yo." Jazz had his hand on his chin.

"Jazz, that's the kid Chook's work. This nigga just came up out of nowhere. He came through the block one day while Rico was spitting in a cipher with a couple of other niggas. When they were done, Chook told Rico if he was serious about rapping, he would introduce him to his man. It was a wrap after that."

"Yo, I got to get Rico's album, son. You know I'm gonna support anything from around the way. When do his joint come out?" Jazz asked.

"It's in stores next week, but I'll get you one from Rico later on."

"When are you gonna get me in contact with Chook, Du? I'm ready to make this move A.S.A.P."

"Let me get dressed and I'll come pick y'all up, then we'll go see him."

"That's peace. Let me call Mutt and tell him that you'll be here in a short. You know I'm over Mom's crib, right?"

"Come on, son, where else you gonna be?" Du said sarcastically.

• • •

"Chook, this my man Jazz I was telling you about, and this is his man Mutt. They used to have my block before they moved to Ohio to start getting money," Rhondu said as he made the introductions.

Chook looked at the two men and started. "I know you Jazz, you're Curt's lil brother, God bless the dead. Your brother was my man, yo. I went to the funeral, that's where I remember your face from."

"Chook, I ain't been the same since he been gone, yo. I think if he was still living, I never would've had the heart to leave New York, son."

"Sometimes change is good, Jazz. From what I hear you're making the best of it, kid." Chook raised his brow.

"Yeah, Chook, me and my man Mutt here trying to cop some bricks. Rhondu said you got some butter for the low low. What you talking 'bout, son?" Jazz tapped Chook's arm as if to say, *"What's the deal?"*

"I got 'em for nineteen a piece. That's love nowadays especially since *they* been on everything coming in since that 9/11 shit jumped off."

Jazz took a pause to compute Chook's figures. It was $500 cheaper than what he was paying uptown, and he knew his man Rhondu wouldn't put no shit in the game, so he decided to spend some serious paper with Chook.

"Can we get thirteen joints, kid?"

Chook looked from Jazz to Rhondu before he responded. He didn't think Jazz was copping that kind of weight. Rhondu didn't have a clue either.

"Yeah, son, I can handle that. Since you buying so many, I'll drop the price to $18,500 for you, kid. Du, don't worry, son, I'll look out for you too."

"Alright then, Chook, before I leave, me and my man will get that up off you."

For the first time, Mutt jumped in the conversation. All Mutt could see were the dollar signs he was gonna see at them prices. "Yo, Jazz, let's pick them up now while Chook still got 'em, son. By the time we bounce, he might be out."

Jazz shot Mutt a look that could shoot daggers through his heart. He then realized that what his man had said made a lot of sense. "Yeah, ahight, Chook, we gonna get them today if it's cool, yo."

"Y'all niggas give me a couple of hours and I'll get them to you. I just don't keep that kind of work laying around."

"Just get with us when you're ready. Here's my number, Chook." Jazz scribbled his number on a piece of paper for Chook, then all three men gave Chook dap and a hug before they pulled off in Rhondu's M.P.V. heading back to their hood. The men later conducted their business in a professional manner and with that concluded, they were able to use the rest of their time in New York to relax and spend money.

CHAPTER SEVEN

"**H**ere's what it is, dog, we gonna ride down on them niggas today. The bullshit ain't nothing. We gonna try and do it without busting our guns 'cause Champ made a lot of sense. But if they resist for any reason, tear their asses up." Nell had his entire squad gathered. Champ, Kai, Bo and the twins, Larry and Gary.

Champ spoke. "Kai been in the projects all day. Mack and Ron are in their spot and they got a couple of other cats outside hustlin'. Me, Kai and Bo are gonna take care of all the niggas outside. Nell, you and the twins roll up on their apartment."

Nell began, "What are you gonna do with the niggas you round up outside on the block, Champ?"

"We gonna bring them inside so we won't attract too much attention, but if we have to resort to gunplay, I'm shooting to kill, ya heard?"

"Peep this, Champ, when we get to the projects, let me and the twins out in the back. We'll slither our way through. I know Edgewood better than anybody, plus it's dark now. Ain't too many people gonna be outside. By the time it takes you to go all the way around, we'll be in position."

"Alright, Nell, even if you don't make it in time, we're gonna secure the niggas outside. I ain't taking no chances and let one of them bitch ass niggas get the drop on me. Now go get the pieces so we can load up," said Champ.

With that, Nell went into his basement and came back up with a duffel bag full of weapons. He took a Beretta 9 mm and a Mack-10 out of the bag for himself, then passed it along. After everyone secured their weapons of choice, it was time to roll. The destination, Edgewood Projects.

• • •

"Craps, nigga, pay me. You can't hit shit tonight," Mack shouted to his lil man, Kirky, who was shooting the dice.

"Mack, before we leave tonight, I'm gonna get my money back, dog," Kirky shot back.

Mack pulled a fat knot out from his pocket, then unraveled it saying, "Your paper ain't long enough, lil nigga. You keep pulling out that teeny bopper bankroll against this big boy shit, you can't win like that, dog."

Mack, Ron, Lil Kirky and a couple of the other crew members were all in front of their spot shooting dice. Edgewood Projects were a bunch of two-story attached apartments. Most blocks were one-way streets that had speed bumps in them to make sure people didn't drive crazy when the kids were outside playing. Everybody was all into the dice game never paying attention to the black Chevy Express Cargo van that came creeping up on them. The van pulled up on them as the back doors flew open.

"Lay down, niggas, y'all know what it is!" Kai yelled with authority in his voice. He had his hammers ready and aimed.

Everybody fell to the ground simultaneously, shaking and praying that their captors wouldn't shoot them. Mack, the first to look up from the ground, recognized Kai along with Champ who was hopping out of the van. "Yo, Kai, what the fuck are you doing, dog? I thought we were cool?" Mack questioned.

Champ chimed in, "All you bitches get up real slow and walk into the apartment. One wrong move and that's your ass."

By this time, Nell and the twins came through from the backside, weapons drawn, with Nell saying, "Yeah, this is better than we expected. Everybody was out on the block."

All the men went inside the apartment. Once inside, the twins started ransacking the place while Bo and Kai were looking at their captors like they were crazy. The twins were hoping to find some drugs and cash for themselves. Nell already told them that whatever they found, they could keep. The twins rest assured were gonna shake everyone's pockets down before it was all said and done.

"As of now, y'all niggas can't sell another grain of work in these projects. If I catch y'all anywhere near here, your ass is mine. When them New York niggas get back, tell them the best thing for them to do is go back home. Edgewood Projects now belongs to Champ and Nell. Ho, ass niggas!" Champ yelled proudly.

Mack took all he could take, sitting on the floor watching the twins turn over everything that wasn't nailed to the ground.

"Nell, you know I ain't going for this shit, yo. You might as well tear my ass up now 'cause I'm coming back with my peoples, dog."

Nell gave Mack a quick look then squinted his eyes. "Mack, I wouldn't like nothing else better right now than to slay your ass, but since you coming back, I'm gonna give your bitch ass a real reason to come see me."

Nell took his pistol and commenced to whip Mack all upside

his head. Mack started screaming for Nell to stop. Champ went to grab Nell so he wouldn't kill Mack up in the apartment. Mack's head was leaking juice from at least three different places. Nell's temper was full blown now and he went to Mack's man, Ron, and gave him a couple of smacks upside the head as well. Nell gave the little workers a look like he was gonna give them a beatdown also, but Champ saved them by telling Nell he had already made his point. The twins went all through Mack and Ron's pockets and took all their loot. Kai and Bo followed suit and shook the workers down. The twins didn't like that one bit, especially when they saw Kai and Bo extract a nice sized bag of rocks off of one of them. The twins decided to give the apartment one more looking over in case they missed something and stumbled upon a package with eleven ounces in the septic tank. Larry stuffed the work in his underwear; they didn't want Nell to see how much they had come up with 'cause they still planned on hitting him up for some cash for helping him.

By the time they made it back down the stairs, Champ and Nell were ready to bounce. Nell kicked Mack in the stomach and warned him and Ron that they better be gone from the projects for good when he got back. On the way out the door, Champ looked at Mack's workers, mainly Kirky, who he watched grow up, and told them to holla at him if they wanted to, their beef wasn't with them.

After Nell and them pulled off, Kirky had the other men help him carry Mack and Ron to his car and drove them to Good Samaritan Hospital where Mack had to have surgery since he had lost a lot of blood.

CHAPTER EIGHT

"**C**hamp, I'm telling you, dog, I would be feeling a whole lot better, dog, if you would've let me put all them niggas to sleep. Never in my life have I let a nigga walk away from my work," Nell stated.

"Nell, what do you think would've happened if I let you kill them cats in that apartment? I'm gonna answer it for you. Our black asses would be gearing up for the penitentiary, nigga. Somebody in them p.j.'s would've snitched on us, dog. I'm telling you, we did the right thing," said Champ.

"Champ, I hope you're right. I just pray this shit don't come back and bite us in the ass." Nell was unloading his weapon.

"Nell, first thing in the morning, me, Kai and Bo are gonna have Edgewood going crazy. I'm gonna come out the gate with some jumbo ass rocks, you'll see."

"Be careful, Champ, don't let them fools catch you slippin', dog."

• • •

"Yo, Larry, we got a nice piece of change off them cats. Nell looked out for us on this one. We didn't even have to pop a nigga," Gary said.

"I got about four thousand out that nigga Mack's pockets alone, dog. I say we go to the Bass and sell them ounces to one of them niggas for about seven hundred a piece. That's a buck cheaper than what they're going for. They should jump on this product for that price," Larry replied.

"Nell said he's gonna look out for us also. I just hope it don't take him forever. Sometimes he be spinning niggas, dog."

"Gary, we ain't got to sweat it, cuz even if he play games, we still gonna have seven or eight gees a piece once we sell this shit, nigga, we're straight."

"Ahight then, Bruh, let's go through the Bass now and see what we can come up with." With that, the twins took off.

• • •

"Yo, Ron, you alright, dog? That was some foul shit Champ and Nell put down on us, dog," said Lil Kirky.

"I'm alright, Kirky. Where's Mack at though? They kind of fucked my man up, dog," Ron replied.

"They had to give him a blood transfusion or some shit. They said he lost a lot of blood, Ron. I hope Mack'll be alright so we can go and handle our business."

"Kirky, I ain't fuckin' with them cats. They can have Edgewood. We'll just find us somewhere else to open up shop."

"Ron, you on some bitch ass shit, dog? Your main nigga who you been hustlin' wit forever just got his ass punished by them cowards. And you just gonna let it ride? Get your bitch ass up!"

Lil Kirky couldn't take no more. He hit Ron with a two-piece right there in the emergency room parking lot. *Mop! Mop!* Ron dropped on the spot. Kirky had the name lil 'cause he was short, not 'cause he was small. Kirky was diesel with his. He had been in juvenile lock up for three years for popping his step-father after he caught him beating on his moms. Kirky used the entire three years working on his once puny stature. He had only been home for about a year to date, and he still worked out on a daily basis. Ron was lucky they were at the hospital. Had they been anywhere else, he would have really given Ron the business.

"Get your bitch ass away from me, Ron, 'fore I stomp your ass out, nigga. Matter of fact, give me a number for Jazz or Mutt so I can let them know about Mack." Kirky was still heated.

"Mack probably knows how to get in touch with them. Mack is the one who calls when we need to see him," Ron said, trying to recover.

"I can't fuckin' believe you, dog, talkin' 'bout you ain't messing with them. A nigga like you would've gotten fucked in juvie if you would've let a nigga get off on you like that. Ron, you need to find you another line of work 'cause you got this game all fucked up." Kirky walked away, pissed.

• • •

"Jazz, I know you said you wanted to stay here in New York for a couple of weeks, but all that yeyo we holding onto is burning a hole in my pockets. I'm ready to get back to the Oh-10 and get this money," said Mutt anxiously.

"Mutt, I still haven't taken my girl anywhere yet. We went to Justin's last night to eat and she was loving that shit, yo! I'm gonna take her downtown later on and let her shop till she drops on Fifth Avenue, ya heard?"

"Nigga, fuck that Fifth Avenue shit. My bank can't stand that shit yet. I'm still a Coliseum type nigga myself. I can get all the designer shit I need right there on Jamaica Avenue, son," Mutt retorted.

"Mutt, you got to treat yourself sometimes, son. You steppin' your game up when you hit the stores on Fifth, kid. It's like you on a whole different level. My brother, Curt, showed me that before he passed, and you know he stayed on some fly shit." Jazz was beaming again.

"Jazz, I guess you ain't heard a word I said, son. My bank ain't up to par for that shit yet. Trust me, when I get it to where as I feel I'm ahight, son, then it's on."

"Tell you what, Mutt. Let me take Drea shopping and shit today, then I wanna take her to Central Park tomorrow. After that, I might make up an excuse for us to go back 'cause ain't nothing really popping off here for me anyway." Jazz was giving in to Mutt's request.

"Jazz, have you tried to call Mack since we've been here?"

"Nah, I ain't had no reason to. I figured we'll see him when we get back. I know for a fact by the time we get back, he's not gonna have any more work left. All I had left was a brick and a half and he bought that off of me with his own money before we bounced."

"Yeah, that ain't shit to move. We definitely got to get our asses back, son. Hurry up with all that tricking you got planned so we can go get this money, yo. Holla back."

CHAPTER NINE

"Mack, you had me worried there for a minute, dog. You ain't said a word to a nigga in two days."

"Kirky, they been having me on so much medication that I've been like a zombie up in this bitch. They're talking 'bout releasing me tomorrow though. I can't wait to go see Nell and them, dog."

"I had to drop Ron's bitch ass the other night in the parking lot. Nigga had the nerve to say he was gonna leave the situation alone and we just find another place to hustle."

"You bullshittin'? I know he didn't say some shit like that out his mouth. He better be glad he didn't tell me something like that the way my shit is all swolled up. Nell fucked me up, dog, got me looking like the fuckin' elephant man."

"I know Ron is your man, Mack, but he ain't ready for this shit for real. He can't take no heat, dog. Beef comes with this shit and as soon as things get ugly, he wants to stay pretty and bounce."

"Kirky, fuck that nigga Ron for right now. I already know he ain't got no heart. I'll figure out what to do with him later. Do Jazz and Mutt know what happened yet?"

"I don't think so. Ron said he didn't know their numbers and that only you know how to reach them. They had you in here on dumb dumb status so I couldn't ask you shit. If you got their numbers, I'll go call them for you though."

"You know what, dog, we'll just wait till they get back to tell them. That way I can probably be healed up, 'cause I know they're gonna be ready to go and handle these cats when they hear this shit."

"That's cool with me, Mack, but let me know if you change your mind, dog. I'll make the call for you. I'm about to bounce so you can get some rest. Looks like that medication is wearing your ass down again." Kirky was looking at Mack's I.V.

• • •

"Nell, it's been three days since we ran them dudes up out of here. You ain't heard nothing, have you?" asked Champ.

"I better not hear anything, Champ. Them suckas better keep playing their position and stay as far away from these projects as possible."

"We been moving crazy product the last couple of days too. Them niggas was moving some shit through here. I ain't never seen Edgewood roll like this. I got all them lil niggas around here that be trying to hustle out on the block slinging packs for us and keeping their eyes open for some crazy shit."

"It's all good then, Champ. I'm on point for whatever, dog. You take care of the money side and I'll handle the rest. Oh, yeah, give me three gees when you get a chance so I can hit the twins off. Them niggas keep sweatin' me about some paper. I already know they came off that night we ran through here. My man told me he heard they were giving away dope in DeSoto Bass that next day," said Nell.

"Nell, I ain't got that much on me right now. I'll call you later and you can come and pick it up."

"That's cool. I want to keep them lil niggas happy just in case we need them again, know what I'm saying?" Nell gave Champ a pat on the shoulder.

• • •

"Yo, Mutt, I've been calling Mack's cell phone all morning while we been on the road. I can't catch him, son," Jazz shouted while they were on their way back to Ohio.

"Have you tried the apartment in Edgewood yet?" asked Mutt.

"I don't know the number by heart. I can't find it in my phone either. I thought I had it locked in."

"I got that shit in my cellie, Jazz. I'm gonna call over there and see if I can catch 'em."

Mutt dialed the number to the apartment and a stranger answered.

"Hello." The voice was feminine, like a woman.

"Yo, I think I got the wrong number, can I speak to Mack?" Mutt asked.

"Yeah, you called the right number, but Mack and them ain't been around for a few days," the woman answered.

"Yo, who the fuck is this anyway?" Mutt said, raising his voice.

"This is Lisa. I'm the owner of this apartment. I come by every morning to clean up for Mack."

"Didn't nothing happen to my man, did it? It ain't like him not to check in over there."

"I ain't sure, but word in the projects is Nell and Champ came 'round here and ran them off. When I came the morning after it happened, the place was ransacked and there was a lot of blood on the living room floor."

"Have the police been over there? Did anyone call them?" Mutt questioned.

"Ain't nobody 'round here calling no police. I'm glad they didn't 'cause they would've locked my ass up. I got some warrants," the lady said.

"Lisa, if you hear from Mack, tell him Mutt and Jazz are on their way back and to call us. I'll look out for you when I get there too, good lookin'," said Mutt.

"Alright, but I doubt if I'll see him. Champ been out here with a bunch of guys serving it up. They all over the place too."

"Ahight, thank you," Mutt said before hanging up.

After hanging the phone up with Lisa, Mutt caught eye contact with Jazz who could sense something wasn't right by the sneer on his man's face.

"Yo, Jazz, it's going down when we get back. That was the base head bitch whose apartment Mack was using. She told me them niggas Nell and Champ from the other side of the projects came and stepped to Mack and them on some gangsta shit and ran them off, son."

Jazz looked at him. "You playing games with me, right son? I know them country ass niggas ain't play themselves like that. We gonna show them niggas how New York put it down, yo. I know Mack ain't just let that shit ride like that."

Drea was listening to the conversation in a state of shock. She knew her cousin Mack well enough to know that if what Mutt had just said was true, something really bad must have happened to him, 'cause there was no way, only over his dead body, would he leave Edgewood. Mack was the reason the projects had a name in the first place.

"Oh, shit, Jazz," Mutt started, "we got to hurry the fuck

up. If we don't catch up with Mack, who's gonna be able to pick up shorty at the Greyhound station with that work?"

"We'll be able to make it in time, Mutt. Her bus won't be in Dayton till later on tonight. We'll be there way before her."

"Jazz," Drea chimed in from the back seat.

Jazz glanced over his shoulder. "Yeah, baby girl, what's up?"

"I couldn't help but overhear your conversation. I got a bad feeling about Mack. He wouldn't leave Edgewood for nothing in the world. Nell and Champ, they know how Mack feels about them projects, that's his home."

"Drea, I've been thinking the same way. Let's just pray that he's alright. I'm sure we'll find him when we get back."

CHAPTER TEN

" **M**utt, you got everything squared away with shorty? And did you take the work to the stash?" Jazz asked. The trio were back in Ohio.

"No doubt, Jazz. I think its time we go and see what's up with Mack though. I knew we shoulda had some wolves here from New York at all times. This shit would've never happened, son."

"We don't need no wolves, Mutt. If them niggas really violated, we gonna tear this whole fuckin' town up. Never will I let some Bama's get out on us.

"Jazz, I'm telling you, that crackhead chick said them niggas are posted all over the projects, son. We ain't gonna be able to do shit by ourselves. Try Mack over his house again. Maybe we can catch him."

• • •

"Mack, I know you wish you had a chick staying with your ass now, dog. You can hardly move and shit. I still can't figure out why you ain't wanna go over your people's crib 'till you got better."

"Lil Kirky, I don't want my moms seeing me like this. Old girl will have a heart attack. I pray none of her old friends from Edgewood find out about this and tell her."

The phone began ringing and Lil Kirky picked it up.

"Hello," he said.

"What's up, Mack? This Jazz."

"Nah, this Kirky, dog, what's up?"

"Put Mack on the phone for me, kid."

Kirky gave Mack the phone and told him it was Jazz.

"What's up, Jazz?" said Mack.

"Nigga, we been trying to get in touch with you. You alright, son?" Jazz was excited to hear his man's voice.

"Jazz, I'm just getting out of the hospital, son. Them niggas Champ and Nell rode down on us. They fucked me up pretty bad, kid. They call themselves making a power move for the projects."

"You ain't get shot up, did you, son?"

"Nah, that nigga Nell beat me down with his pistol. He opened me up pretty good, yo. I had to have a blood transfusion 'cause I lost so much blood, son. I'm swelled the fuck up like balloon man, dog."

"Mack, don't worry. We gonna handle them niggas, I promise. Matter of fact, me and Mutt gonna get their asses tonight!"

"No, Jazz! Wait till I get better, dog, the way that ho ass nigga Nell did me, I got to have him to myself. You best believe I told that nigga I was coming back if he didn't take me out."

"Your cousin, Drea, is worried to death about you, Mack. Why don't you call her when we hang up so she'll know you're still with us. Me and Mutt are on our way over there to your crib now. We'll see you then. Peace!" They hung up.

• • •

"Yo, Mutt, them kids really did punish Mack. He just got out the hospital earlier today, son. He's kind of lumped up right now. One of them niggas pistol whipped the shit out of him."

"We got to go see them niggas then. Let's go strap all the way up and show these Bamas how our guns bust, kid," Mutt replied as he fingered a bullet.

Jazz paced the room. "Mack wants us to wait till he gets better so he can get revenge personally. I kind of feel him there too, kid." He stopped, turned around and looked at Mutt.

Mutt was sitting on his sofa. He stood up and began pacing as well. "Ahight, yo but if we gonna wait, I'm going back to N.Y. and I'm getting the wolves together. You bullshittin', Jazz."

"Mutt, if we go up there with some dudes we rounded up, they gonna think we getting' soft, kid. Once niggas start thinking like that, we're gonna start having all types of problems when we go back up top," said Jazz.

Mutt was getting frustrated. "Jazz, fuck it. We'll do it your way, but I'm telling you, son, I don't agree with you on this. I know and you know our peoples will run through them projects and dead everything moving."

Jazz and Mutt went to see Mack and they all decided to wait until he got better before they retaliated. Kirky let everyone know that when it went down, he would be there, guns blazing with the rest of them. They decided they weren't gonna take care of no other business until they took care of Nell and Champ. The plan was for everybody to lay up at the crib until Mack got healthy, then it was on.

CHAPTER ELEVEN

"**N**ell, you keep this dro, dog. Every time me and Larry get with you, we get high as a motha fucka," Gary said. He was at home with his twin brother and Nell.

"I'm getting hungry now, Gee, munchies starting to kick in, dog," Nell answered back. The air was just thinning from the smoke Nell just exhaled.

"Fuck it, let's go down on Riverview and Broadway and hit Church's Chicken. That's my shit," said Larry, the other half of the twins.

"There it is then, after we eat, we can ride through Edgewood. I need to go see my man Champ anyway."

• • •

"Drea, me and Mutt will be back in a minute. I'm gonna go see your cousin, then stop and get us something to eat on the way back. I'm gonna use your car. Where're your keys?" Jazz asked, looking around their apartment.

"The keys are on the nightstand in the bedroom. I got a taste for some chicken or something," Drea answered.

"I got you, baby girl. Let's ride, Mutt." Jazz nodded for Mutt.

Mutt stopped in his tracks. "Yo, Jazz, don't forget your heat, son. We can't get caught slippin'."

"I'm a step ahead of you, Mutt." Jazz pulled up his shirt brandishing a chrome plated nine. "Give me some love, Drea. I'll be back in a short." Drea walked over, kissed Jazz on the mouth and allowed him to exit her home and be the man he was built to be.

Jazz and Mutt hopped in Drea's car and went to see Mack. Mack was starting to feel better, but he was still having migraine headaches from the beating he took. He figured it would at least take another week before he would be able to move on his enemies. Mutt was getting very impatient because none of them were making any money and just the mere thought of Nell and Champ thinking they had run them off made him sick. On the way out the door, Jazz and Mutt gave Mack some dap and a hug and told him to call if he needed anything.

"Nell, this chicken is hitting the spot, cousin," Gary said while he, Nell and his brother were sitting down inside Church's Chicken eating dinner.

"Yo, that car pulling in looks familiar. I just can't place it right now, dog," Nell said, squinting his eyes at Drea's car pulling into the parking lot of the restaurant.

• • •

"Jazz, when we get back to your crib, I'm gonna fuck me some chicken up, son. Make sure we get the works—coleslaw, macaroni salad and whatever else they got. I'm gonna chill here in the car while you get it."

"Yeah, Mutt, this chicken do be bangin', kid. I wish they had Church's up top," Jazz said as he was stepping out of the car to head into the restaurant.

Jazz was not paying any attention to his surroundings so

he never noticed Nell and the twins sitting at a table in the dining area. He walked straight up to the cashier to place his order. Nell was sitting at the table kickin' it with his cousins when he noticed Jazz standing before him ordering food. Nell reached in his waistband and pulled out his gun. The twins saw Nell pull his joint out so they followed suit. Nell whispered to the twins that Jazz was one of the New York dudes that they had beef with. Without saying a word, the two knew it was time to put in work. They all got up from their table with their pistols drawn and walked toward Jazz. Mutt was chilling in the car and noticed the three men get up. He spotted a pistol in one of their hands. He sprung into action, gun in hand, safety hitch off, knowing that the three men were moving on Jazz. Jazz was still immune to the situation, but finally turned around after his order was filled. He looked straight into the eyes of Nell who was now around ten feet away from him and was slowly raising his pistol in his direction. Jazz knew it was the end because he didn't have time to reach for his piece. Mutt was the first to start busting. *"B-dap. B-dap. B-dap. B-dap."* The front windows of the restaurant started shattering. Nell started busting back, first at Jazz who tried to jump over the counter getting caught with two slugs in the side, then in the direction of Mutt, who was hiding behind a car. The twins let their trey eights go. *"Pop-pop-pop-pop."* They were trying to distract Mutt long enough so they could make it out of the restaurant. Jazz was sitting behind the backside of the counter. He crawled further to the rear for cover. He slid his pistol out in case somebody came to get at him. The female workers were all screaming and the place was total chaos. Mutt looked from the car he was hiding behind. *"B-dap. B-dap. B-dap. B-dap."* He wanted to make it inside so he could see if

Jazz was alright. Nell and the twins started busting back in Mutt's direction long enough to get him to take cover so they could make their move out of the store. Mutt heard the men running. He let off his last bullets hoping that he hit something. He watched the threesome get away, running up Broadway. He ran into the restaurant to check on Jazz.

"Jazz, where are you, son?" He was looking around.

"In the back," Jazz yelled back with pain in his voice. "I'm hit, yo."

Jazz made it over the counter to where his man was and saw blood pouring from his stomach. The cashier was hysterical. She ran straight to the phone and dialed 911. The manager helped Mutt carry Jazz to the car and Mutt laid him on the back seat. Mutt sped off to Grandview Hospital where he made sure his man was being helped. Mutt disappeared before the police got there because he knew he couldn't take any chances of being taken into custody. He drove Drea's car over to Mack's house. He had to call Drea so that she could make it to Grandview to be by her man's side. With his man in the hospital, there was nothing left to do but handle the beef his own way. Mutt called Dayton International Airport to book a flight for the next thing smoking to New York City. It was time to bring in the wolves.

CHAPTER TWELVE

"**D**amn, Mutt, what the hell are you doing back in the city already? I know y'all ain't moved that shit you bought already," Rhondu said with enthusiasm. They gave one another some dap.

"Yo, Rhondu, Jazz got wet up out there last night. I just flew in a little while ago. I'm trying to get some of the crew together so that we can go down there and handle them Bamas. Whoever is willing to come will be compensated very well for their services." Mutt looked at Du.

Du smiled. "Count me in, nigga. Jazz is my ma'fuckin' man, fam. If it wasn't for him, I wouldn't even have this block on smash, son. I'm gonna go get Craig, Link and my black ass cousin Cris from Brooklyn. You know that bugged out ass nigga dick get hard for some beef, yo!" Rhondu was hyped up.

"How long will it take you to get them all together, Du? I'm trying to get back at them clowns ASAP, son." Mutt looked at his watch.

"Give me a couple of hours and we'll be ready, Mutt. I got to catch Black Cris, but Craig and Link are right here in the hood somewhere. I saw them earlier. Do we need to take some heat with us or what, son?" Rhondu asked.

"Me and Jazz got an arsenal down there, son. I wouldn't

ride down no highway dirty like that anyway. Just call my cell phone when you're ready, Rhondu, and hurry your ass up."

• • •

"That shit that happened been all on the news all day, dog. They said the nigga got hit twice and he's in critical condition. I'm mad that you didn't kill that nigga, Nell." Champ was heated. He spoke what was on his mind.

"Trust me, Champ, I tried, but his man must've been looking at us the whole time, 'cause as soon as I was gonna blast dude, his man started firing at us," explained Nell.

"I bet they'll take their asses home *now*. When them hot balls hit your ass, you get smart *real* quick. Ya feel me, Nell?"

"I had to have my girl call her car in stolen, dog. I ain't know if they linked my car to the shooting or not. Champ, that was some crazy shit, dog. My cousins had them bullshit trey eights. When them niggas ran out of bullets, they were scared to death."

"I *bet* that was some crazy shit. Man, I hate that I missed out on that shit, Nell. What are we gonna do now, dog?" Champ was looking for some action.

"It's a wrap now. We put our work in. Ain't nothing else to do but get this money. We'll be on point for anything if it jumps off, but I doubt that very seriously," Nell said confidently.

"I'll be here in the projects, Nell. You know I don't go nowhere. When are you coming back?" Champ looked at his surroundings.

"I'm going over to my girl's house for awhile, then I'm gonna go swoop up the twins and probably come back through."

"Ahight then, Nell, I'll holla later on." They gave each other a handshake and a hug and moved out.

• • •

Ring. Ring. "Hello!" It was Rhondu.

"Yo, Mutt, this is Rhondu. We're ready, son. My cousin just got here, yo." Rhondu couldn't stop thinking about the drama.

"I'll be over at your crib in a short. I'm getting a van for us to ride back in. I'm at the rental place now."

"Ahight then, we're here waiting on you son. Out."

• • •

Mutt made it back to Rhondu's crib with a rented Chrysler Town and Country van. Craig and Link, two other members of Jazz' New York crew, went along to support their longtime friend. Like Du, they went way back with Jazz and felt loyalty to him and anyone who came from the block for that matter. Black Cris, Rhondu's cousin from Flatbush, Brooklyn, was another story. He was a gun for hire, notoriously known throughout the borough of Brooklyn for putting in work. People from Brooklyn knew when he came through with the screw face, it was time to scatter because once he flipped, he didn't give a fuck who got the business. The ride to Ohio was mainly quiet except for when Mutt told them how Jazz got hit up and everything he knew about the enemy. They pulled into the city limits of Dayton, Ohio, a little after midnight and headed straight for Mack's house.

• • •

"Mack and Kirky, these are my peoples from up top, Rhondu, Craig, Black Cris and Link," Mutt said as all the men gave dap and hugs to one another.

Mack started. "Yo, Mutt, I just got off the phone with Drea. She said Jazz is doing alright. They were able to get that bullet out of his side. It just missed his kidney, too, she said."

"I hate that them Bamas were able to touch my man up like that. I saw them moving on him a second too late, but I *was* able to save his life. If I wasn't there, they definitely would've murdered my man. Mack, I know you wanted to be in on this, but I can't afford to play no more games with these niggas. We're going looking for them tonight, son," Mutt said matter-of-factly.

Kirky jumped in. "We can probably catch them niggas out somewhere tonight, too. Especially that nigga Nell. He really do think he's untouchable." He folded his arms.

"Yo, Kirky, do the twins still be in the Bass trying to hustle?" Mack asked. He had his hand under his chin trying to think.

"Damn, yeah, I almost forgot about them lil niggas. If they ain't out clubbin', they definitely gonna be somewhere over there," Kirky replied.

"Fuck it," Mutt said, "let's go catch them little bastards first. Mack, get that caché case with all that shit we got from the gun show. Let's go tear some shit up." Mutt was motioning with his hands.

"Yo, Mutt, how the fuck do all of y'all plan on getting around, dog? I know you ain't using that van with them hot ass New York tags," Mack interjected.

"You're right, yo. I never thought about that. You're gonna have to let us use that Explorer you be taking care of business in. Ya heard?" Mutt replied. Mack continued. "That's cool with me. I don't give a fuck, just tear them nigga's asses up. *Damn*, I wish I was in better condition to go." Mack's adrenaline was up.

Mack went and got the case with all the weapons from his bedroom closet and brought it into the living room where everybody was relaxing. Mutt came and took the case and opened it.

All of his boys' eyes widened with amazement. The black steel of the multiple tecs glistened. There was even one AK in the mix and Black Cris scooped that up off the rip. Everyone grabbed their weapon of choice except for Kirky. He knew he was gonna be the driver for the mission so his lil 380 he had been keepin' on him since the beef started would do him just fine.

Mutt told his boys to each grab one of the pistols just in case one of the larger weapons jammed up on them. Mutt made Rhondu stay back with Mack because there was no room for him in the Explorer. Five was enough anyway. Rhondu hated that he wasn't gonna be able to bust off on the niggas who tried to flatline his main man, Jazz. Kirky started the truck up and headed in the direction of the DeSoto Bass housing projects. They were going to pay the twins a much needed visit.

CHAPTER THIRTEEN

"Yo, Gee, let me hit that blunt with you, dog. It's kind of slow out here tonight. If it don't start picking up soon, I'm about to bounce," said Ricky, a little hustla from the Bass. He and Gee were standing outside of their spot kicking it.

"When my brother comes back, I'm a spark it up. Oh, shit, here he comes now." Gary spotted his twin approaching.

They embraced. "What's up, Gary? I just got off the phone with that nigga, Nell. He's down in Edgewood chillin'. He said he might come through and check on us a little later. I told him I'll call him back if we bounce though."

"That's cool, Larry. I'm staying right here. Ain't nobody really out but us three, so we should be able to move some of this package Nell gave us earlier. Here, Lar, light up the El, dog." Gary passed his other half the blunt.

"Kirky, we gonna tear all these nigga's asses up tonight. After we find the twins, we're going to Edgewood and hold court on them niggas," Mack said breaking the silence in the truck just as they were approaching the Bass.

"Y'all niggas be ready. We're about a block away. I'm gonna ride through where all them niggas be serving cars at. If they out, that's where they gonna be," said Kirky.

Black Cris said his first words of the evening. "Just point them niggas out. I got this."

The SUV entered the Bass and crept through slowly. Everyone in the Jeep were fully focused. Coming into view further down the street were three individuals looking as if they were in a deep conversation. From a distance, Kirky wasn't sure if it was the twins or not. Mutt was sitting in the front passenger seat praying to God that it was them. His hands were sweating profusely from the nervous energy he had from the prospect of death approaching. Kirky got closer to the trio and noticed that it was the enemy. The twins and Ricky noticed the Explorer creeping from down the street, but thought it was some fiends looking to score. Their guards were all the way down due to the fat juicy blunt they just got through taking to the head. Kirky mashed on the gas pedal and Mutt and Black Cris sprung into action. The twins tried to run, but Mutt and Black Cris were on them. *Pop. Pop. Pop. Pop. Pop. Pop. Pop. Pop. Pop. Pop. Cack-cack-cack-cack-cack-cack-cack.* Flames were shooting from the passenger side of the Explorer. All three men fell on the side of a building. Larry was screaming in pain. Both of his legs were shredded. Gary was heaving heavily, gasping for air. He had a hole straight through his torso. Ricky was a done deal. His skull exploded from the AK Black Cris was spitting.

"Stop this bitch! Come on, Cris, let's make sure we got them niggas," Mutt yelled, as the large vehicle came to a stop.

Kirky stopped the Explorer immediately and reversed a few feet. Cris and Mutt hopped out before the truck came to a complete stop. Semi's in hand, they ran straight up on the twins. They pumped a few more slugs into each one of them. At such close range, their bodies were mangled from the high caliber slugs. Neither of the men would be able to have open caskets for their funerals. Mutt and Black Cris hopped back in the truck and Kirky sped off.

"We're going to Edgewood, son!" Mutt said half out of breath. The adrenaline was going through his body at a high rate of speed. "Kirky, call that smoked out bitch Lisa and ask her if them niggas are out over there," Mutt added.

Kirky dialed Lisa's number. It was his old stomping grounds.

"Hello," Lisa answered.

Kirky spoke up. "Let me speak to Lisa."

"This Lisa, who's this?" she questioned.

"Yo, Lisa, this Lil Kirky. I got somebody that wants to talk to you, hold on." Kirky handed Mutt the phone.

"Lisa, what's up baby, this is Mutt."

"What's up with you, Mutt? I thought you were gonna come and see me." She was blushing.

His game kicked in. "I got you, girlfriend. I need you to do me a favor. Go outside and see if them niggas are in the projects."

"I was just outside on the other end earlier. Nell, Champ and a couple of their boys were standing in front of their spot. Ask Kirky if he knows Rebe's apartment," she said.

"Here, talk to him." Mutt handed Kirky the phone.

"Yeah, Lisa," said Kirky.

"You know my girlfriend Rebe, don't you?"

"Yeah, of course. Who don't know Rebe in Edgewood?"

"Well, that's where them niggas were posted up about an hour ago. She let's them use her apartment as their spot."

"Can you go and make sure for us. I promise we'll make it worth your while for helping us." Mutt was wooing her.

"Call me back in about five minutes, Kirky. You better take

care of me, too. Y'all motha fuckas fucking up my high with this bullshit." The thought of some dope made her middle moisten.

Kirky hung up the phone and let everyone know that Lisa was on her way to check things for them. He was now only a couple of blocks from Edgewood so he decided to pull over on a side street until he made contact with Lisa again. He wanted Nell and Champ to be there so they could handle them fake ganstas once and for all. Black Cris was so nervous just sitting still that he wished he had a Newport to help calm himself down.

"Kirky, call that bitch back, son. All this sitting ain't kosher, yo," Black Cris spoke up from the back seat. Craig and Link shook their heads in agreement.

"Ahight, dog. I'm on it," Kirky said. He dialed her number.

Lisa answered on the first ring. "Lisa, did you take care of that?" Kirky asked.

"I just walked back in. They're still out there. You better hurry up though. I heard Nell say he was about to leave."

"How many of them were over there?"

"Champ, Nell, and some more dudes, I don't know their names though."

"Is your girl Bebe over there?" Kirky asked.

"She left, but they're all sitting in the front room smoking and drinking," she said.

"Thank you, Lisa. I won't forget this."

Kirky hung up the phone and pulled off without saying a word. The rest of the men in the vehicle knew by his actions that they were getting ready to put their work in.

Kirky started, "They're over there, dog. I know exactly

where they are too. The apartment is on the corner, like a town-house and shit. I'm gonna pull this truck straight up in front and we all rush the door, guns blazing, dog."

Black Cris jumped in. "With this AK, that door should turn into shreds. Let me lead y'all niggas and follow me in. Shoot anything moving and we should be outta there in less than two minutes."

Kirky pulled up in front of Rebe's apartment. As soon as he put the car in park, all the doors flew open. They opened fire. *B-dap. B-dap. Cack. Cack, B-dap. B-dap. Pop. Pop. Pop. Cack-cack-cack-cack.* The door to Rebe's apartment exploded from the fuselage. Nell, Champ, Kai and Bo didn't have a clue what was happening. They all simultaneously ducked to the floor. All types of hot balls were whistling past their heads. Black Cris was the first through the door followed by Mutt, Link, and Craig. Kirky was the last one to run in.

Kirky started. "You niggas thought it was over. Here we are you bitches!"

Nell, for the first time in his life, saw death staring him in the face. He had the look of a defeated man. He looked at his crew and saw tears coming out of Champ's eyes as he was lay-ing on the ground frozen with fear. Kai was laying on the ground shaking as if he was having a seizure. One of the many slugs tore into a major artery in his leg and he was slowly bleeding to death.

Black Cris shouted, "Mutt, hurry up, son. Take these Bamas out so we can get the fuck out of here!"

Mutt walked up to Nell and remembered the look on his face when he tried to creep up on Jazz in Church's Chicken. No words were needed. He let his Mac-II spit on his man's attacker, then kept on squeezing in the direction of the others. He didn't stop spraying until his clip was empty. Craig and Link were shook witnessing the enemy take all of those slugs at close range. Kirky had to pull them away from the carnage and into the truck. They took off in the direction of Mack's house. They saw at least seven police cars heading in the direction of Edgewood. They got away in the nick of time.

When they reached Mack's house, Kirky gathered all of the weapons, wiped them down real good and went to dispose of them. Before he left, he gave Mutt and his crew from New York some dap and a huge hug. He knew by the time he got back from his mission, they would all be on their way back home. Mutt pulled Mack aside.

"Yo, son, it's a wrap. Don't worry about a thing. Make sure you look out for your girl, Lisa. She helped us a lot, yo."

"I got that covered. You gonna go see Jazz before you leave, Mutt?"

"As bad as I want to, I can't. I'm getting my ass as far away from this town as possible. I don't know when I'll be back, Mack. This town is gonna be hot as fire, dog."

"Well, I'll be here, Mutt. Get with me."

"That's for sure, yo. We're still gonna get this money together. Ain't no doubt about that."

Black Cris yelled, "Let's get the fuck out of here, Mutt."

"Alright, Mack, we out, baby boy. Be good."

CHAPTER FOURTEEN

R ing. Ring. Ring.

"Hello, Drea." It was Mack.

"Hey, Mack, what's up?" she was beaming.

"I see you made it to the hospital early this morning. Is Jazz up yet?" he asked.

"Yeah, he's watching *Jerry Springer*."

"Tell him to turn on the news real quick and pass him the phone," Mack said.

Jazz heard his friend and immediately flipped to the news channel. News crews were all over Edgewood Projects interviewing tenants. They were wondering if anyone had information in connection with the quadruple homicide. Then Jazz heard the anchorwoman speak about a triple homicide in DeSoto Bass, which she said may have been related. Tears of joy streamed down his eyes. He told Mack he would call him right back. He knew Mutt had taken care of business. Mutt must have gone home and brought back the wolves.

Kevin (Polo) Taylor is an up and coming writer from South Jamaica, Queens. His soon-to-be-released debut novel *All About the Paper* is a gritty street tale depicting inner city street life. Definitely be on the look out for that and more to come in the future from this star on the rise.

Temptations

Vincent Warren

CHAPTER ONE

By Vincent Warren

Bang. Bang. Bang. "Boy, wake your ass up. Your coach is on the phone. It's 4 o'clock in the afternoon. We should've been out of here five minutes ago.," Ms. Jackson shouted.

"Mom, I got the phone. Hello, Mr. Johnson, I'm on my way," said Speedy, getting himself together.

"Listen, Speedy, you should've been here already. Get your ass down here. This is the championship and you need your warm up," answered his coach.

"Okay. See you later, Coach," replied Speedy. He hung up the phone and put on his shoes.

Tyshaun "Speedy" Jackson was the all-state point guard. He had received a scholarship for his basketball abilities. Every important college coach and scout was calling him, writing him, and attending his games.

Speedy first woke up at 2:30 p.m.. He took his shower and dressed himself in a sweat suit. He fell back to sleep until his mother, Tamara Jackson woke him up. Speedy tied up his sneakers and grabbed his book bag with his basketball outfit and hygienic utensils inside. He brushed his teeth soon after, and he and his mother quickly walked out of their house. Tamara locked the door and caught up to Speedy. His mother drove a black

BMW. Tamara couldn't help but smile as she glanced over at her son, while they marched towards the BMW. Tamara punched the alarm button on her key ring. The car made a beeping sound and all four doors unlocked. Tamara walked around to the driver's side, as Speedy opened the passenger side door, sat down and closed the door behind him. Tamara locked herself in, turned the key in the ignition, and then the car came to life. She pulled out of the driveway and made a right heading south.

"Boy, your father would've been proud of you. You better not mess up all that you got going for yourself," Speedy's mother said.

"Come on, Mom, I know what I have to do," replied Speedy.

"Yeah, but them boys you hang with are trouble." His mother glanced at him.

"Come on, Ma, do we have to go through this today?" Speedy sighed.

"Okay, since you know it all, just remember that temptations will get you in trouble in this world," responded Ms. Tamara.

Speedy's mother talked and talked as she drove. Speedy let her words go in one ear and out the other through the passenger's side window. Speedy and his mother lived in Saint Albans, Queens. All the houses were beautiful. Speedy's father died a year earlier from lung cancer. Warren Jackson was Speedy's mentor and best friend. Speedy promised his father that he would bring the title home during a visit to his father's grave. It was after his team, the *Mad Lions* won the District Conference. The Mad Lions were ranked number one in the State of New York.

The black BMW pulled in front of Saint Clark's College. There were a hundred cars in the big parking lot. Tamara drove her car to a spot that was occupied by Speedy's teammates. The twelve young men sat on the ground between the yellow lines and as the BMW got close, the team got up and moved out of Speedy and Ms. Tamara's way. When Tamara parked, one of the guys approached her door. He opened it for her.

"Thanks, Tommy," said Ms. Jackson, smiling.

"No problem, Ms. Jackson," responded Tommy.

The twelve boys crowded around Speedy and started roaring like Lions. They all laughed then headed inside the college. A security guard directed Ms. Jackson to the gymnasium. Speedy kissed her and told her he would see her soon. He and his teammates headed for the locker room. They walked, silently, since it was a serious moment. Entering the locker room, their coach said, "Okay, you stink little girls, take a seat. Tommy, you're starting center. Speedy, you're the one guard. Curtis, you're the two. Derrick, I need you at power forward today, and Bryan, you get the small forward spot. I don't want to see a one man show," the coach looked at Speedy. "I want team ball. The first one to argue is on the bench. Now let's get out there and take some shots," said the coach excitedly.

The players and the coach jogged out of the locker room after the twenty-minute speech. They jogged into an already packed gym. The gym was huge. The basketball court was surrounded with fifteen row bleachers in three directions, leaving the west wall as an exit and an entranceway. This was the biggest high school game of the year.

As Speedy and his teammates, along with his coach, reached the center of the court, Speedy spotted his friend, Tymel "Fly Ty" Lamont, on the bleachers.

"Hey, Player, get busy, my nigga," Fly Ty screamed to his

homie.

As Speedy looked up at Fly Ty, Speedy did a little turn around dance. When Speedy turned, he spotted his mother and never returned his gaze back at Fly Ty.

"Yo, Fly Ty, you see that?" questioned a sixteen-year-old spectator sitting next to Ty.

"Yeah, Speedy's moms got his ass shook," Fly Ty answered.

The lights in the gym went low.

"Nowww, for your starting line up!!" the M.C. sounded.

•   •   •

"Damn, Pat, we got a flat tire," shouted Ann.

"What the hell you mean, Ann? Speedy's gonna kill me if I miss his game."

"What the hell, Pat, we caught a fucking flat," responded Ann angrily.

"Yo, I'm going to find a cab," Pat suggested.

"Bitch, you just gonna leave me right here? You don't know what could go down," answered Ann. She was stuck in the middle of nowhere, frustrated.

"Listen, Ann, I'm sorry, but I have to go," said Pat.

"Damn, at least help me get someone to put on the spare tire," shouted Ann.

Antonelle "Ann" Phillips and Patricia "Pat" Brown got out of the red Range Rover and tried to flag down a passing car on the busy Grand Concourse in the Bronx. The Jeep they were in was parked on the side of the road with its hazard lights on.

"Yo, Ray, stop the car. Yo, stop, son!" Damon said, eyeing the two ladies.

"Damon, you don't even know them bitches, gee," Ray replied, pulling over.

"Yo, Ray, they got a truck family, *and* they look good, play boy."

"Damn, that's probably some nigga's shit."

Damon pulled his Navigator over, stepped out, leaving the motor running and headed toward the Range with Ray right behind him.

"So, what seems to be the problem, ladies?" asked Damon.

"We have a flat and we need help changing the tire," replied Ann.

"Damon, hold on. I'll get a jack and some vice grips from the truck." Ray took off.

Ray came back as fast as he left. In twenty minutes, the spare tire was on and the flat tire was in the huge trunk of the Range.

"Yo, Ray, someone's taking the truck," shouted Damon.

Ray and Damon ran towards the Navigator. The Navigator pulled off fast. Ann and Pat got inside the Range and drove off.

"You slut bitches," screamed Ray.

"Yo, you foul, Pat," said Ann.

"Fuck 'em," replied Pat.

"Pat, I got to see my boo's game. Damn, slow down a little. You ain't see that cop car on your left side?" asked a nervous Ann.

"Shit, they just put their sirens on. We're pulling over," said Pat.

"Oh, fuck me, what a fucking day. Speedy is gonna flip," shouted Ann.

The patrol officer walked over to the driver's side window and said, "Miss, do you know that you were doing sixty miles an hour in a thirty-five mile an hour zone?"

"No, sir. I wasn't paying attention," replied Pat.

"Well, do you have your license and registration?" asked the cop.

"Yes, sir, one second," answered Pat.

Pat reached up with her right hand and pulled down the sun visor. She retrieved her registration papers, then reached in her pocketbook with her left hand for her wallet.

The Game

"This has been a great game. Speedy has one promising future," said the commentator.

"Well, Dick, I would have to concur with that. The kid is amazing. Ooh, here he comes with the ball up the court. He's being double teamed. Speedy dribbles left, oh, he crosses over and kicks it to Curtis. Curtis pulls up for the three, he misses, ooh. Bryan dunks it as it comes off the glass," the commentator screamed excitedly.

"It's twenty seconds left in this fourth quarter. It's a tied score, 98 to 98. The Rochester Devils are taking the ball out," the commentator continued.

"Now this guy has a handle, Larry. Here comes Douglas, he brings it up..." *Bang, bang, bang.* "Aaaahhh! Aaaahhh!" *Bang, tat, tat, tat, bang, bang, pop, pop.* People were running and shouting.

When Douglas was bringing the ball down, a young man, early twenties, named *Low Down* spotted another young man named Daquan that shot and killed Low Down's older brother, Varney. Daquan tried to creep through the crowded bleachers to get Low Down. "Excuse me, excuse me," Daquan said as he walked past a few people. Low Down followed Douglas with his eyes as Douglas dribbled the ball down the court. Low Down spotted Daquan creeping with a gun. Low Down grabbed his knapsack off the floor, unzipped it, reached into it, and pulled out a Mac .10 semi automatic Uzi. He then inserted the clip. Daquan saw Low Down load his weapon so with only a second left, Daquan raised his 21 shot Berretta, twisted his wrist sideways and pulled the trigger, ducking as he approached his enemy. Low Down dove on the floor before Daquan could hit him.

Low Down cocked his Uzi. *Click, click*, aimed it at Daquan and squeezed. *Bttaatt.* Daquan pulled a young lady in front of him. She got caught in the neck and head. Innocent people were being hit. The yelling and screaming intensified. Ms. Tamara made it off the bleachers. *Bang. Bang. Bang. Cack. Cack. Cack!*

"Mom!! Mom! I'm over here. I'm over here," Speedy screamed for his mother. Tamara raced over to Speedy while his friend Curtis fell on the floor and got trampled to death. Tamara and Speedy made it out of the school. People were running out. Police cars were everywhere.

"They're still inside, Officer," said a security guard. The police charged into the school.

Low Down was standing over Daquan with his Mac aimed at Daquan's face. Daquan ran out of bullets and had three holes in his stomach.

"Freeze," yelled one police officer.

Low Down turned, aimed his gun at the policeman and pulled the trigger. He banged off four shots then dove onto the bleachers, trying to hide between the seats. *Bang, bang, bang, pop, pop, pop!* Bullets were chipping away the bleacher seats. Low Down raised the Mac from between a seat and fired. *Blah, click!* Click, click, click. "Fuck," Low Down yelled. His gun was empty.

"Ayo, Pat, what the fuck is going on, oh my God!" Ann yelled.

"Dammmnn, yo Ann, there goes Speedy's mother's car," Pat replied.

Ann unlocked the truck door and jumped out before the truck fully stopped. She stumbled and fell against a parked car. Ann raced over to Mr. Tamara's BMW and spotted Speedy and Ms. Tamara jogging to the car. "I'm sorry for missing your game," Ann said.

Speedy raced over to the car when Ms. Tamara hit the alarm button. The doors unlocked. "Get in the car, Ann, hurry up," yelled Ms. Tamara.

Pat parked the truck and was looking for Fly Ty. *Knock, knock.* "Yo, open the door," Ty yelled as he stood outside the passenger side window. Pat opened the door. Fly Ty got inside of his truck that Pat was driving. The Range Rover pulled off and so did the BMW.

As for Low Down and Daquan, they were arrested and charged with eleven counts of murder and five hundred counts of attempted murder. They would eventually receive the death penalty.

In front of Pat's house

"Pat, stop playing games. Just give me some throat before you go inside your house."

"No, Ty, you take too long to cum," answered Pat.

Fly Ty sat in his Range Rover while Pat massaged his sex

organ which was sticking out his zipper. Pat went down on him and took him into her mouth. Her head went up and down for about ten minutes, until the cream filled her mouth. She rose up, looked at him, and swallowed everything. She stuck her tongue out and smiled.

"Damn, I like when you do it like that. Thanks, Ma. I'll pick you up tomorrow for the movies at like 6 o'clock. I love you." Fly Ty kissed Pat on her forehead.

Pat kissed him back on his cheek and climbed down from his jeep. She jogged to her house and once she was inside, he drove off.

Fly Ty was from South Jamaica, Queens. He drove his truck to his main drug spot on the strip. He parked his truck and stepped out with his keys in hand. Fly Ty was twenty-years-old and living on his own. His mother was a social worker and his father was a mailman working for the Postal Service. Fly Ty was a disgrace to his family. He was a twenty-year-old criminal. Fly Ty was 6'1", brown skinned, 180 pounds, was in shape and had all the right moves. The strip was a street corner that held ten stores—a pizza shop, barbershop, Chinese restaurant, grocery store, a bar and four vacant buildings. He was a two-time felon, mack baller, weed smoking, black gangsta. Fly Ty walked towards the pizzeria. The strip was packed. Young women and men roamed the street. Fly Ty reached in his pants pocket and drew a knot of money.

"What's in the bank, Justice," asked Fly Ty.

Justice was part of a circle of guys rolling dice. "Whatever's in your hand," Justice replied.

"Yo, Ty, it's thirty-five hundred dollars in it. How much you want to put up?" asked Nat.

Fly Ty dropped his money on the floor and placed his left foot on it. "Whatever's under my foot," said Tymel.

"Na, fuck no! Fuck, hell no. I want to stop this bitch," said Fats, a fat dude with greasy hair.

"Okay, Fats, do your one, two thing," said Tymel.

Justice rolled the dice after he shook them in his hands. Justice had a special trick he would do. He would have the three dice displaying 4-5-6 in his hands, and would pretend to shake them, but would hold his hands tight, giving the dice no space to move in his palm. He'd toss the three dice at the pizza shop wall and the dice would not roll—they would spin.

"Oh, shit, 4-5-6, nigga! Pay that note," Justice called out.

"Motha fucka, that's like the fourth Celo you rolled. Damn!" shouted Fats.

Fats paid Justice the thirty-five hundred dollars and left to go get some more money. Fly Ty whispered into Justice's ear. "Yeah, nigga, I know what you doing. I'm not going to say shit. I'm not going to blow you up, but I want twenty percent," Fly Ty whispered.

Justice looked at Fly Ty and nodded in agreement. "What's in it? What's cracking?" yelled Justice.

"Yo, Killer Black, there goes a vic, son," said Bones observing the dice game as he drove by.

"Yeah, Bones, we gonna park around the corner," replied Killer Black.

Killer Black and Bones parked their black 1993 MPV, turned off the ignition, and exited the van leaving its doors unlocked. They both clutched 16 shot glocks. They pulled their hoods over their heads and jogged down the block. As soon as they turned the corner, Killer Black yelled, "Nigga, everybody put their money on the floor, now!"

"Ayo, Killer Black, what the fuck's up, my nigga?" questioned Fly Ty.

"When you get released, Ty? Matter of fact, respect the game, Bee, run that," replied Killer Black.

"Yo, K.B., you ain't getting shit. Break out, son," Fly Ty answered boldly.

Bang. Killer Black shot Fly Ty in his kneecap. The rest of the men immediately dropped their money on the ground. Ty fell to the ground and held his knee with both hands. An audience of people watched the robbery from a distance.

"All you niggas got ten seconds to pick this buster up and bounce," shouted Bones.

Justice picked Fly Ty up, wrapped Ty's right arm around his shoulders and walked off slowly. The rest of the dice players took off like a track meet. Bones and Killer Black took all the money off the floor and ran back to the van.

● ● ●

"Ty, stop screaming like a bitch. You ain't gon' die, my nigga. We're going to the hospital," said an angry Justice.

"Yo, Jus, this shit is burning, man. Take my truck," Fly Ty said in agony.

"You ma' fuckin' right. Your blood won't be all up in *my* damn car," replied Justice.

A crowd of men and women raced over to Justice and Fly Ty.

"You ma' fuckas spread out," shouted Justice.

Someone had called the cops. Three squad cars arrived at the scene. A young female went to flag one of the cop cars.

"Butch, if you call that cop, I'ma smack those fake eyebrows off ya forehead!" shouted Justice.

"Fuck you, Just," she yelled back.

The doors to the truck were unlocked. Justice helped Fly Ty into the passenger side, closed the door and jogged over to the driver's side. Justice got inside, slammed the door and said, "Ya, Ty, pass the keys." He had his hand out.

Ty dug in his pocket and pulled out a set of keys. Blood was all over them.

"Yo, Ty, nigga, you have to put the key into the ignition," said Justice.

"Like I got AIDs, nigga," Fly Ty said in a painful voice. He turned the key in the ignition and the truck came to life. Justice pulled off slowly and after the police were far behind, he pressed the peddle to the metal. "Rummmmm."

"Yo, Jus, I'm gon' kill that nigga, son, I swear, dawg," shouted Fly Ty.

"Yo, homie, don't talk. Just keep the pressure on your knee," replied Justice.

Fly Ty pulled off his Coogie sweater and tied it around his knee. Eight minutes later they were in front of Saint James' Hospital. Justice opened the door, got out and slammed it shut, then jogged around to the passenger side. Fly Ty opened the door after he reached over and took the key out of the ignition. Justice helped Fly Ty out of the truck, slammed the door and held Fly Ty's arm as Fly Ty hopped into the hospital. The truck was parked at the emergency entrance's side. As soon as they reached the emergency room, Justice yelled, "Get me a doctor. This man is shot."

Fifteen seconds tops, three nurses were racing toward the

duo with a stretcher. They told Fly Ty to lie down. The nurse pulled the bed railings up on the sides of the stretcher and cut the sweater off his knee. One of the nurses started cutting his pants leg while another nurse checked his pulse. Fly Ty passed out from loss of blood.

"Sir, you can't come back here. Could you please have a seat out in the emergency room," said a nurse.

Justice about faced with his head down, walked into the emergency room and found himself a seat. He covered his ears with his hands and bent forward. The emergency room was loud from babies crying, adults crying and talking simultaneously. A woman rocking a child in her arms turned and looked at Justice. She said, "He's gonna live. He looks like a strong man," the woman said with assurance.

Justice took his hands off his ears, sat up and spoke to the woman. "Excuse me, what did you say?" he asked.

"I said, he's gonna make it, he looks like a strong brother," said the thirty-something-year-old black woman.

"Yeah, I guess so," Justice replied solemnly.

A nurse came out into the emergency room and walked over to Justice. "Excuse me, sir, were you the one with the male who was shot in his knee cap?"

"Yes, I am," replied Justice.

"Well then, can you please follow me," said the nurse.

Justice rose up and looked at the woman he spoke with before he was interrupted by the nurse. She spoke in a low voice. "Be careful. You know the nurse might be bringing you to the 5.0!" said the woman.

"Thanks. I be knowing," replied Justice. They smiled at each other and Justice walked off following the nurse. Once they walked through the emergency room doors, plain clothed detectives were waiting for him. Justice smiled to himself and made a mental note to get the woman's phone number who was right about the police.

CHAPTER TWO

April 5ᵗʰ, 12 p.m.

Tap! Tap! Tap! Tap! Someone was knocking on Speedy's door. "Who is it?" he shouted. He headed for the door.

"Who are you expecting to see, Speedy?" asked Ann. She was tapping one of her feet.

Speedy recognized the all-so-pleasant voice and opened the door. Ann opened the screen door and walked past Speedy looking like she had an attitude.

Speedy walked out of the house and scanned the area to make sure no one saw her enter the crib. He closed the screen door, locked the inner door and walked into the living room. To the left of the living room was a large kitchen with a dining table and sterling silver chandeliers. Near the entrance sat a staircase that lead to the attic where Speedy had a large bedroom, a studio and workout room. To the right of the ground floor by the steps was a long hallway that held photos of historical African American figures on its walls. At the end of the hall was the master bedroom where Ms. Jackson took comfort. At the other end of the hall were two nicely decorated guest bedrooms. Mr. Jackson was a judge before he passed away one year ago.

Tyshaun "Speedy" Jackson looked at Ann and as always, was turned on by her beauty. Ann was 5'5, 135 pounds. Her skin was so light that it looked reddish. Her hands were small and soft, and her face was very pretty. Her figure was a perfect 8 and people sometimes said that she resembled a model.

Speedy didn't look bad himself. The young man was nine-teen-years-old and already 6'2. He was often asked if he was any kin to Denzel Washington.

"So, what took you so long to get here?" Speedy asked. He was playing in Ann's hair.

"I had a phone call from Pat and she said that Ty had got-ten shot in his knee last night. That was my ride, so I had to call a cab," Ann replied.

"That means you waited two hours for a cab?" Speedy asked smiling.

"No, dummy, Pat had me on the phone for almost an hour."

"Listen, my moms should be here in about three hours, so take all that tight shit you got on off, and let's get to fucking," Speedy said excitedly.

Speedy sat next to Ann and they began kissing one another. Speedy pulled her onto him and the couple enjoyed each other's company for the next two hours.

• • •

Pat's house

"Pat, hurry up in the bathroom, shoot," Pat's seventeen-year-old sister Wanda jumped up and down outside the bath-room door. She had to move her bowels and she couldn't hold it.

"Wanda, use Mommy's bathroom. I'm taking a shower," Pat shouted.

Wanda pushed the bathroom door open, closed it and pulled her pants and underwear down and sat on the toilet.

"Damn, Wanda, did something crawl up your ass while you were asleep? That shit stinks. Flush the fucking toilet," shouted Pat over her water running.

"Pat, I hear you cussing in that bathroom."

Before Ms. Brown could finish her sentence, Pat yelled, "Mom, I'm sorry."

"Alright, child, watch your mouth. I'm telling you, just because you're eighteen-years-old, don't think I won't slap your mouth," shouted ms. Brown.

"Ooh, Lord Jesus," said Pat's grandmother.

"Sorry, Momma, that child thinks she's too grown, you understand."

"Wanda, you better not ever do that shit again or I'll beat your ass up. I don't give a fuck what Mommy says," Pat told her sister in a low tone.

Wanda paid her no attention. Her deed was done. Wanda wiped, flushed the toilet and washed her hands. She spoke in a low tone. "I don't know what the fuck you been drinking, Pat. You're only one year older than me and I won't just let you do me dirty."

Pat responded to Wanda in a calm manner, "Wanda, I love you, yo. Now could you please get out?"

Wanda walked out of the bathroom, closed the door and walked down the steps. She made a right into the kitchen.

"Hey child, how you doing?" Ms. Betsy asked.

"I'm okay, Grandma, I didn't know you were here yet."

Pat entered her room and hung her towel on a hook that was behind the door. Pat's hair was thick, dark and lovely. It was past her shoulders. Pat was what most guys would call a dime. She stood 5'7, 135 pounds, perfect shape with a set of breasts that looked too round to be real. She had a golden complexion with no blemishes and smooth skin. Some said she resembled Pop Diva Janet Jackson. Pat sat down on her bed, reached through her bed curtains and took the cherry body lotion from the top of her dresser and lotioned up.

Tyshaun's crib

"Ooh, yess, fuck me, Daddy!" shouted Ann in complete ecstasy.

"Um, I... I'm... cum... cumin'" Speedy was laying on his back with Ann sitting on top of him.

When Ann felt him shrink inside of her, she rolled off of him and laid on her stomach. After three minutes of silence, Ann spoke up. "About time, Speedy. I don't even know why they call you Speedy." She was referring to their lengthy love making so she laughed.

"Come on, let's get in the shower, Boo," Speedy suggested.

Speedy and Ann walked to the shower, still naked, and hopped up into it.

"What are you doing, Speedy?" asked Ann. She turned to face him as the water beat in her face.

"I'm looking for my *Isley Brothers* tape. Here it goes." Speedy put the tape in the tape deck and pressed play. *Voyage to Atlantis* sounded throughout the bathroom.

"Pick your neck up, Ma," said Speedy. He was washing his girlfriend's chest and shoulders.

"I love when you wash me up, Baby," replied Ann.

• • •

179

Fly Ty's house

The *Ten Crack Commandments* by Biggie Smalls played loudly in the background.

"Yo, Pat, pass me some more baking soda, and get me some from out of the freezer," Fly Ty shouted.

"Nigga, I'm not going to help you ruin your life. Bad enough I don't like for you to be selling this shit. Fuck I look like helping you cook this shit, nigga!" yelled Pat.

Fly Ty was cooking up some coke. He also had four of his friends over playing poker in his dining room. Two others were playing Play Station in his living room.

"A yo, Ty, I know you gon' ride on that buster who shot you, cuz," said Justice.

"Nigga, you know retaliation is a must, family," responded Fly Ty.

"Then what are we waiting for. Let's get it shaking, player," shouted BoBo.

"Ayo, Bo, time is everything, God!" said Fly Ty, shaking a large coffee pot full of coke over the stove.

"Nigga, you know..."

Blong! Blong! Blong! Blong! Bullets were crashing through Fly Ty's window stopping him in mid-sentence. Fly Ty dropped the coffee pot on top of the stove, breaking it. Pat was forced to the floor by Fly Ty. As he fell, he drew his 40 caliber 16 shot Glock from his waistband. The dudes who were playing poker were on the floor with their guns drawn. One of the cats that were playing the video game was shaking on the floor with a gunshot wound to the side of his head.

Errrr! The car merked off. It was a drive by. Fly Ty hopped to his door, opened it, and limped towards the street. He took aim at the blue car, but it was already turning the corner.

"Fuck!" shouted Fly Ty. Pat ran out into the street crying and shaking. Fly Ty hugged her. The sound of sirens told them that the police were on their way.

"Shit, the coke," said Fly Ty. Fly Ty pushed Pat to the side and hopped into his apartment. He limped toward the kitchen, stepped over the table that was now in pieces on the floor, grabbed a dishtowel and began wiping away the coke.

"Pat, get the fuck out of here," Fly Ty screamed.

Pat ran out of the house and ran towards her place which wasn't too far.

"Yo, somebody get the guns out of here," yelled Justice.

"BoBo, take my gun," shouted Fly Ty.

BoBo ran into the kitchen, grabbed Fly Ty's gun as well as everybody else's, and took off out the door.

"Freezzeee," shouted a detective as BoBo exited the apartment. BoBo turned to his right, jumped over a small gate and faced the back of the house which was connected to the studio. BoBo had seven guns wrapped up in a coat. He ran into the back yard, tossed the coat over the gate, hopped the gate, picked up the coat and kept running. The detective knew he wouldn't catch him so he gave up the chase.

CHAPTER THREE

The precint, 6 p.m.

"So, I am going to ask you one more time, who was the guy that ran?" asked Detective Johnson.

"I told you, if you're not going to arrest me, let me go!" replied Fly Ty.

"Okay, you want to play hard ass. Get the fuck out, and if somebody kills you, I hope your family will be happy," said Detective Hellberry, the assisting officer.

Fly Ty grabbed his coat off the table, stood up and pushed his chair back with his good leg. He looked the two detectives in the eyes and walked past them.

Pat was waiting for him in the station with Ann and Speedy. The four of them walked out together, with nobody saying a word.

"So what are we gonna do, Ty?" asked Speedy. The quartet was standing in front of the precinct.

"Let's go to the fucking movies," Fly Ty suggested.

"The movies?" Pat questioned.

"Yeah, why not?" Ann interjected.

"Okay, let's all split up and get dressed. Fuck it, let's get Fly Ty out of these streets for a few," said Speedy.

* * * * * *

Pat's house

"Mom, I'll see you later. Bye, Grandma, and Mom, where is Wanda?" asked Pat.

"She went to the store," responded Ms. Brown.

"Okay, tell her I'll see her later," Pat said then walked out of the house.

She raced down the porch steps and towards the truck. Fly Ty took his left hand off the steering wheel and pressed the lock button on the driver's side down. The door unlocked. Pat opened it, climbed inside and closed the door behind her. She leaned her upper body over towards Ty with teary eyes and they kissed. She then repositioned herself and Fly Ty drove off.

Pat looked back at her house and noticed her mother and grandmother staring through the living room window at her. She turned her head to face the road and Ms. Brown and Ms. Betsy closed the curtains.

"So, Debra, where do you think that boy got the big ol' car from?" said Ms. Betsy.

"Well, his family has a lot of money and they live in that big ol' house up the street," Debra replied.

• • •

"So, how's your knee feeling?" asked Pat.

"It's cracked and has a hole through it," answered Fly Ty.

"Well you need to hurry up and kill them guys before they kill you, Baby," said Pat now crying. She was still a little bit shaken up.

"Don't start. Just put my cane in the back seat, Baby, please," he begged.

Pat reached on the truck's floor, picked up his cane and placed it on the back seat. "Do you want me to drive?" Pat asked.

Fly Ty looked at her then slowly pulled the truck over. They switched seats. They headed to Tyshaun's house. Speedy and Ann took cabs home. Ann got dressed and took a cab to Tyshaun's house. He was also dressed so they waited together for Fly Ty and Pat to pull up.

• • •

Tyshaun's house

"Come on, fix your face. You look cute," whispered Speedy in a romantic tone.

"No, Speedy, I had these clothes on earlier, you know," replied Ann.

Speedy looked at Ann with a sad tone and spoke. "Ooh, poor baby," said Speedy.

Beeppp. Fly Ty beeped his horn.

"Come on, Ann, that's them." Before he left, Speedy wrote a quick note and placed it behind a magnet on his refrigerator, telling his mother that he and Ann went out to the movies.

"So what up, bird man, holla at cha dude and pop ya collar, young scholar," said Speedy.

"Ain't shit, Speedy, a little stressed about earlier, nah-mean?" replied Fly Ty.

The truck pulled off. Everyone got silent when Fly Ty told them the story about him being shot the night before and how Justice knew the guy.

"How I look over there, Ty?" asked Pat, referring to her parking skills.

"You're good, Ma," answered Fly Ty.

The doors opened and the group exited the SUV. They walked into the theater and approached the window.

"Good day. Welcome to Sunrise Multiplex. May I help you?" asked a portly white lady at the ticket booth.

"Can I have four tickets for *Hoezetta*?" replied Fly Ty.

The lady told him that the next movie plays in fifteen minutes. Fly Ty paid the thirty dollars for the tickets. The foursome headed upstairs where their movie was showing.

Speedy pulled his wallet out of his pocket, opened it and drew out a fifty-dollar bill. He gave it to Ann and spoke. "Listen, you and Pat get the popcorn and soda. Cop two big popcorns, some candy and two large ass sodas. Get four straws too."

"Word, me and Pat gonna share a soda and popcorn, and y'all two do the same. I doubt it if one person can eat one of those buckets or drink one of those big ass sodas by themselves. Tell her not to put too much ice, more soda, less ice. The *Hoezetta* movie is playing over here, okay?" Fly Ty said as he pointed. "Me and Speedy will get the seats. We'll meet y'all up there," said Fly Ty. Fly Ty and Speedy kissed their females.

"Yo, Pat, I think I'm pregnant," said Ann sadly.

"Bitch, you don't use condoms or birth control?" Pat asked.

"The pill be blowing bitches bodies up and I always forget to tell my man to use a condom, plus I think he might get mad at me if I asked him to wear one," said Ann.

"Girl, your moms is going to kill you if she found out you were pregnant. That nigga got no job and he don't hustle. His ass lives off his momma," said Pat.

"At least he don't sell drugs like Tymel, getting himself and his house all shot up and shit," said Ann.

"But we ain't talking 'bout Tymel, besides, do you even want a baby?" asked Pat.

"I don't know. I mean, he has a chance to be an NBA star

for Christ sakes. I'm going to become a doctor. We should be ahight in the future," Ann said skeptically.

"Yeah, I believe that, but a baby might slow you and him down. So that's something to think about.

CHAPTER FOUR

"Tyshaun. Tyshaun, are you home?" Ms. Jackson shouted into her house. She locked her door and walked into the kitchen to put her orange juice in the refrigerator. She spotted the note hanging from the refrigerator and grabbed the note and read it to herself. She walked out of the kitchen and into her room. She took off her clothes, folded them on her bed, took her bathrobe off a wall hook by her closet, and swung it around her back like a cape. She stuck her arms through it and walked back to her bed.

Ms. Jackson flopped down on her bed and picked her phone up. She punched in the number and a voice came on. "Ooh, yes Baby, if you want to talk to a big, well-hung brother, punch in your credit card number. I'll be waiting for you." Ms. Jackson punched in her credit card number and twelve seconds later, a man came on the line.

"Hey, Love, what do you want to hear?" asked the man.

"I... I want you to spank the phone with ya thing," Ms. Jackson replied.

The man did what he was told and Ms. Jackson pushed her right pointer finger inside of herself. Ten minutes into the conversation, she was shaking, reaching her climax. Ms. Jackson hung the phone up without saying bye. She got off her bed and headed to the bathroom inside her room to take a shower.

Tamara Jackson was thirty-seven-years-old. She stood 5'9, and was so pretty that she intimidated men. Sometimes she desperately needed a lover, but Tyshaun probably wouldn't understand. His father hadn't been dead two years yet, so his mom moving on with someone else would be too much for him. She closed her eyes and thought about her son's father. She spoke to herself in a low voice. "Damn, I need you. I miss you and won't ever forget you.

• • •

Sun Rise Movie Theater

"Yeah, you're right. Whatever the case may be, I'll wait till I'm sure, then I'll sit down with him, his mother and my mother."

Ann responded to Pat concerning the possibility of her being pregnant.

"May I help you?" a lady spoke with a Middle Eastern accent from behind the counter.

"Um, hum, yes, can I have two large popcorns, not too much butter, two large Sprites, not too much ice, and three Star Bursts...make that four Star Bursts," answered Ann.

"That will be twenty-four dollars and five cents," the cashier told Ann. Ann handed the lady the fifty dollar bill. The lady gathered up Ann's change, gave it to her and said, "Have a nice day. Enjoy your movie."

"Thank you," replied Ann.

"One second. Hey Bobby, two large popcorns, a little butter, two large Sprites, a little bit of ice and four Starbursts."

"Ain't that Speedy coming our way?" asked Pat. She was looking through the crowd.

"Yeah, Pat, don't say anything about the baby."

Pat looked at Ann angrily. "Come on, girl, how the fuck I look telling y'all's business," Pat spat.

"What up, y'all two. I knew y'all would need some help. Pass me the sodas and candy. Ann, grab a popcorn." Ann passed him the sodas and candy and Pat passed her one of the buckets of popcorn.

Pat opened the door, stepped in and walked down the aisle. The movie was just about to start. Previews of other movies were playing on the huge screen. Almost all of the seats were occupied. Speedy lead them to a middle seat on the right side. Fly Ty sat in the spot close to the wall. Pat sat next to him, Ann sat next to her and Speedy took a seat next to her.

"Ah, shit, Ann," said Pat.

"What happened, Pat?" asked Ann confused.

"We forgot the straws," Pat and Ann said at the same time.

"Pop the top and act like we're in the ghetto," Ty interjected.

"Say no more," replied Speedy. Ann held the popcorn in her lap. Speedy placed his right arm over her shoulder and she leaned on him until her head was on his chest. He then kissed Ann on her forehead. Ann held the popcorn in her lap with her left hand and held her belly with her right. She felt a small lump when she pressed her hand into her flat stomach. Her eyes became watery as she tried to fight off her tears. She told herself that everything was going to be alright.

• • •

Jamaica Avenue, Queens

"Damn, Wanda, you see that 600?" Desiree asked her friend.

"Yeah, Desiree. I would suck his dick to ride in that thang,"

Wanda answered.

"That nigga probably financing that bitch and here you are talking 'bout sucking dick," said Glenda.

"Yo, Wanda, where you going?" asked Glenda. Wanda was walking off.

"I'm going to see what this nigga getting into," she answered.

Wanda's friends were just as gorgeous as she was. They were just less classy. Wanda looked just like Pat, just a little shorter with shorter hair.

Wanda walked over to the 600 Benz and the window came down. Wanda bent down and leaned into the window.

"What up? How you doing? My girlfriend thinks you're cute and she wants your phone number," Wanda said, batting her lashes.

"How about giving me yours?" said the guy.

"Damn, you ain't even ask me my name."

"My bad, Shorty. My name is Elijah, and yours, if you don't mind?" he said smiling.

"My name is Wanda. Give me your number. I'll put it in my two-way," replied Wanda.

"Yo, Glenda, what you think that bitch over there telling him?" asked Desiree.

"Who gives a fuck. She probably ran that *my friend wants your number* bullshit."

"Here she comes now. Look at her chicken head ass, switching and shit," said Desiree.

Elijah pulled off.

"So what happened, Wanda?" asked Glenda.

"What you think? He fell for the *my friend shit* and asked

for my number instead."

"Niggas don't want no shy bitch. They take too long to give up the ass."

"What up with Pat, Wanda?" asked Desiree.

"I almost beat that bitch up today," replied Wanda.

• • •

Ms. Jackson's house

"Who is it?" yelled Ms. Jackson answering her door. She opened it.

"Bitch, if you scream, I'll blow your fuckin' head off," said a masked man pointing a gun at Ms. Jackson's face.

"Please don't hurt me. I... I... I'll give you anything you want," she replied nervously.

The gunman had been watching her house for three hours. He was released from prison three months earlier after serving time for burglaries and a rape. He stepped into Ms. Jackson's house and closed the door behind him.

"Bitch, take off all your clothes and get the fuck on your hands and knees," said the gunman in an aggressive tone. The gunman was a white male, 300 pounds, and 6'6. Ms. Jackson complied. The gunman undid his zipper, got on his knees and forced himself into Ms. Jackson's rectum. He brought the butt of his gun down forcefully on the back of her head, leaving her unconscious. After he had his way with her, he got off the floor and walked into her kitchen and found a steak knife. He walked back towards her as she laid on her stomach looking up at him. As soon as she rolled over onto her back, the assailant turned her over and sliced her throat. He picked up his gun and left her house.

CHAPTER FIVE

Sun Rise Movie Theater

"That was a good movie," said Speedy.

"Hell, yeah, those two bitches, *Hoezetta* and *Shanta* were crazy," answered Pat.

The two couples walked towards Fly Ty's Range Rover. Fly Ty walked around to the driver's side and pressed the alarm button. The Jeep beeped twice and all four doors unlocked. Fly Ty opened the door and hopped in. Pat got in the passenger seat and Ann and Tyshaun sat in the back.

"Yo, Fly Ty, drop Ann off first, then me, then you and Pat can do y'all's thing," said Speedy. Fly Ty nodded his head and kept his eyes on the road.

As Fly Ty drove, he noticed the light turned yellow. He tried to catch the light before it turned red, but "errrrr," a tractor-trailer rammed right into the Range Rover, flipping the Jeep over six times. The damaged SUV landed on its roof and skidded down the street crashing into a parked car. Fly Ty's head was sitting outside the windshield with a chunk of glass sticking through his neck. Pat's face was crushed when it hit the dashboard. Ann broke her neck. Speedy was knocked out with both legs and arms broken. When he woke up six months later, he wished he had died along with his friends.

CHAPTER SIX

Eighteen months later

"Yo, nigga, this is the third time this week that you came buying guns, Speedy. Nigga, this is gonna cost you, God! What the fuck you gonna do, son, kill up an army?"

Speedy stood in an abandoned lot talking to Tonny Shine, the gunrunner. Speedy had the stolen Toyota Camry trunk open, loading the guns inside of it. He checked out the Mac 10 he just bought from Tonny. Speedy pushed the loaded clip in the gun, cocked it, raised it to the gun dealer's head and pulled the trigger. *Boom!* Tonny fell to the ground, his body shaking. Speedy shot him four more times in his face. *Bang! Bang! Bang! Bang!* Speedy closed the trunk of the stolen car, got inside with the Mac on his lap and drove off. "Errrrr."

Speedy drove to a local drug spot where they sold Angel Dust PCP. He got out of the car and walked into the bakery. Speedy walked to the counter of the empty store, purchased three bags of Angel Dust and one Philly cigar. Once Speedy got outside, he looked around, got inside the stolen car and headed to the 86th Precinct. Speedy parked a half a block away and opened the Philly with a razor blade. He placed the three bags of PCP in the Philly, rolled it up and smoked it as he listened to Biggie Small's *Ready to Die* off the *Ready to Die* CD. After he smoked the Philly, he packed three 9 mm, 21 shot Rugers in his Army jacket pockets, and kept the Mac in his hand. Speedy got out of the car and headed into the police station. He entered the building at around 7:30 that evening when the place was alive. Speedy drew one of the Rugers from his coat pocket, tapped his bullet proof vest, pushed the glass door open with his feet, and the police officer standing near the entrance took Speedy's first bullet to the head. *Boom!* The cop's hat flew off his head, sending his brains to the floor. Speedy aimed his nine to his right towards the counter. *Bang! Bang! Bang! Bang!* The cop at the counter desk was shot two times in his face. Twelve cops ducked and ran. Speedy squeezed the trigger on his Mac, sending bullets flying everywhere. He turned around and headed back out of the station's door.

Bang! Bang! Pop! Pop! The officers fired back as Speedy raced through the glass door. The door shattered, but Speedy made it across the street. He headed for his stolen car. The cops ran behind him shooting. *Pop! Pop!* Speedy made it safely behind the stolen car as bullets tore through its frame and windows. Speedy raised his Uzi over the hood of the car and returned fire. *Bttattt!* Two cops got hit but their vests saved them. Speedy was on a suicide mission. He wanted to die, but he wanted to take as many cops as he could with him. He wanted to kill the cops for not killing the rapist that killed his mother. Speedy came from behind the Camry and stood out in the open with his Uzi and P.89, both guns hollering. *Blatttt, pop, pop, pop. Blatttt!* Speedy was knocking down cops like they were bowling pins. He was struck in the leg, but was numb of the pain. He walked towards the cops firing his guns. When his guns emptied, he dropped them and drew his last two weapons. He squeezed the two nines. *Pop, pop!* He was then shot in his shoulder, then his chest, but the vest he wore held him steady. He kept firing until his guns clicked. As Speedy held his empty guns, aiming and squeezing the triggers, he started to cry from rage. He cried because he was out of bullets. Speedy killed ten cops and wounded five. When the cops saw that his guns were empty, they walked toward him. One cop yelled, "Bastard, put the fuckin' guns down, now!" Speedy could not hear; he was in a trance. The cop aimed at Speedy's head and pulled his trigger. *Bang.* Speedy's head burst open and he fell backwards, dead.

He looked down at himself and noticed his body mangled on the ground.

"Yo, Speedy. Yo, Speedy," Speedy recognized the voice. He knew he was dead, but looked around and didn't see anybody.

"Up here, nigga!"

Speedy looked up and he saw his boy Fly Ty, Ann, Pat, his father and his mother.

"Jump, Baby. Come with us. We're at a better place. Come on, Baby," said Ms. Tamara.

Speedy couldn't resist the temptation. He lept into the air and was once again reunited with his loved ones.

End

Quiet Town

Thomas Glover

CHAPTER ONE

"Yo, son, what up?" Ty was talking to his homie Rashawn (Ra), who was sitting on the bench. It was a hot and muggy summer afternoon in their Red Hook housing projects in Brooklyn, New York. Ty was about 5'10, light skinned, with a low-cut ceaser and a muscular build courtesy of a recent bid up north. As he approached Ra, he gave him dap in the form of a half-handshake/half-hug.

"What up, Ty Nitty?" Ra said releasing his embrace from his childhood friend. Ra was tall, about 6'3, slim, with long hair braided in cornrows. "Long time no see, my nigga! You got brolic, son!" Ra said stepping back to examine Ty.

"You know I been hittin' that iron baby! But it ain't been that long, son. Only like a couple joints. I got hit wit' a lil' two to four. I did about a deuce off of that up Clinton. Then when I got out, I went straight to PA."

"PA?" Ra said more in the form of a question rather than a statement.

"Yeah, nigga, PA! Tryin' to get that O.T. (outta town) money, son!"

"Oh, yeah! So what's poppin' out there?" Ra asked now seeming more interested in what Ty had to say.

"Son, it's crazy cake out there!"

"Word?"

"Word! You remember my lil' cousin Corey, right?"

"Yeah. He used to stay in my man Murder Mike's building. Where that lil' nigga been at anyway?"

"He in PA, son! Him and my aunt moved out there some-time last year. They in a little spot called Lancaster about an hour outside of Philly. It's wild money out there, son!" Ty explained. "You know Corey only like seventeen right now, so he be goin' to school and all that shit, but he still from the city, nah' mean! He still faster than them lil' country niggas out there. He be gettin' a little bit of paper on some part-time shit, makin' like $500 off an 8-ball," Ty concluded.

"What?" Ra said not believing what he'd just heard. "Hold up, son. You mean to tell me that off of three and a half grams, you can make $500 out there?" he asked still in disbelief.

"Yeah, son," Ty replied.

"That's like $4000 an ounce," Ra quickly calculated.

"I know, my nigga! That's why I came to holla at you. You know a nigga just came home and you always been getting' money, my nigga," Ty said more serious now.

"No doubt, son. So what's on your mind?"

"I just wanted to know if you could help a nigga get on his feet, so I can make this power move O.T.," Ty asked Ra humbly.

"Look dog, you know you been my nigga from the cradle. So of course I'm a look out for you. But I got an even better proposition for you."

"I'm all ears, doggy."

"Why don't you let me go out Lancaster wit' chu, and we can flood that bitch and get money for real. You and Corey can punish the blocks and I'm a sell some weight out there so we can really get this shit poppin'."

"Son, that's the move right there," Ty agreed with Ra's plan. "'Cause Corey be coppin' his weight out there, and he be payin' like a buck fifty for an 8-ball."

"Word, that's what's up. That means they probably payin' anywhere from a gee to $1200 for an ounce. That's love right there. I'm a holla at my connect and get everything situated so we can get out there as soon as possible. When you gonna be ready to leave, son?"

"Whenever, my nigga! I'm ready!" Ty said all hyped up and excited.

"Aiight, son, chill," Ra said laughing at his partner. "We gonna get it poppin'. We'll be ready to move out by this week-end."

"No doubt, baby," Ty said giving Ra dap. "I'm a holla at Corey and let him know we comin' out there, son."

"Aiight. Tell 'em that Murder Mike comin' out there wit' us too."

"Damn, son! What we bringin', the whole Red Hook wit' us?" Ty asked concerned that the more heads involved would equal up to less dough for him.

"Nah, son. Murder's my man. He hold me down at all times. He ain't even gonna be hustlin' out there. He just there to watch a nigga back and all that, know what I'm sayin'? In case niggas start actin' funny and whatnot," Ra said to reassure Ty that Murder wouldn't be steppin' on his toes.

"*Them* niggas? Them niggas ain't even thinkin' about actin' funny, son! Them niggas is pussy out there, for real! I was out there for like two weeks for dolo and them niggas ain't even look at a nigga crazy. *And* I was fuckin' them niggas' bitches and all that," Ty said convinced that he was untouchable. Ra just shook his head.

"Are there any other niggas from New Yitty out there?" Ra asked using Ty for a quick background check of Lancaster.

"Yeah, there's a couple cats out there from the city gettin' a couple of dollars. But they won't be able to fuck wit' us once we bring that raw out there."

"I know that's right. But I don't care how sweet you say it is, I'm still bringin' Murder wit' me. You can't sleep on them country niggas too much, son," Ra warned Ty.

"Them niggas is mad pussy, son! Believe me when I tell you! They don't wanna see Ty Nitty flip and start whilin'!" Ty said patting the gun tucked in his waistline.

"Aiight, baby! I hear you. I'm a holla at you tomorrow and let you know what's good," Ra said raising up from the bench where he was sitting.

"Aiight, son. Get at me tomorrow."

"For sure, my nigga. One."

"One."

As they both headed off in opposite directions, Ty just knew he was about to get rich as soon as they reached Pennsylvania. Ra, on the other hand, knew that there was definitely money to be made in Lancaster, but he also knew that there was more to be discovered in PA than Ty realized. He also understood everything wasn't always what it seems.

CHAPTER TWO

The rest of the week, Ra handled his business to get prepared for the move O.T. He had estimated that he should only take one kilo of cocaine to Pennsylvania to start. He felt he needed to see at how fast a rate that the product would move. He didn't want to take too much coke and get stuck sitting on all that work in unfamiliar territory. He calculated that it should take about a week to two weeks at the most to distribute all of the cocaine with him selling weight and Ty and Corey moving small packages.

By week's end, Ra had rented a black Ford Expedition from Hertz Rental Car Service. On Saturday morning, Ra and his man, Murder, picked up Ty in front of his building and they were off to Pennsylvania.

"Yo, what up, son?" Ty said as he hopped in the back passenger seat directly behind Murder. "So, this is how we rollin' huh?" Ty said inspecting the interior of the truck. "Shittin' on them niggas right away."

"You know, son. Brooklyn style!" Ra said also amped up to finally be heading out of town as well. "You remember my man Murder, right?" Ra motioned to his man in the front passenger seat.

"Yeah. What's good, son?" Ty reached over the front passenger seat and shook Murder's hand.

"Peace," replied Murder as he shook Ty's hand. Now Murder was an official right-hand man. He was huge, 6'4, 300 plus pounds, and black as a ma'fucka. He was immensely intimidating without ever saying much at all. But one thing for sure, the whole Brooklyn knew he clapped that heat. Hence his namesake, Murder.

"Now, son, you gonna have to gimme directions. You know I ain't never been out here a day in my life," Ra told Ty.

"It ain't nuthin', son. We can go across the Verazano Bridge into Staten Island, then hit the Jersey Turnpike from there. I'll give you the rest of the directions how to get to PA once we get on the turnpike," Ty said directing them on the appropriate course.

"Aiight, son. Just don't get me lost out this bitch. We dirty as a muthaphucka. We can't be takin' no unnecessary chances and end up out in West Bubblefuck somewhere," Ra explained, emphasizing the seriousness of their moves even though he was smiling.

"I got chu, baby!" Ty assured him.

"Yo, roll somethin' up, Murder," Ra said to his man riding shotgun in silence.

"I'm already ahead of you, son. I got this blunt of purple already twisted," Murder said raising his freshly rolled trees of haze to show Ra he had it all under control.

"My nigga! PA here we come!" Ra screamed as he weaved through traffic rockin' to *I Love the Dough* by *B.I.G. & Jay-Z.*

Three hours later, Ty had safely guided them on a successful journey. They drove past a sign that read "Welcome to Lancaster, Pennsylvania!"

"I told you I got you, son! We here now!" Ty beamed as they entered the small municipality. "Find a quiet town and tie it down," Ty said quoting a verse by *Beanie Sigel.*

"Yeah, that's exactly what we gonna do too, tie it down," Ra said surveying his new surroundings. The city of Lancaster was lined with lots of trees and plenty of small, one-way streets complete with tight row houses. It was a drastic contrast to the numerous large skyscrapers and gritty landscape of their native New York City.

"Yo! It's mad Puerto Rican chics out here, son!" Murder said sounding amazed. "You see this shit, Ra?" he continued as he peered out the window of the large SUV.

"Yeah, son, I see. It could be a lovely summer out here in Lancaster," Ra replied confidently.

"I told you, I was fuckin' wild bitches out here, son! These bitches love a nigga from the city," Ty boasted.

"Well, there goes a Days Inn right there. Let's get situated and stash this work before we see what's really good out here," Ra suggested.

"That's what's up, kid. Let's be smart about everything," Murder agreed.

They pulled into the parking lot of the Days Inn. After renting a double occupancy room for the weekend, they unloaded their bags from the truck and secured all of their drugs and belongings in the hotel room. Ty called his younger cousin Corey to let him know that they would be coming past his house within the next half an hour to pick him up.

Corey and his mother stayed in the Hillrise housing projects located in the southeast section of Lancaster city. They were different from the hi-rise projects in New York City. They were an assortment of low-budget townhouses and four-story apartment buildings that spanned over a three block radius. Corey and his mother stayed in an apartment building on the South Duke Street side of the complex.

Ra parked on South Duke Street, across from a Spanish restaurant called "La Familia." There was a small group of black and Puerto Rican guys from the neighborhood standing in front of the restaurant. They watched attentively as Ra, Ty and Murder exited the truck and walked up the steps that led to the walkway to Corey's building.

"Yo, son, we gonna wait out front," Ra said to Ty. "See if we can catch some bitches or somethin'. Grab your lil' cousin so we can roll through the hood."

"Aiight. I'm only gonna be a hot minute, anyway. I just gotta say what's up to my aunt real quick," Ty said as he entered the doorway to his cousin's building. Ra and Murder sat on the wall out front of the building and got the attention of a Puerto Rican girl and a black girl who were walking by.

"Yo, ma! Come here, let me holla at you a second," Ra said convincing the Puerto Rican girl and her friend to talk to him. The girls walked over to Ra and Murder and began having a conversation.

Meanwhile, across the street...

"Yo, Benny! You see them clowns over there?" Gito asked his partner, who was coming out of the restaurant drinking a mango juice. Now Benny was a big nigga *and* a big nigga in the hood. He stood 6'5, was brown-skinned with wavy hair and he stayed fresh from head to toe. The chics in the hood called him a pretty boy, even though he was 280 pounds, built like an NFL linebacker *and* a certified gangsta. He was born and raised in

Lancaster, and was one of the city's favorite sons.

Benny's crew was called the Young Kings. They were noto-rious throughout the city and controlled the southeast section of the city as far as the drug trade was concerned. They were also well known for robbing out-of-towners who tried to infiltrate their side of the city. Whether you knew them for being grimy or for getting money, if you were in Lancaster, you definitely knew of the Young Kings.

"Who you talkin' 'bout, Gito?" Benny asked his homie as he surveyed the area, while taking a swig of his drink. "Them nig-gas over there?" he said as he fixed his eyes in the direction of the two guys talking to a couple of girls, whom he knew to be Tanea and Moya, across the street.

"Yeah, man!" Gito said sounding thoroughly disgusted with the whole situation.

"What about 'em?" Benny asked nonchalantly.

"Them clown ass-niggas just got out of that black Expedition over there wit' the New York plates. It was three of 'em. The other funny-looking nigga went inside A-building. He looked kinda familiar, but I can't place where I know that nigga from right this second," Gito finished as he shook his head at the scene taking place across the street.

Now Gito was a boss in his own right. He was a chubby, Puerto Rican kid with a low-cut. People said he resembled the rapper Cuban Link. He was a couple of years younger than Benny, but they had known each other since they were kids. Their mothers worked together and were close.

Over the years in Lancaster, there were more than a couple of street wars between the Puerto Ricans and the blacks. But, as time passed, the two diverse ethnic groups began to co-exist with each other more peacefully. Through it all, Benny and Gito had remained tight, not letting the racial bullshit come between them. They figured that they were both minorities who didn't have shit. So when they came of age and it was time for them to start getting money in the streets, it was only natural that they fucked with each other. Benny had all the younger brothers in the hood on his team, and Gito had all the boriqua niggas under the wing. Gito's squad was called the Yayo Stars. With Gito's uncle firmly in place as their connect, they quickly became young legends in the city of Lancaster.

They saw two other cats emerge from out of A-building.

"Ain't that lil' Corey over there?" Benny asked.

"Yeah, that's him. And that funny lookin' nigga, too," Gito said as he recalled where he had seen Ty before. "That's where I remember him from. He's Corey's cousin or somethin'. He been out here before, but he was by himself though."

"And now he brought some of his lil' homies out here," Benny said as he pondered the situation. "So they Corey's peoples, huh? I thought lil' Corey was alright, too. Used to cop his little 8-balls and sevens. I guess he got tired of payin' our prices, and tried to put his peoples onto some O.T. money," Benny figured.

"We should air them niggas out, B, before they even think about gettin' some paper out here!" Gito fumed ready to let loose.

"Nah, G., chill out. We don't even know what it's hittin' for yet. They might just be a couple of ounce niggas frontin' in a rental," Benny pointed out, then continued, "Let 'em get comfortable, while we find out what they workin' wit'. You know word travel fast 'round here. Look who they hollerin' at, Tanea and Moya. A couple of smeezes. And they think they found a couple of dimes or somethin'. Give them niggas a few weeks and we'll know their whole M.O. Then we can do to them what we do to all the nut-ass dudes from outta town who come out here thinkin' they found somethin' sweet," Benny said matter of factly, as he watched all four of the New Yorkers hop into the Expedition and pull off.

"Yeah, I guess you right. At least we can get some cake out of it," Gito mentioned.

"Exactly. We gotta make it worth our while. It won't take that long, trust me. Just tell your peoples to keep an eye out for that black Expedition with the New York plates. Pay attention to where they playin' at and tryin' to set up shop. All we gotta do is give 'em enough rope and they'll hang themselves," Benny reasoned, as he and Gito got into Gito's black S500 Mercedes Benz. They left the block, knowing all they had to do was remain patient and their mark would set itself up.

CHAPTER THREE

Over the next few weeks, Ra, Ty and Murder got acclimated to the way things worked in Lancaster. The first thing they found out was that it was too hot to be staying at a motel. Two drug busts had occurred at different motels in the short time they had been in Lancaster.

No longer willing to take the chances of staying at a motel, they began posting up at Moya's crib. Moya stayed on High Street in the southwest quadrant of the city. Ra had already made Moya his shorty, and was paying her bills, buying her daughter pampers and the whole nine. But, those were minor things considering he was now moving almost two kilos of crack a week.

It had only taken Ra a little over a week to move the first kilo of cocaine he had come with to Lancaster. Ty and his cousin Corey had begun selling jumbo-sized twenty dollar rocks on the Howard Avenue side of Hillrise Projects. They were hustling just around the corner from Benny's strip on the South Duke Street side of the PJ's. Ty and Corey had it poppin', going through packs like clockwork. And since Ra was over in southwest, he found that it was a little more outta town friendly over there as opposed to southeast.

There were a couple of other hustlers from New York he

had run into over in southwest, but they were only half an ounce, and ounce type of niggas. Nevertheless, they were cool with Ra because he was from *"up top"* like them. Most of them hung out and hustled at a bar called *The Manor*, a couple of blocks up the street and around the corner from Moya's house. But, more importantly, Ra was glad that there weren't any real crews in southwest to terrorize shit like the Young Kings.

Ra had also come across a few dudes from Lancaster who were coppin' anywhere from four-and-a-half to nine ounces, at least once a week. Before he knew it, he had established loyal clientele that were coming through on the regular. As a result, he and Murder had to troop back and forth to New York every week to re-up on at least two bricks. Shit was lookin' really lovely in PA. Or at least they thought it was.

"Yo! I got jumbos money! One for twenty! Two for thirty if you're thirsty!" Corey hollered at the fiends, tryin' to divert them from going around the corner to cop off of somebody from Benny's squad. The two crackheads kept on walking. *"Fuck 'em,"* Corey thought to himself. Shit had been going well for him ever since his big cousin had come back to the town with Ra and Murder.

Things were so good, Corey had decided to say fuck school altogether. He had only been going half of the time anyway. And besides, there was just too much money to get. He had become accustomed to pulling all-nighters with Ty, gettin' that money. *"Where the fuck is Nitty at anyway?"* Corey thought. *"Fuck it, more cake for me,"* he assumed as he checked out his reflection in a parked car window.

Corey examined his slim, light skin frame covered in baggy Sean John blue jean shorts and an oversized white tee. His crisp, all-white Air Force 1's and Yankee fitted hat completed his attire. *"I'm doin' it out here, son!"* Corey mused to himself as he looked down at the iced-out cross attached to his *rose gold* link chain. He had just purchased it on a recent trip to New York with Ra and Murder. He was comin' up.

Around the corner...

"Yo, come here, Fletch. What chu workin' wit'?" Butter asked one of his favorite customers as he walked onto their South Duke Street strip.

"I got fifty," Fletch said. "I need three nice ones now too, Butter. I'm on the come-up! If I can get this whitey started, I'm a be comin' back to you all night!" Fletch said trying to gas Butter up, while displaying a crisp fifty dollar bill.

"I got chu, Fletch. But let me not see ya ass no more tonight, and I'm a fuck your black ass up when I catch you!" he warned Fletch, recognizing his game.

"I ain't playin', cousin, I'm for real! All night," Fletch said as he accepted the rocks, and began scurrying off down the darkened street.

"Aiight, I'm a be out here," Butter yelled at him.

Butter was one of Benny's top lieutenants. He ran the night shift on the strip. Butter was about 5'10, dark skinned with a stocky build. Butter grew up in Lancaster right around the corner from Benny. He stayed with his grandparents until his mother moved him and his younger brother, Mil, to Newark, New Jersey about seven years prior. They only returned to Lancaster on holidays and summer vacations over this time period. While they were in Newark, Butter mastered the art of stealing cars and eluding police in high-speed chases.

Butter and his family moved back to Lancaster about two

summers ago. Upon returning to the city of their birth, Butter and Mil immediately hooked up with their cousins, B.O. and Bear, who had started Young Kings with Benny. Essentially, Young Kings was a family affair so the loyalty was unquestioned and always there.

On this particular night, Butter was on the block with Angie. Angie was basically like one of the fellas, except for the fact that she was bad as a muthaphucka. She had a pretty, smooth, high yellow complexion, long-ass, curly, black hair, even though it didn't matter because she always wore a fitted hat to the back, some pretty-ass lips and a tattoo of a butterfly underneath her right eye. She was a slim chic about 5'5, with a decent little frame, but she always wore baggy clothes like a dude so you never could tell. And to top it all off, she liked pussy. A cold-dike. But she always rode out for her niggas, bust her gun, and got money. What more could you ask for from one of your homies?

"Yo, Angie, you got that?" a skinny, young, pale Puerto Rican girl asked her.

"Blanca, you know I got that muthaphuckin' work! Why else I'm a be out here? Now bring ya' smokin' ass over here!" Angie screamed on her, and the young fiend walked over to her with her head sunk down.

"I only got seventeen," Blanca said softly as she looked into Angie's face for sympathy.

"Aiight, bitch," Angie conceded. "I'm a bless you this one time. But you better get on your job and start hustlin' up some dicks to suck or somethin' 'cause I ain't gonna keep takin' these shorts from ya' ass!"

"I know, but it's slow right now. I'm waitin' on a trick, but I just need a quick eye-opener."

"Aiight," Angie said tired of hearing the sob story as she broke her off one of her smallest pieces.

"Thanks, Ang," Blanca said gratefully.

"Just bring that trick money through when you get it, lil' hooker."

"You know I will. Oh, Angie, I almost forgot to tell you. It's some kid around the corner tryin' to catch all the custies before they can come down here," Blanca informed Angie.

"Oh yeah? What he look like?"

"Some lil' light skin kid. I seen him around before, but he talk like he from New York or somethin'," she assumed.

"Aiight, Blanca, good lookin'," Angie said as she gave her another tiny rock in return for that little bit of information.

"Oh, I'll definitely be back. Good lookin' out," Blanca said as she hurried down the block.

"Yo, Butter!"

"What up, Ang?" Butter asked as he appeared from the alley where he had his stash.

"Yo, Blanca said there's some non-descript ass nigga around the corner over on Howard tryin' to stop our flow. Flaggin' down all the custies and whatnot."

"Well we gonna have to go see about that. You got your ratchet on you?" He asked if she had her gun with her.

"You know I keep my thing on me," she replied as if it were common knowledge.

"Aiight, hop in the whip. We gonna circle the block and see what's good over there," Butter said as they hopped into an older model black Jaguar that he had rented from one of his white friends. They proceeded to drive up South Duke Street and turned right onto Howard Avenue driving up the slight hill.

"There he go right there," Angie said as she noticed Corey in between the buildings making a sale.

"Oh yeah! Well we got a little surprise for that nigga," Butter said as he turned off of Howard Avenue onto Rockland Street. He parked the car in the diagonal parking spaces that lined the Rockland Street side of the projects.

"Yo, Ang, check it. We gonna creep right down Howard and I'm a ask that nigga for the time. As soon as he go to check for the time, you just put the joint to him. Aiight?" Butter asked his partner in crime.

"I got chu, my nigga," Angie responded confidently, ready to put in work.

Butter looked out of his window to make sure that they wouldn't look suspicious. When he saw the coast was clear, he turned to Angie.

"Let's rock!" he said giving her the cue to move. They quietly slipped out into the night, shutting the car doors lightly. They moved stealthily down Howard Avenue to where Corey was posted up in the middle of the block, oblivious to what was going on around him.

"Yo, what up money? You got the time?" Butter asked Corey as he jumped back startled by Butter.

"Damn, son. You scared the shit out of me. I ain't even see you," Corey said as he looked down at his watch.

"It's cool, dog," Butter laughed falsely reassuring Corey.

"It's eleven twenty..." Corey never got a chance to finish his sentence before Angie's gun was directly in his face.

"You now what it is nigga! Let me hold somethin'!" Angie said as Butter began to remove Corey's chain and watch.

"Damn, dog, it's like that?" Corey asked still tryin' to sound like a man as Butter continued to search his person, taking his package and about $700 from him.

"Shut up, nigga!" Butter said as he smacked Corey in the face with his gun, cutting him below the eye before tumbling him to the ground. "Bitch-ass nigga, had a hammer on him and didn't even reach for it. You see this shit?" Butter said as he displayed Corey's gun for Angie. She just shook her head. "You fuckin' coward!" Butter kicked Corey in the stomach as he curled up into a ball on the concrete sidewalk. Angie delivered another blow to his skull with her gun and Corey let out a feminine scream.

"And tell your peoples don't even think about gettin' no paper 'round here, ya heard? Lil' G-pack nigga. Come holla at me when you wanna step up!" Butter said as he spit in Corey's battered and bloodied face. He continued to squirm on the ground in pain as his attackers fled off into the night.

CHAPTER FOUR

The following day, Benny was having lunch as usual at the La Familia restaurant with his right-hand man, B.O. and his man Bear. Now B.O. was the quiet, brain type nigga of the crew. He was always formulating a plan. He was about 5'9, a buck sixty, brown skin, with a low-cut ceaser with waves. Bear, on the other hand, was almost identical to B.O. in height and weight except for the fact that he was a midnight black complexion. Bear was what you would call the 'loose cannon' of the crew. Ready to flip at anytime. B.O. and Bear were like the opposite sides of the same coin. They balanced each other out and they worked perfectly together. They were also first cousins. Benny's son's mother was also B.O. and Bear's cousin. They had known each other their whole lives.

About three years ago, the three of them decided to form Young Kings after Benny returned home from a three-year bid up north, with the idea of forming a team. They had grinded up from the bottom together. Combined with Benny's solid connections with Gito's uncle and the Spanish community, they put together one of the most feared and respected organizations the city had ever seen. They were businessmen as well as hustlers and killers. They had formed a music promotion/entertainment company as a vehicle to launder their profits from the drug game.

Over lunch, they were discussing the possibility of promoting a concert at *The Chameleon* nightclub the following month. Butter entered the restaurant.

"What up, Young Kings!" Butter announced as he embraced each member of his family.

"What up, Butter? What's good?" B.O. asked his younger cousin.

"Ain't nuttin', B.O. You know, doin' what I do," Butter said pulling up a chair to join the trio at the table. "What y'all into? I see the paperwork all over," he asked referring to the numerous files spread across the table. "What's the plan?"

"We throwin' a show next month at "The Chameleon." We tryin' to decide who we should bring out here. I was thinkin' we should bring Beans and them SP niggas," B.O. said.

"Nah, man. We gotta bring Kiss and them niggas, trust me! That's who the hood wanna see. Niggas is tired of them SP cats. D-Block is hot right now!" Bear debated adamantly about his point of view.

"Yeah, I'm wit' Bear on this one, B.O. Bring them D-Block niggas through. The hood gonna go crazy for that. Maybe a couple shootings, a fight, a stabbing or two. You know, the regular," Butter said laughing.

"I know that's right. Niggas gonna act stupid regardless. But as long as we get that money first, I don't care what they do. They can set that muthaphucka on fire for all I care," Benny interjected, emphasizing the bottom line, to make a dollar. "But anyway, how the nightshift go, Butter?"

"Shit was a little slow. But it was all gravy. I still did my usual numbers. I even caught me a little jooks last night," Butter said as he untucked the rose gold chain that he took from Corey from under his white t-shirt and let it hang around his neck displaying it for his peoples.

"Oh, that shit aiight too," Bear said as he appraised the necklace. "That shit cost at least a couple stacks. Who you get, Butter?"

"Some nut-ass, young boy from New York. I don't know him, but he was hustlin' over on Howard tryin' to cut throat. So me and Angie caught that nigga slippin' for this chain, a cheap-ass watch, about 7 cent, almost a G-pack and a burner," Butter summarized his heist.

"Damn! That shit sounded like a hustler's starter kit!" B.O. joked.

"What he look like?" Benny asked.

"Some lil' light skin nigga. Angie said he stay in A-building," Butter said shrugging his shoulders as if to say it didn't matter to him either way.

"Oh, that must a been lil' Corey then," Benny figured. "He was out there for dolo?"

"Yeah. I told you he was slippin'," Butter laughed.

"Well, that serves his little-ass right. He done brought them faggot-ass niggas from New York out here almost a month ago, and he ain't cop shit off me since. Actin' like he tryin' to come up and shit. He shoulda' known better than to be tryin' to get money on this side of the hood anyway," Benny finished.

"Well, he ain't gonna be tryin' no more. You can bet that! Angie pistol-whipped the shit outta that nigga, B. You shoulda' heard that nigga scream like a bitch!" Butter reenacted Corey's girlish squeal and they all burst into laughter.

Across town at Moya's house...

"Yeah, son, them muthaphuckas robbed me!" Corey was

explaining to Ra, Ty and Murder how his face had gotten all fucked up and why his pack money was short.

"Who gut chu, son?" Ty asked him, looking confused.

"Some nigga, I don't know who the fuck he is. But he kinda dark skin wit' cornrows and he missin' a front tooth. But I do know the shorty though. Some rah-rah ass, yellow bitch named Angie."

"What? A bitch! Son, tell me you ain't let no bitch stick you up?" Ty asked his little cousin in disbelief as Ra and Murder just shook their heads.

"Yeah, nigga! A bitch! If you woulda' been holdin' me down like you was supposed to, instead of chasin' some dust-bomb ass bird, maybe I wouldn't a got stuck the fuck up!" Corey said fully displaying his anger.

"Aiight. Both of y'all be easy," Ra said trying to calm the situation. "Son, what else happened?" he asked Corey.

"Nuttin' really. After they took my shit, they just told me not to be tryin' to get no money around there no more. And to tell my peoples, don't even think about getting' no paper 'round here," Corey finished looking to Ra for answers.

"Well, Nitty, I told you. Everybody ain't as sweet as you think. They challenging your block where you set up shop at. How you gonna handle it? It don't matter to me. They ain't fuckin' wit' my flow," Ra said, now shifting the pressure on Ty's shoulders to show and prove.

"Nigga, you know how Ty Nitty get down!" Ty said taking out his pistol and cocking it. "You know where they be at, son?" he asked Corey.

"Yeah. Right over on South Duke across from my building," Corey said to his big cousin, scared of what was about to happen next.

"Well, let's go. I got the custie's whip right outside. Don't nobody know whose it is, we can go get busy right now. Get it poppin' in broad daylight. Let's go, now!" Ty said to Corey as he headed towards the front door.

"This is the type of shit I been waitin' for, son! I love it when my gun go warm," Murder said as he left the house with Ty and Corey. Ra simply fell back on Moya's couch and wondered how many of his peoples would return.

Back at La Familia...

Benny and his team were just finishing up their lunch and were getting ready to roll out.

"Excuse me, Jimmy, can I get the check please?" Benny said to the owner of the restaurant who had watched him grow up from a little boy, shoveling sidewalks, to a well- respected young boss.

"No check for you today, my friend," the Spanish man who was in his mid-forties said to him in a thick Latin accent.

"Gracias, my friend," Benny replied thanking him for his hospitality. He then turned to his crew. "Yo, I'm about to go to the bathroom real quick," he informed them.

"Aiight. We'll be right out front," B.O. said.

"I need a cigarette after that meal right there," Bear said as he, B.O. and Butter exited the restaurant.

"There he go right there, son! That's him! That's him!" Corey said excitedly as he drove past La Familia.

"Aiight son, be easy," Murder said from the passenger seat trying to keep the youngster calm. "Just circle the block. When we ride back past 'em, we just gonna start lightin' shit up, Nitty."

"You know it, son!" Ty said checking his weapon one last

time, knowing it was time for action.

The dark blue, late model Ford Taurus turned left onto North Street before making another left onto Rockland Street. Corey then steered the vehicle onto Howard Avenue completely circling the projects before finally turning left onto South Duke Street.

Butter, Bear and B.O. were among the crowd of midday people who were casually loitering in front of the restaurant.

"Yo! Which one of y'all grimey-ass niggas got me for my lighter?" Butter asked knowing he wouldn't get an honest answer out of either of his cousins. "It's a red one," he clarified so there wouldn't be any misunderstanding what his lighter looked like.

"I don't got it," B.O. said laughing. "You need one?"

"Yeah," Butter said as B.O handed him a red lighter. "Yo, this is my shit right here!" and the music of the streets rang out, piercing the joyful mood of the early afternoon. Pop, pop, pop! Pop, pop, pop!

The rounds came rapidly in a hail of gunfire that buzzed above and beside the people gathered on the corner. A window of the La Familia establishment was shattered as everybody hit the deck for cover.

Benny ran out of the restaurant and started to return fire at the dark blue sedan, as were Bear and Butter from behind a parked car. The Taurus slowed down briefly but after a few slugs pierced the body of the car, it accelerated in an effort to escape down the street. The vehicle then made a sharp right turn down Chester Street and sped off until they were out of sight.

"Yo! Everybody aiight?" Benny asked as he examined the scene.

"Yeah, I'm straight," B.O. said picking himself off the concrete and dusting off his clothes.

"Yeah, I'm cool!" Butter responded. "Them pussy-ass New York niggas must call that retaliation or somethin'? All them shells and couldn't hit nobody. Pullin' a drive-by like we in Cali' and shit," Butter laughed lightly to himself.

"Nah, man, fuck that!" Bear screamed.

"What's the matter, dog, you hit?" Benny asked concerned for Bear's health.

"Nah, dog. I'm aiight. It's just the fact that them pussy-ass niggas just sprayed up our block like somethin's sweet! Somebody gots to die, B. That's my word!" Bear fumed while he was pacing. And everybody thought the same exact thought, *why'd they get this nigga started.*

"Aiight, my nigga. I feel you. They want a war, we gonna bring the war to they front door. But right now, we gotta bounce," Benny said as the sirens could be heard closely approaching in the background. The four then dashed around the corner and jumped in Benny's white Yukon Denali that was parked on the side of the restaurant. Benny proceeded to pull off down the tiny side street, safely escaping before the police arrived to canvas the area. As Benny drove, he knew in his mind that the war was on! And a slight smile came across his face.

CHAPTER FIVE

Over the next couple of weeks, nobody had seen Corey, Ra, Ty or Murder anywhere in the hood. They were obviously laying low since the *'shootout in broad daylight,'* as the newspaper headline had read. Being as though Lancaster was such a small city, the incident garnered more attention than necessary. As a result, Ra and his peoples had been playing Moya's crib real tough in the southwest section of the city. They assumed they were relatively safe over there because they were out of Young Kings' territory. The money was still flowing strong for Ra, who was still serving his loyal customers.

Benny, on the other hand, was frustrated that he couldn't put his finger on his adversaries' exact whereabouts, even though he knew the background on all the players in this game. He was aware that the big, black nigga in the New Yorker's crew was Murder. And he was supposed to be the muscle of the group. He already knew Corey, and classified him as minimal to no threat at all. He also knew that Corey's cousin was a doldier-type, stupid, follower dude who chased pussy and popped off at his mouth a lot that they called Nitty. Studio gangstas. But, the individual who intrigued him the most was the tall, brown skin kid with the braids named Ra. He was the brain, the nigga that really mattered. Benny had heard from various sources that Ra had been moving a little weight over southwest and that was all Benny needed to know to sick the wolves on him. His only objective at that point was to find out exactly where Ra laid his head, and to take him for all he was worth.

Benny had talked to Gito and told him to put out an APB on the niggas from New York they had seen across the street from La Familia, and to also find out where they were residing, by any means necessary. Seeing as though Gito had a few members of the Yayo Stars who played over in southwest heavy, Benny figured they should be able to find out something. Gito said that if Ra and his peoples were anywhere in southwest, his young boys would find them in a matter of days. Benny knew that all he had to do now was keep his niggas from doing anything stupid or irrational and they would be just fine. He was determined to make sure that all of his moves would be made based upon precise and calculated decisions. He got off on that war shit like a seasoned general, for real!

On one particular evening, Benny, Bear, Mil and Butter were over B.O.'s house, the official chill spot, playing X-box, smoking trees and cooking up coke.

"Yo, I got next on that Madden!" B.O. yelled from the kitchen to Mil and Butter who were playing the game in his living room.

"Aiight, B.O., I got you. I'm bustin' this nigga's ass 14-0. I'm about to 21 point mercy rule this nigga," Mil replied, laughing at his older brother.

Mil had just come home from a short skid-bid. He did thirteen months in the county prison. He was only nineteen and the youngest member of the Kings. He was also the wildest. Mil was about 5'10 like his brother, but he was skinnier and had shoulder length dreads. Mil was accustomed to the gang-bangin' lifestyle he had adopted in Newark. He had yet to master the art of outthinking his enemies. He just had that *clap on-site* mentality. No plotting, no planning, no nothin', *just see a muthaphucka you don't like and get it poppin'.*

Benny was in B.O.'s small kitchen working hard at the gas stove. He was cheffing 125 grams of powder cocaine. His goal was to bring back 175 grams of crack. He was showing B.O. a few tricks of the trade when it came to the art of stretching oil-based cocaine to the hardened form of crack cocaine.

"See B.O., when this shit bust down to the oils, that shit can hold more baking soda while it's in a complete liquid form before you let it cool down and rock the whole way up," Benny said as he showed B.O. the contents of the glass Pyrex pot melting together. He added more baking soda and stirred the mixture with a butter knife to whip and blend it all together.

"Yeah, I see. That shit look like it's some butter, too!" B.O. said complimenting and admiring Benny's work.

"You heard what Jigga said. '*I'm new in town, I don't know my way around, but I got some soft white that's sure to come back brown.*'" Benny recited a quote by *Jay-Z* from the song *1-900-Hustler*. "Peanut butter, my nigga," Benny said as he sat the pot of tan colored crack underneath a fan to finish cooling off.

"Y'all niggas got that cheffin' shit down to a science," Bear commented, pullin' on his blunt while sitting at the kitchen table. "But I'm more concerned wit' these niggas who new in *my* town," he said referring to their newfound enemies from New York.

"Look, cousin, just breath easy right now. I wanna get at

them niggas just as bad as you do. But them bitch-niggas been in hiding ever since they pulled that homo-stunt, drive-by bullshit a couple of weeks ago. Ain't nobody seen or heard from 'em since. I got a feelin' they still in the town, but I need to know exact locations so we can do this shit right! I ain't on no faggot-ass, drive-by shit like them cats. You dig me?" Benny said thoroughly expressing his feelings about the situation.

"Yeah, I dig you cousin. But I'm out for revenge, B., for real! I see blood right now! Them niggas violated, straight up and down!" Bear said still heated and still pullin' on his blunt.

"I feel you, my nigga. But I also see the big picture. That shit they pulled didn't hurt none of us. Not a scratch on any of us. But when we hit them niggas, we gonna hit 'em where it hurts. They pockets. Snatch the head and watch the body drop. That nigga Ra is the head. The rest of them dudes is peons. Once we get a hold of that nigga and do the damn thing to him, them niggas'll be outta here on the next thing smokin'. Believe me!" Benny said addressing Bear's concerns and calming him down at the same time.

"I know that's right! Money over bitch-ass niggas. I need a couple dollars off of them niggas anyway," B.O. added.

"Aiight, B. You call the shots. Just let me know when I can pop off some shots at them niggas' heads," Bear said as he listened to reason. But as always, he was ready to go. He had been trained in that manner since childhood.

"I got you baby! You'll be the first to know," Benny said giving his man dap. "Now pass that *L* you been steamin' on for the past half-hour!" They all laughed together.

"You know I be chiefin', B.," Bear said as he finally passed the blunt to Benny.

"Yo, B.O.! This shit is over," Butter yelled from the living room.

"Aiight, my nigga! I'm comin' right now. And don't try to start a new game either, Mil!" Slick-ass, lil' nigga, B.O. thought as he weighed out the finished product of Benny's work on a small, black digital scale.

"Damn, B.! That shit came back to 182 grams," B.O. announced in amazement.

"I told you, baby! They don't call the boy 'Bricks' for nuthin'." Benny said referring to one of his nicknames, as he watched B.O. divide the crack into two 90-gram packages and place them in clear plastic sandwich bags.

"Yo, I'm a give half to Mil and the other half to Butter. Let them niggas slaughter the nightshift and get they money up," B.O. said to Benny.

"That'll work," Benny agreed, and the three of them walked through the dining room to the living room to join Butter and Mil.

"Here," B.O. said tossing a package to both Mil and Butter who were sitting on the grey cloth couch in front of the big screen television.

"Damn, B.O. Good lookin'!" Mil thanked his cousin with large eyes from having in his possession the most narcotics he'd ever held.

"Good lookin', cousin. How much is it?" Butter asked B.O.

"I gave both of y'all 3 o's. Just holla at me after the weekend's over and y'all better come up!" B.O. stressed to his younger cousins.

"No doubt!" Butter replied confidently.

"Aiight. Now pass me that stick, nigga," B.O. said refer-

227

ring to the X-box controller.

"Yeah, B.O., that nigga was talkin' all that shit, and I came back and bust his ass 28-21," Butter boasted of his come from behind victory over his younger sibling as B.O. sat down on the couch in between him and Mil. Bear and Benny were sitting together on the matching loveseat watching the game. Just then, Butter's cell phone started to ring indicating an incoming call.

"Hold up a second, B.O.," Butter said as he paused the game to answer his phone. "Hello. What up, Angie? Where you at? We over B.O.'s crib. Aiight, just beep the horn when you out front. One!" Butter hung up his cell phone. "Yeah, Mil, that was Angie's hot ass. She said she right around the corner. She tryin' to go out to *The Breeze*, and she want a nigga to hold her down. You tryin' to roll wit' us?" Butter informed and asked his little brother.

"No doubt! I'm there. You know it be bitches in "The Breeze" on *Thirsty Thursday*, my nigga!" Mil said emphatically. He had just started to go out and hit the club scene since he got released from the county. But he was already addicted to the easy broads and drama that accompanied the club atmosphere.

The Breeze was a Haitian owned club/bar that every hood rat, hustler and wannabe hustler in town frequented on the weekend in Lancaster. If you wanted to find something in the hood, you would find it at "The Breeze."

"What up, Bear? You tryin' to roll?" Mil asked him.

"Hell, nah. You know I don't fuck wit' Angie like that. That's y'all homegirl." Bear frowned at Mil's question.

"Why you don't fuck wit' Ang?" Benny asked him out of curiosity.

"She got beef wit' my girl over some silly shit. So I don't

fuck wit' that bitch 'cause she be frontin' and shit. Bitch pulled a burner out on my girl and everything," Bear said.

"I told you that bitch go hard! I fucks wit' her," Benny said, "but I feel you on not goin' to "The Breeze" though. It be a lot of dickhead bullshit that be poppin' off down there. And besides, them hatin' ass bitches be just waitin' to run back and snitch to my girl. I can't even push up on nuthin'. I'm cool. If I go out, I gotta go outta town. We'll probably go to Philly this weekend anyway, so I'm a chill."

"Word! I ain't for that bullshit neither," B.O. echoed Benny's statement. "Besides, if I try to go out now, wifey'll kill me."

"I know that's right!" Butter said laughing, just as a horn started to beep out in front of B.O.'s house. "That's Angie right there," Butter said peering out the front window. "I'm a holla at y'all niggas later," he finished as he went over and gave B.O., Benny and Bear all a hug.

"Aiight, my niggas," Mil said as he gave them all the same goodbye gesture as his brother.

"Y'all niggas be safe," Benny said.

"You know it, my nigga," Mil responded as he and Butter headed for the front door.

"Call me if anything," B.O. said.

"Definitely, my nigga," Butter said as he and his brother started to walk out the door. "One."

"One," B.O. said closing the door behind Butter and locking the double lock and chain on his front door. He then went back to his seat on the couch.

"Them lil' niggas wild," Benny commented, "but I love 'em to death."

"I know. They still young though, B.," B.O. reasoned. "They

gotta run loose and have they fun."

"I understand that much. But I just want everybody to be extra careful, ya' heard. We still at war. And 'The Breeze' be a trap sometimes. You know we done had to get it on, or pop somethin' up more than a couple of times down that mutha-phucka. And right now ain't the time for no mistakes. Every move we make gotta be calculated. We can't afford no slip ups," Benny said with all the seriousness in the world.

"I feel you, dog. But they'll be aiight. They in the hood. Plus, they know we only a call away if anything jump off," Bear added.

"If y'all say so. But one day a nigga might not be able to make that call. Ya' feel me?" I ain't tryin' to lose none of my niggas. Ya' heard?" Benny said exhaling the smoke from his lungs as they all solemnly reflected upon the loved ones they lost. "But anyway," Benny said snapping them all out of their momentary daze, "I got a buck on this game right here."

"I got chu, my nigga," Bear said grabbing the other X-box controller as he dug inside his pocket and slapped a crisp Benjamin Franklin on the glass coffee table.

And for those few moments at least, all the pain of the streets and the harsh realities of their lives were temporarily forgotten. They were kids again. Having fun with one another, playing a game, not caring who won or lost because Lord knows, the game that they played everyday of their lives on the streets only had a few winners, and the losers rarely survived to play again. That was the cruel, hard facts of the game of life.

CHAPTER SIX

"The Breeze" was basically no more than a nice-sized bar/restaurant that also doubled as a small club on the weekends. It was a normal, small, ordinary establishment that had an added Caribbean feel. There was normally reggae music playing on the jukebox during daytime business hours when the midday crowd consisted of business people who worked in the downtown area who had come to sample the Caribbean cuisine offered on the lunch buffet menu. And also the local Jamaican, Haitian and other people of Caribbean heritage patronized "The Breeze" during the day because it was the only place that reminded them of their culture and heritage in Lancaster.

"The Breeze" had one long, wooden surfaced bar on the lower level of the establishment. It was lined with about twenty stools and spanned almost the complete length of the first level. The opposite wall was filled with six, double-sided, padded seating booths. You had to go up exactly three stairs to reach the second level of the club. The only thing separating the first level from the second level was a waist high wooden railing located by the edge of the second level overlooking the bar area. The second level of "The Breeze" consisted of a small sitting area that was used for dining in the daytime with a few round tables and chairs, a long wooden table where the DJ set up his turntables and sound system, and a small dance floor. The back entrance that led to the large rear parking lot and the kitchen area was on the opposite side of the dance floor.

The club was located close to Lancaster's center city. It was easily accessible and located at a central location where as though everybody in the city felt comfortable going there. It wasn't much, but with all the other clubs in the area having been shut down by overly frightened ownership following numerous brawls and a handful of shootouts, "The Breeze" was all the hood had.

As normal, on Thursday through Sunday, The Breeze had transformed from a quaint little Caribbean bar into a hip-hop bangin' hot spot. On this Thursday, Butter, Angie and Mil parked in the rear parking lot. They decided to enter the spot through the back entrance by the kitchen, seeing as though the security was more relaxed as opposed to the bouncers who manned the front door. As always, they still had to pay the bouncer a couple extra dollars to get Mil in since he was still under age.

Inside, the club was packed to capacity with the usual cast of characters. Women wearing next to nothing, some who needed to put some more clothes on, niggas who were getting' money and niggas fakin' like they were gettin' money even though they were wearing imitation throwback jerseys. The dimly lit dance floor was jammed with people dancing to a new Jadakiss banger.

"You hear dat shit, Butter?" Mil hollered over the extremely loud music. "They playin' my shit! *The Champ is Here!*" Mil screamed the chorus to the song as he walked through the crowd. They made their way to the lower level and posted up at the bar. Butter got the attention of the extra sexy barmaid, Michelle. Michelle was one of those women who God had blessed with eternal youth. She was in her mid-thirties but her body was that of a twenty-year-old who had never had a child, while her face held the innocence of a five-year-old little girl. She stood 5'3 and her frame held a perfect 130 pounds. Her light carmel complexion was accented by her naturally curly brown, shoulder-length hair, and beautiful big brown eyes. Her smile could melt ice.

"Can I help you?" she spoke to Butter.

"Yeah. Let me get three shots of Henny, and three Incredible Hulks." Butter requested his normal drink of Hennessey, also a mixture of Henny and a blue liquor Hypnotiq to create the David Banner named mixed drink. Michelle went to the liquor shelf behind her to fill his order. She placed all six drinks on the counter in front of Butter who was sitting at the bar. Mil and Angie were standing behind him. He passed the drinks over his shoulder to them.

"That'll be twenty-four dollars," Michelle said as she returned from the register.

"Aiight," Butter said as he handed her a fifty.

"You need change?" she asked Butter, being smart.

"Nah, that's for you. But I do need your number," Butter said flashing his one-tooth smile.

"Boy, stop playin'. You know you just a baby. I went to school wit' your aunt. Sorry," she said apologetically as she moved down the bar to serve another customer.

"Damn, she always playin' you dog," Mil said laughing at his brother. "But I know one thing, these Incredible Hulks be havin' me bent," Mil said as he continued to drain his drink.

"She gonna give in one day," Butter said self-assuredly.

"Mil, you were right. These Incredible Hulks are strong as a muthaphucka, but they good as shit, though," Angie said.

"Michelle, lemme get a whole bottle of that Hypnotiq!" Butter yelled to the barmaid. A minute later, she produced the bottle from the display refrigerator.

"That'll be forty-five dollars," she told Butter, who paid her with another fifty and simply turned away to talk to Mil and Angie.

"I don't know what y'all gonna do, but it's some freaks in this bitch," Butter said looking in the direction of the dance floor. "I'm about to go up there and try and catch me somethin'."

"Aiight, I'll be up there in a little bit," Mil said as he returned to the conversation he was holding with a slim, light skin girl standing next to him. Angie had pushed up on a red-bone sister who was sitting at the bar, next to where Butter had just left his seat.

When Butter made it to the second level, he posted up on the wall on the edge of the dance floor. He made sure that he was close to a corner as well, and lit up the blunt he had rolled before he had come inside the club. He knew in the cut where he was at, he was cool to blaze up because it was so crowded and them damn Haitians who ran the joint really didn't care what one did, as long as you tried to be discreet about it.

What Butter failed to notice was Murder, Ty and Corey coming through the back entrance and making their way to the dance floor area.

"Yo, son. I told you this is where all the chickens be at!" Ty said to Murder.

"Yeah, son. You was right, this time. I'm about to bag a few chics up in here!" Murder said as they continued to navigate their way through the overcrowded dance floor.

"Yo, Nitty!" Corey said to Ty in a loud whisper, and Murder took notice to the alarmed tone in Corey's voice. "That nigga who robbed me is up in here," he said as he noticed Butter on the wall dancing with a slim, brown-skin girl.

"Over there on the wall, dancing wit' that big bottle of Hypnotiq in his hand," Corey described.

"You sure, son?" Ty asked him, partly because he never really got a good look at Butter when they were shooting at him and partly because he wanted complete confirmation before they moved out. He continued to strain his eyes trying to see in the poorly lit club.

"Of course, I'm sure son! He wearing my muthaphuckin' chain!" Corey said pointing out the fact that his iced-out pendant was danglin' from the cable draped around Butter's neck. That was all Ty needed to hear to proceed into action.

"Yo, Murder. He dolo. Let's move on this nigga now!" Ty said and the trio began to move in Butter's direction. At that moment, Butter glanced up from the shorty he had been grinding on to notice that the same little nigga he had robbed was headed towards him with two other cats he didn't know. At that point, he pushed the girl he was dancing with to the side and positioned his back against the wall preparing to go all out. When Murder, Ty and Corey were within reach of Butter, Ty spoke first.

"What's good, son!" Ty said ice-grilling Butter.

"Ain't nuttin' good, you fuckin' clown-ass nigga!" Butter said as he smashed Ty across the face with the bottle of Hypnotiq, shattering the bottle and leaving him with only the jagged neck of the bottle. The result of Butter's first blow left Ty on the floor leaking and grabbing for the wound on his face.

All them Fifty Cent muscles for nuthin'! Murder then rushed Butter, putting him in a bear hug. The commotion on the dance floor caused the DJ to stop the music and for all the lights in the club to be turned on. As usual, the pussy-ass bouncers were slow to react to the scuffle.

"Yo, these dudes up there on the dance floor tryin' to jump your brother," the brown skin girl that was dancing with Butter had run to tell Mil.

Mil and Angie then ran up onto the dance floor and saw Butter wrestling with Murder and Corey and an already bloodied Ty trying to swing on him. Mil was able to sneak up on Ty from behind and connect with a sucker punch to the side of his face that crumbled him to the floor. Angie, even though she was a chic, could rumble with the best of them. She hit Corey over the head with a Heineken bottle that staggered him, but he quickly regained his faculties and squared off with her as they shot a fair one.

With Ty knocked out completely unconscious on the floor, Mil went to help Butter break free of the chokehold Murder had on him. Once Butter was free, they tried to attack the much bigger Murder, but he was proving to be a formidable opponent.

By this time, security had finally gotten up the nerve to intervene in the battle as they tried to separate the combatants. Butter then pulled Angie toward the back entrance and told her to go start the car. Butter and Mil were quickly following behind her out the back entrance and retrieved their pistols out of the vehicle. Then they eased on behind opposite sides of the bar's rear entrance door.

Unaware of their surroundings, Murder tried to help Ty to

his feet as the commotion was coming to a halt. They tried to make it to the nearest exit.

"Yo, son. Them niggas bounced already. Let's get the fuck outta here!" Corey stated still shook up from his tough rumble with a female.

"Aiight, kid. Be easy! Just clear a path and lead the way out the back while I help this nigga," Murder said as Corey immediately started pushing his way through the throngs of people while Murder helped the semiconscious Ty toward the back exit supporting his dead weight on his shoulder with his arm draped around his neck.

"Here they come, Butter," Mil said as he saw Corey through the small, square window in the door about to exit the club. Corey brushed past the bouncers who were standing guard by the rear exit so he could hold the door open for Murder to half-carry/half-drag Ty's limp body through. When Corey stepped outside the frame of the backdoor, Mil raised his battle-worn pistol level with Corey's shocked face and fired a single, fatal shot. Pop!

The startled expression on Corey's face would be the last emotion that his young grill would ever hold. As the single bullet from Mil's rusted .38 long revolver crashed through his face, his lifeless body tumbled backwards crashing onto the ground.

Butter emerged from the other side of the entranceway and fired several shots from his black porcelain Glock 9mm pistol. One slug struck one of the bouncers, who was standing in the doorway, in the chest. Another shot hit Murder in the lower leg causing him to drop Ty to the floor while trying to take cover inside the rear entranceway of "The Breeze."

Amidst the chaos and screaming of the people who were

running throughout the now human-flooded parking lot, Butter and Mil then retreated to the late model, gold, rented Chevrolet Malibu where Angie was waiting at the top of the parking lot with the engine running.

"Hurry up, Ang, pull off!" Butter instructed her as he and Mil slammed the car doors behind them. Angie peeled out making a screeching sound with the car's tires as she raced the getaway vehicle down a narrow alley before turning off onto Plum Street and blending into the late night traffic.

"What the fuck happened?" Angie asked as she tried to get them a safe distance away from the scene of the crime.

"We tried to murder them niggas!" Mil said. "I got that nigga too, Butter! I got 'em," he gloated, both excited and proud of his first homicide.

"Yeah, them niggas never even saw it comin'," Butter replied. "Now we gotta find somewhere to get low at. Yo, Ang," he turned to her from his passenger seat and said, "you just gotta keep driving out Route 30. We just gonna go far outside the city to some lil' telly and chill," Butter insisted.

"Don't worry 'bout nuthin'. I got chu, my nigga!" Angie replied confidently. "You know I'm a wheel this muthaphucka to where we gotta go."

As they continued to ride in silence, Butter thought how his kid brother had grown into a total monster, almost as cold-hearted as himself. He also wondered how that night would change their lives or possibly come back to haunt them one day. Tired of the endless possibilities and scenarios running through his mind, he said, *"Fuck it! Better them than us,"* he reasoned as he turned up the radio, leaned back in his seat, closed his eyes and listened deeply as the song *Many Men* by *50 Cent* bumped out the car speakers.

"*Many men, wish death upon me, Blood in my eye dog and I can't see/I'm just tryin' to be what I'm destined to be, and niggas wanna take my life away.*

"*I'll put a hole in a nigga for fuckin' wit' me, My back on the wall now you gonna see/You better watch how you talk when you talk about me, cause I'll come and take your life away.*

"*Many men, many, many, many, many men wish death 'pon me; Lord I don't cry no more, don't look to the sky no more, have mercy on me;*

"*Have mercy on my soul, somewhere my heart turned cold: Have mercy on many men, many, many, many, many men wish death 'pon me.*"

Butter noticed Mil in the back seat smiling, gazing out the window reciting every word to the song. And the only thing that Butter could think to himself was, "*Damn, God help us all.*"

CHAPTER SEVEN

A few days after his crew's latest confrontation with the Young Kings at The Breeze, Ra laid in bed contemplating his current situation. He truly understood in his heart that things had gotten completely out of hand. They had only been in Lancaster for a little over two months and everything that could possibly go wrong, had gone *horribly* wrong.

For starters, Lil' Corey was dead. And now Ty had to console his aunt and help her prepare to bury her only child. Murder had gotten shot. And after the doctors removed the slug from his leg that shattered his left shin, he developed an infection in the wound and had to be re-hospitalized. He was scheduled to be released in two days. *"I'm the last muthaphucka standing',"* he thought to himself.

But, amazingly, through all the bullshit, Ra was still getting money. His flow and clientele were consistent. That was the only constant in his life. During a bad week, he could still move a key and a half for top dollar with no problem. The money was looking lovely. That was the major reason he had decided to stay in Lancaster, no matter what happened. Because normally, after a bad string of events like they'd just encountered, it would be time to pack your bags, cut your losses and leave town. But there was also *another* variable to this equation. Her name was

Moya and she had him open.

Ra looked down at her face as he rolled over in bed beside her. She was a dime, make no mistake about it. She had a smooth, mocha-chocolate brown complexion that was darker than your average Puerto Rican, so some people mistook her for being black. But combined with her long, jet-black hair, chinky eyes and full lips, she was a uniquely, exotic beauty. Moya stood 5'4, 140 pounds, but in all the right places. Ass, thighs and breasts. Just like he liked his women. Ra had wifed her almost immediately after meeting her.

Ra had heard the stories of how she was a freak and a whore before he started fuckin' wit' her, but he didn't care. He felt that as long as it happened before he was involved with her, it didn't matter. He accepted her and her two-year-old daughter, Aaliyah, just as they were.

Ra rose from bed thinking how he had found a gold mine in Pennsylvania. And how he wasn't going to let some country-ass niggas fuck that up for him. Fuck the bullshit, he was going to keep getting money and that was all there was to it. He threw on his grey Rocawear sweatsuit he had on the day before and his grey Nike Huaraches and decided to walk around the corner to the store for some Dutches.

It was a nice, sunny September day as he walked outside. He walked down the little hill from High Street, turned right onto New Dorwart Street and headed for DeJesus Bodega that was located two blocks away on the corner of Manor Street. He made this trip on the regular. He had gotten comfortable on this side of town. Southwest was more laid back, and the out-of-towners weren't frequently getting terrorized.

Ra went into the corner store and purchased a gallon of

orange juice, a pack of Newport 100's, and a box of vanilla Dutch Masters. He figured Moya and Aaliyah would want something to drink with breakfast when they woke up. When Ra exited the bodega, he immediately lit up a Newport. He had been nickin' for his first cigarette of the morning. He retraced the same path he had taken to the store as he started for home.

When Ra turned onto High Street and reached Moya's front door, he noticed a black S500 Mercedes-Benz breeze past him. *Nice whip*. And he thought nothing else of it as he unlocked the front door and disappeared inside the house.

Benny was at B.O.'s house waiting for him to get dressed so they could go to Philadelphia and go shopping. As usual, B.O. wasn't ready when Benny arrived, so Benny was in the living room playing with B.O.'s sons, Kai and Kion, while B.O. finished getting ready. His cell phone rang.

"Yo," Benny answered.

"What up, dog?" Gito asked him on the other end of the phone.

"Ain't nuttin', G.I. What's good?"

"B., you ain't gonna guess who I just saw!"

"Listen, G.I., just lemme know what's good. I ain't got time to be playin' around today," Benny said standing up from the couch and sitting B.O.'s younger son, Kion, who had been sitting on his lap, down on the couch.

"Yo, dog. I just seen that nigga Ra!"

"Yeah? Where the fuck he at?" Benny asked as he walked out of the living room and into the kitchen, so that he could hear better.

"He been right under our noses all this time. That nigga been right in the town. Check it. I was comin' from my young boy Chita's crib when I seen this nigga goin' into Moya's crib. He was carrying groceries and the whole nine! Like he been livin' there forever. Fuckin' house nigga!" Gito joked of his discovery.

"Stop playin', dog!" Benny laughed.

"Word, B! I heard he was fuckin' wit' her but I wasn't sure until today. The Expedition was parked out front and everything," Gito said expressing how serious he was.

"Aiight, G.I., good lookin'. I know how we gonna handle this already. Listen, we gonna make this happen tonight. For sure! So keep your line open. I'm a hit you back, aiight?"

"Aiight, dog. I'm on call. Just holla at me when you ready to move out."

"Definitely, my nigga. One."

"One."

B.O. had just walked into the kitchen as Benny hung up his phone. "What's poppin', my nigga?" B.O. asked as he saw Benny staring reflectively out the kitchen window.

"We got him, B.O.," Benny said quietly, confident that they had finally found their mark.

"Who?" B.O. said not fully understanding exactly to whom Benny was referring.

"Ra!" Benny said in a voice barely above a whisper with a devilish smile on his face.

"Say word."

"Word! Gito found out that nigga been stayin' wit' Moya. After all this time, he wit' the same hood rat I first saw that nigga hollerin' at," Benny reflected.

"That's some shit, right?" B.O. thought as well.

"Yeah. I overestimated that nigga. I thought he woulda' had better sense than to be fuckin' wit' her. But, it's all to the good, I guess. He just made our job a thousand times easier," Benny reasoned. "Call Bear and tell 'em to get over here now! We gotta get this shit mapped out right. The three of us are gonna handle this shit ourselves. We can't afford no mistakes or fuck-ups on this one," Benny stressed to B.O., who was already on the phone calling Bear.

"He's on his way," B.O. said hanging up the phone.

"Aiight, say no more," Benny said as he sat back and began to mentally formulate the plot for his enemy's demise.

That night around eleven o'clock, Benny was ready to initiate the first stage of his master plan. He, B.O., Bear and Gito were just about to leave B.O.'s crib for Moya's crib.

"Yo, G.I., you know what you gotta do, right?" Benny asked him again to make sure he understood his instructions.

"Yeah, dog. Just circle the block and make sure it's safe of police while y'all in the house. And call you if I see somethin' ain't lookin' right," G.I. said on-point as always.

"That's it, my nigga. 'Cause we gonna go right through the back door, but still one of them nosy-ass neighbors might call the cops. I ain't tryin' to get caught up on some old okey-doke, unexpected shit," Benny continued. "B.O. and Bear, you know what it is. We been here before," he said looking at his two closest niggas in the world. "Duck tape, masks and gloves. Let's roll!"

G.I. left first in his car. Benny, Bear and B.O. hopped in an older model, black Ford Explorer that they used specifically for shit like that. They were enroute to Moya's house.

When they reached Moya's house, they noticed that the television was on in the front room of the house as it illuminated the room through the curtains. All the other lights in the house were off. B.O. then drove down the block and turned onto New

Dorwart Street and parked the weathered SUV. They exited the vehicle and crept up High Street before slipping into the alley that separated Moya's house from the row house beside it. They traveled through the alley to Moya's backyard and stopped just outside her back door.

"Aiight, my niggas. I can see shadows on the living room wall moving around in the light from the TV," Benny whispered to his comrades while peeking through a window at the rear of the house. "Now, when I kick this door off the muthaphuckin' hinges, we go straight through the kitchen to the living room and on whoever's ass is in there. I'm a secure the upstairs, quick and to the point. So, we got everything?" he asked. B.O. and Bear just nodded in agreement under their ski-masked faces as B.O. pointed to the black bag he had over his shoulder.

"Aiight then, on the count of three, we in there," Benny finished, knowing there was nothing left to say. One," he whispered, "two, three!" BOOM!

The back door came crashing off the hinges and the frame, flying into the darkened kitchen. Benny was a master at kicking in doors. His legs were as big as a horse's and he always dismantled them with one strike. Bear and B.O. were through the door before it even completely fell down. They were smooth and quick as they moved through the stealth of the house.

Ra was unprepared, without a gun in reach, caught off guard, butt-naked and in mid-stroke. He was lying on top of a nude Moya in front of the television on the living room floor. Before he could even attempt to get up, B.O. held his crispy, chrome, Smith & Wesson .40 caliber pistol to the back of Ra's head as he looked down into Moya's terrified eyes. She let out a silent scream.

"Nigga, you know what it is. Don't Fuckin' Move!" B.O. said slowly and precisely to Ra, who obeyed, putting his hands straight out to his sides and not moving a muscle.

"Oh, my God!" Moya screamed aloud this time finding her voice.

"Shut up, you stupid bitch!" Bear said as he smacked her in the mouth with his black semiautomatic .45.

"Yo! My girl ain't got shit to do with this, son!" Ra pleaded.

"Shut up and stand up, you faggot muthaphucka!" B.O. ordered him as he kept his gun firmly embedded at the base of Ra's neck and guided him to sit down on the floor away from Moya. "That ain't your bitch, anyway. That's everybody's bitch!" B.O. said as Moya curled up in front of the black leather sofa crying and missing her two front teeth courtesy of the blow he had delivered with his gun. Benny casually strolled into the living room and observed the scene.

"Got caught wit' your pants down, huh, big guy?" Benny teased Ra. "That's what happens when you shit where you lie. Anyway, the upstairs is clear. Ain't nobody else in here but the baby. And she fast asleep," Benny informed Bear and B.O. "I was tempted to R. Kelly her lil' ass, but I figured it wasn't necessary. Now, to the real shit. I only found about twenty stacks up there, all neat and organized in a nightstand next to the bed, and this faggot's punk-ass jewels," Benny said holding up a pillowcase in his left hand that contained the loot. "Nigga, where it at?" he screamed violently at Ra.

"I don't know what chu talkin' bout..." Ra never finished his statement before he felt the butt of Bear's .45 smack him square across the face. Bear was getting a kick out of the shit.

"Stop lyin', nigga! Where the coke at?" Bear asked, tired of playing games with him.

"I don't got it. Y'all already got the money. Why don't y'all just leave, son," Ra pleaded holding his bloodied face.

"Aiight, nigga. I see you wanna do shit the hard way," Benny said sounding disappointed. "I know how to get chu to give it up. Yo, pass me that duct tape," Benny said to B.O., who then handed him the roll of grey tape. The two of them then proceeded to hog-tie Ra, taping his wrists together behind his back, then taping his ankles together before taping his ankles to his wrists. When they were finished, Ra was completely immobilized and helpless, convinced he'd never make it out of there alive.

"You cool now, money?" Benny asked Ra laughing. "You want a square?" Benny said as he pulled out a loose cigarette from his pack and placed it between Ra's lips, not even waiting for him to answer. He then lit the cigarette for him. "Smoke, nigga!" Benny instructed him.

Ra began to smoke the cigarette, inhaling the smoke until he started to choke and his eyes turned red and watery from the clouds of mist. Benny then removed the burning cigarette from Ra's mouth and proceeded to place the smoldering cancer stick on his face leaving red burn marks and blackened ashes on his skin.

"Ahhh!" Ra screamed unable to withstand the unbearable pain. "I don't got nuthin' else, son! Please, chill!" Ra begged.

"Nigga, stop lyin' to me! I look stupid to you?" Benny asked him incredulously, as he continued to burn Ra all over his back, chest and face with flaming cigarette butts.

"Chill, son, chill!" Ra screamed out in anguish. Then Benny motioned to B.O. to hand him the black bag he had brought with them. Benny reached inside the bag and produced a five-gallon gasoline can. Ra's eyes grew large when he realized what was about to go down.

"What the fuck you gonna do with that?" Ra asked trembling as Benny just smiled.

"Bring that stupid-ass bitch over here, too!" Benny instructed, and Bear grabbed a handful of hair from the back of Moya's head and pushed her down on the floor next to Ra's tortured body. Benny then proceeded to douse Ra and Moya with the contents of the gasoline can.

"Chill, son! What the fuck is that?" Ra asked, already knowing from the stench that it had to be gas.

"Hell on Earth. And if you don't tell me what the fuck I wanna know in the next sixty seconds, you and this bitch both gonna feel eternal fire," Benny said, meaning every word he uttered.

"Son, I ain't got nuthin'. You took all my paper, I swear," Ra said sounding pitiful, still trying to hold out on his stash.

"Yo, you lucky this bitch all used the fuck up or I'd rape this bitch. But, I don't wanna catch nuthin'.'" Bear said as he smacked Moya on the ass. "Get up, hooker!" Bear commanded her. "On your knees."

"Damn, dog! You knocked the bitch fronts all out. I can't even get no head!" B.O. laughed.

"Aiight, bitch, face down, ass up!" Bear ordered Moya as he pushed her face into the beige carpet, leaving her with her ass propped in the air.

"What you doin', son? Please, son, let her be. She ain't got shit to do with this!" Ra said in a desperate plea for his wifey's safety and dignity. Bear ignored him and viciously rammed the barrel shaft of his black .45 handgun into her exposed vagina.

"Aah! My God, no!!!" Moya screamed as Bear ripped through the flesh of her vagina with his pistol.

"Bitch, don't you move again," he said to her as he laid her on her back and again inserted his gun inside her bloody vagina. He continued to menacingly move his pistol in and out of her womb.

"What the fuck, is she on her period?" B.O. asked laughing as he looked down at the messy scene.

"Son, please! Stop!" Ra said, now with tears running down his face. "You got it, son. You got it," Ra finally submitted. He had seen enough.

"You really love this bitch, huh?" Benny asked him, before telling Bear to stop torturing Moya's body. "Aiight dawg, that's enough."

"Damn, dog! She was about to cum, too! I could tell," Bear said as he removed his gun from her bloodied orifice. "It was good, wasn't it?" Bear asked Moya as she curled up in the fetal position whimpering in excruciating pain. "Lil' freak!"

"Aiight, now give it up and I won't have to set y'all on fire after all," Benny said calmly to Ra.

"It's all outside in my truck. Everything. The money is in the glove compartment and the coke is in the center console between the seats," Ra confessed weakly.

"Where the keys at?" Benny asked him.

"In my pants pocket, over there," Ra said tilting his head towards the black leather recliner in the corner across the room. B.O., who was closest to the chair, rifled through Ra's pants pockets and quickly found the keys to Ra's truck.

"I got 'em. I'm a go see and it better be there!" B.O. threatened Ra, as he went out the back door. He returned within a couple of minutes with a brown paper shopping bag.

"I got it, dog!" B.O. said holding up the bag. "It's at least a brick of coke, probably a little more. I ain't even try to count the dough, but it looks to be about thirty or forty!" B.O. said estimating that it was between thirty and forty thousand dollars he had just gotten out of the SUV.

"Aiight, that's cool right there. We outta here," Benny announced.

"Hold up! What about these two muthaphuckas? Can I kill 'em or what?" Bear asked Benny, hoping and praying that he'd say yes.

"Nah. I'm a man of my word. He gave us what we wanted," Benny noted. "You get to live, bitch-boy," he said to Ra, "but I suggest you get outta this town A-sap. Take it as a lesson. You live and you learn," Benny said matter-of-factly as he turned to B.O and Bear and gave them the signal to head for the back door. With a pillowcase and a brown paper bag containing all that Ra was worth, they fled out of the house into the wee hours of the morning.

As Moya laid bruised, battered and demoralized on the floor next to Ra, she heard a rumbling come from the middle room between the living room and the kitchen. "Oh, my God, they're back!" she feared. As she heard the soft footsteps approaching, she cowered beside Ra. However, it was her daughter, Aaliyah, who wandered into the living room.

"Mommy, what's wrong?" the confused child asked her injured mother. Ra breathed a sigh of relief while Moya just began to cry even more, sobbing now, wishing she had never met Ra. *Pussy muthaphucka*!

CHAPTER EIGHT

Lancaster city police officer James Bell was patrolling the far-east section of the city, where East King Street turns into Lincoln Highway East heading out of the city before eventually becoming Route 30 East. It was a normal sunny September afternoon in Lancaster, PA.

Officer Bell was from the hood. He grew up in southeast and played football in high school, although he was no superstar. All things considered, he was a lame and never really respected for who he was as a person. This always bothered him. It became almost a permanent chip on his shoulder to prove his worth as a person. After numerous failed attempts at college or any other meaningful career goals, he resorted to a life of civil service. After going through the ranks from traffic cop to bike patrolman, Officer Bell was now in a police cruiser free to terrorize and patrol the hood. He was determined to make something of his life even if it meant harassing, setting up, and imprisoning the same individuals he had grown up with. He epitomized the words Uncle Tom, coon and house-nigga. Rule number one in the hood: *never forget where you came from. You might just have to return one day.*

While sitting in his white patrol car watching for speeding vehicles merging onto the highway, he noticed a gold Chevrolet

Malibu pass by him in a pack of light traffic heading into the city. He eased out into the traffic to tail the car he had spotted. This particular vehicle stood out to Officer Bell because, at headquarters, posted on the most-wanted bulletin board was a notice pertaining to a recent homicide that had occurred at a local bar. A gold Chevrolet Malibu sedan had been listed as a possible getaway car in connection with the crime.

Another reason this automobile specifically struck a chord with Officer Bell was because he also recognized the driver as one Dorian Chambers, a/k/a Butter.

He had known Butter for years. His family had lived only a few blocks away from Butter on the other side of King School. They had even attended King Elementary School together, even though he was at least three years older than Butter. He was also aware that on the bulletin board posted back at the station house that Butter had been named as a murder suspect in the club shooting as well. The bouncer from "The Breeze" who was shot gave a statement implicating Butter as the shooter after picking his picture out of a photo array. He described Butter as the triggerman who shot him and Corey James, the seventeen-year-old decedent.

Officer Bell immediately got on his radio and alerted headquarters that he was following the *murder suspect* in *"The Breeze"* homicide case, and that the suspect was driving a gold Chevrolet Malibu sedan traveling westbound on Lincoln Highway approaching the intersection at Broad Street, entering the city limits.

The Lancaster City Police Station was located only about five blocks from where Officer Bell had radioed his call. Seeing as though this was a lead in a top priority case, his superior officers ordered Officer Bell to tail the suspect at a safe distance, but not to pull him over or make any other decisions until further notice.

The lead detectives at the precinct ordered all available units to proceed to the area of East Orange Street adjacent to Reservoir Park, since it was the only available thoroughfare once Lincoln Highway merged into a dead end and King Street became a one-way road. They knew in order for the Malibu to pass west through town, the direction *they* had been heading, they would have to drive west onto Orange Street. So two blocks away from Broad Street, where Lincoln Highway and East King Street merged, the police orchestrated a roadblock at the corner of East Orange Street and Franklin Street in less than five minutes. They had effectively sealed the entire end of the block.

Reservoir Park spanned the entire two blocks between Broad Street and Franklin Street on the left hand side of East Orange Street. Located directly behind the roadblock on the other side of Franklin Street was the Lancaster County Prison. The police had created the perfect plan, so that their suspect had very limited options once they completely boxed him in with Officer Bell bringing up the rear. Now all they had to do was wait for him to fall directly into their trap.

Butter had noticed the dickhead cop following him as soon as the cruiser pulled out of the parking lot of *Advance Auto Parts*. Butter knew he wasn't speeding when he drove past the cop, so why was he tailing him from about three cars back? *Maybe I'm just paranoid.* He was coming from the Ramada Inn on Route 30, about fifteen minutes outside of the city. He had been laying low there since the night when shit had gone down at "The Breeze." Butter had seen on Newscenter 8 that Corey had been killed and that two others had been shot. But according to the reporter, the police had no suspects or leads in the case. So he figured he was safe. At least for now.

Butter was on his way to meet Benny at Mr. Vic's Family Styling, a hair salon and barbershop, so they could talk face to face. Benny said he didn't want to discuss anything over the phone. And as normal, during the daytime hours, Benny was holding court at the shop. Mr. Vic's was located a half a block away from La Familia restaurant across the street from Hillrise Projects. Butter had left Mil at the hotel with the two Spanish chics they had been fuckin' with the night before while he went to see Benny.

Butter knew Benny had a plan for him and Mil to lay low out of town somewhere. It was getting too hot in the hood. Their names had already started circulating through the rumor mills and gossip circles as being involved with the recent shootings that had plagued the city. And in a quiet town, like Lancaster was supposed to be, that was almost enough to get the murder indictments rolling. So Butter figured he and Mil would probably go down south to NC (North Carolina) or somethin' and get some money down there while shit cooled down. But for some reason, some damn cop kept following him.

Butter switched lanes as the two-lane highway turned into three lanes before the merge point at the traffic light. The two left hand lanes were for left turns only. The far right lane was for right turns only. This was where Lincoln Highway ended if you were traveling westbound. Butter moved over the far fight lane preparing to turn right onto Broad Street. The police cruiser calmly changed lanes, and now there was only one car in between his car and Butter's automobile.

When the stop light turned green, Butter turned right onto North Broad Street traveling exactly one block before making a left hand turn onto East Orange Street heading westbound. Butter noticed that traffic was backed up, but he couldn't see the end of the block. *Maybe there was an accident or somethin'*, Butter thought.

At the end of the block, the police were directing traffic, and steering drivers to turn right onto Franklin Street off of East Orange Street away from Reservoir Park and the prison. Officer Bell transmitted over his radio that the suspect's vehicle had just turned onto East Orange Street and was approximately a half a block or 100 feet away from the designated roadblock. The officers gave him the order to proceed with the traffic stop and prepared themselves for action.

As Butter approached the middle of the block, he could see two police cruisers blocking the entire street. He also saw at least four officers out of their vehicles. Two in the middle of the street, directly in front of the roadblock, one on the right hand side of the street, and one to his left standing on the steps that led to the park, all with their weapons drawn. *"What the Fuck!"* At that moment, Butter knew something wasn't right. As he inched closer to the roadblock, the dickhead cop, who was now directly behind him, turned on his lights and began to speak over his vehicle's loudspeaker.

"Mr. Chambers! Your vehicle is surrounded! Do not try anything stupid. Slowly pull your vehicle over on your left side!" Officer Bell said commandingly.

"Muthaphucker!" Butter thought. *"They on my ass, old-ass dude in the car in front of me. Fuck it! I ain't goin' out like that! They gonna have to catch me."* Butter then slammed his

foot on the gas pedal after his split-second decision, ramming an elderly white man who was driving a silver Buick Park Avenue in front of him. He was about twenty feet from the police officers and the two patrol cars that were blocking the street. He decided to go around them. Butter turned the steering wheel to the left and drove onto the sidewalk next to the park. After making it to the corner of Franklin Street, Butter turned left brushing the park stairs and hitting the officer who was standing on them, tossing him in the air before landing on the grass.

The police were caught off guard by Butter's sudden and irrational actions. Unable to immediately get to their vehicles, the officers opened fire on the gold Malibu trying to impede Butter's escape. A few shots struck the vehicle, disabling the right rear tire and shattering the rear window. As Butter raced down Franklin Street toward the hood, southeast, officers scurried back to their vehicles to join the chase.

Officer Bell had been on Butter's tail from the word *go*. As his cruiser pursued the gold Chevy Malibu, Officer Bell knew they were approaching East End Avenue and the only way they could turn was right because to the left and ahead would be a dead end. He was certain he was about to be a hero, *save the day*, and get a big promotion. Maybe even detective. What Officer Bell didn't anticipate was that when Butter reached the end of Franklin Street and made a hard right onto East End Avenue, narrowly missing a parked car, there would be a large brown UPS truck turning onto Franklin Street over the center line that marked the street.

Officer Bell attempted to make the hard right turn onto East End Avenue in pursuit of his suspect going 80 mph. His cruiser collided head on with the United Parcel Service delivery truck. Officer Bell's body was ejected from the front windshield of his patrol car, instantly snapping his neck. His life was abruptly cut short before his body even hit the black surface of the street at the tiny intersection. He would never get a chance to become the hero he died longing to be.

Butter saw the crash behind him in his rearview mirror and thought he had bought himself a few precious extra seconds, but he was sadly mistaken. By the time he reached the next block, three police vehicles met him at the intersection. When he turned left sharply onto South Marshall Street, all three cruisers were behind him.

As Butter blew by the red brick buildings that were the Garden Court Housing Projects, he knew it was only a matter of time before the chase would come to an end. The police had shot out his right rear tire and he had blown out the left front one when he hit the park steps trying to turn the corner at the beginning of the chase. On two good wheels, he continued down Marshall Street until the street ended and he turned right onto Juniata and past Edward Hand Middle School. Butter had already decided in his mind that when he crossed the next intersection at South Ann Street that he was going to get off the main streets and make the right into the alleyway that ran directly behind South Ann Street.

Butter reached the mouth of the alley and cut his wheel hard to the right, but he misjudged the turn and slammed directly into a utility pole to the left of the alley, hitting his forehead on the steering wheel.

Still conscious but disoriented, Butter hopped out of the car and continued in his efforts to escape on foot. The police officers were out of their vehicles in seconds and the foot chase ensued. Butter ran up South Ann Street through the predominantly Hispanic area of southeast. The residents of the street were all outside to see what the early afternoon commotion was about. Butter ducked into a house that had an open door, but as he tried to escape through the kitchen door, he was greeted by an elderly Puerto Rican man with a 12 gauge double-barrel shotgun.

"Don' ju move, Moreno!" the elderly man said in broken English. The police officers filed into the house and handcuffed Butter leading him out of the house to a waiting patrol car.

Benny was sitting out front of Mr. Vic's on the stoop when his phone rang.

"Yo," he answered.

"Yo, dog. Your man Butter just got bagged on my block." It was Gito on the other end of his phone.

"For real?"

"Yeah, dog! He just had the ill chase wit' the jakes. He banged out in the alley behind my block, then they caught him on foot a couple minutes later," Gito informed him.

"Damn," Benny said in disbelief. "Good lookin', G.I. I'm a hit you back."

"Aiight, dog. One."

"One."

As Benny ended his telephone call, he knew that Butter didn't kill Corey. He also knew that it didn't matter what really happened. The Lancaster police would make it so. They were starving for a conviction and Butter would be their sacrificial lamb. It was the dirty reality of the game. Benny understood that. He also understood he had lost one of his best solders, possibly for life.

CHAPTER NINE

Ra had finally had enough. As he sat on the couch in Moya's living room nursing his facial wounds and his bruised ego, he knew that it was time for drastic actions. He had experienced more heartache and pain over the past few months in PA than he had in his entire life in Brooklyn. And at the hands of some bitch-ass country niggas at that. It was too much for his mind to fathom. He was in complete awe of what had transpired. What was left of his team was now there with him in Moya's living room.

Murder, with his one good leg, was sitting next to him on the couch. He was released from the hospital two days after his rival had run up in Moya's spot, punished his man and depleted their stash. Ra was convinced that if Murder had been there, shit wouldn't have gone down the way it did.

Nitty was frantically pacing about the living room, smoking back-to-back Newports. He'd just returned from New York. He had accompanied his aunt to the city so she could lay her only son to rest next to his grandmother. Nitty came back strapped for war. He brought an AK-47 and a .45 caliber Desert Eagle back with him prepared to avenge the death of his little cousin. Seeing his cousin get murdered right in front of him and him not being able to do anything to prevent it was really fuckin' with him emotionally. Mentally, Nitty was ready to snap.

Moya had heard from her girl Tanea that the Young Kings were the ones who had run up in her crib. Not like it was any secret. The whole hood was talking. Ra had known immediately who was responsible for everything that had happened to him and his peoples since they had been in town. Now Ra had decisions to make.

Was it really worth it to stay in Lancaster after almost losing his life and the life of the woman he loved? He still had almost twenty thousand dollars in New York. He could easily take Moya and her daughter, pick up and go back to the city. Or maybe go to some other small town, in Virginia or somethin'. *"Nah, fuck that! I had enough of these quiet towns! Hatin'-ass niggas tryin' to fuckin' murk a nigga. Hell no! Never again,"* he thought.

Ra had decided to leave Lancaster and go back to New York, for good. But before he left, he had a plan to leave a permanent mark on the town.

For the Young Kings, everything was business as usual. On one particular afternoon, Benny, Bear and B.O. were posted on the block in front of Mr. Vic's across from Hillrise Projects. Mil and Angie were just pulling up in a blue Honda Accord.

"What's good, my niggas!" Mil said as he hopped out of the passenger seat while Angie remained in the car behind the wheel.

"Ain't nuttin', lil' nigga. What's up wit' your brother?" Benny asked him immediately.

"He ain't even get no bail. They tryin' to charge him up all crazy and shit. He got the murder charge, from that lil' faggot nigga I popped at the club. Then they gave him two counts of attempted homicide for the bouncer and the other New Yorker who got hit that night," Mil informed them.

"That's fucked up, cousin," Bear said.

"What's fucked up is that that ain't it. For the police chase, he got another murder charge for that cop he banged out that died. And another three counts of aggravated assault for the old white man and his seven-year-old grandson who Butter rammed in the car that was sitting in front of him, *and* for the cop he hit wit' his car. They tryin' to kill my brother, dog," Mil finished as he threw his half-smoked cigarette on the sidewalk.

"Damn, dog. That's fucked up, right there," B.O. said.

"Yo, Mil, tell your moms we got Butter's lawyer and everything else. Just have her contact the lawyer and get at me," Benny assured him.

"That's good lookin', B," Mil thanked him appreciatively.

"That ain't about nuthin', my nigga. We family."

"Yo, B., you see any of them New York niggas lately?" Mil inquired.

"Nah, cousin. I think them niggas skipped town," Benny said laughing.

"Yeah, after that shit, that's what a smart man would do," B.O. concurred.

"Well, I better not catch 'em. I can't wait to rock me another one of them niggas. I think that kid Murder snitched on my brother, anyway. Pussy-ass nigga! How he get a name like Murder?" Mil said shaking his head.

"You know them niggas be on that video bullshit. Think they rappers and shit. Call me Murder, Killa, Capone, Fake mobsters, ain't killin' nuthin'," Bear joked.

"I know that's right, 'cause when we popped off at them

niggas, I seen the bitch come out of all of them," Mil said.

A silver Lincoln Town Car with tinted windows drove past them and turned into the Kentucky Fried chicken parking lot on the next block.

"Aiight, son. They right up there on the next block," Ra said from the passenger seat to Nitty, who was in the back seat. Murder was the driver, one bad leg and all.

"I'm ready to paint this town red, son!" Nitty said as he pulled the hood of his sweatshirt over his head. He had his Desert Eagle gripped tightly between his gloved hands.

"No drive-by shit this time, son. We gonna walk up on these niggas and handle this one up close and personal," Ra told Nitty plainly. "Now, Murder, you sure you straight to wheel this whip?"

"Of course, son. I only need one leg to drive. I'm just mad I can't go wit' chall," Murder lied. In all actuality, Murder was really scared to death. Although he had been in numerous shootouts and even killed a few niggas, he had never been shot until the night Corey was murdered. The feeling of hot lead burning through his flesh, causing inflaming sensations to run through his body, was enough to have him petrified of ever feeling that type of pain again. He was glad to drive, but still he wasn't thrilled about being so close to the action. His feelings started to shine through his phony tough-guy exterior. "You sure you wanna do this now, son?" Murder questioned.

"What the fuck you mean, son?" Ty snapped at him.

"Look, son, it's 3 o'clock. The kids are comin' out of that school over there," Murder said pointing to Martin Luther King Elementary School which was located on South Duke Street directly across from the KFC parking lot where they were sitting.

"So the fuck what, son!" Nitty continued to flip. "Them

niggas killed my cousin! And they still standing right across the street from my aunt's building, where she cry herself to sleep every night. Nah, son. Fuck that! We gonna hit them niggas now!"

"Murder, what's really good wit' chu? Look at my face, son. Them niggas put bogies out in my grill. Tortured me and my girl. This is the perfect opportunity and they ain't expectin' it. Them niggas gotta die today!" Ra said passionately.

"Aiight, son. If you wanna do it now, we'll do it now," Murder conceded.

"Aiight then, Nitty, I'm a leave the 'K' in the car," Ra said referring to the AK-47 assault rifle in the front seat with him. "We can't sneak up on them niggas in broad day wit' that. I got my Glock, seventeen should do the job!"

"I don't give a fuck son! Let's just do it!" Ty said restlessly.

"Just keep the engine runnin'," Ra said to Murder as he pulled his hoodie over his head and gave Ty the signal to exit the car. They both stepped out into the crowded afternoon street.

The corner of South Duke Street and North Street was in between the KFC and the block where Mr. Vic's Family Styling was located. As the hundreds of school children filed out of King Elementary School, they waited at the intersection of South Duke Street and North Street for the crossing guard to direct them safely across the street. Ty and Ra blended in with the crowds of parents and children milling back and forth on South Duke Street and calmly crossed over North Street onto the block where Benny, Bear, B.O. and Mil were standing in front of Mr. Vic's in the middle of the block. They were about thirty feet away from their designated targets. Angie, who was still sitting in the parked Honda Accord, was the first one to recognize the imminent danger.

"Yo, Mil! Watch out!" she screamed from the automobile.

Nitty's eyes had been focused on one target and one target only. The skinny nigga with the dreads that killed his cousin. Mil was the closest one to their approaching foes. The shots from Nitty's .45 caliber Desert Eagle made traffic stop and small children scream out in fear as they scrambled to find shelter. Pop! Pop! Pop!

Mil never got a chance to reach for his rusted, trusty, thirty-eight tucked in his waistband. Nitty's first two shots were accurate, catching Mil high in the chest, knocking him backwards as his dreads swung in the air. He crashed to the pavement. Ra had opened fire as well. B.O. and Bear who were standing behind Mil, dove behind the car where Angie was sitting. Benny fell into the alley that separated Mr. Vic's from the row house beside it. He readied his weapon.

Angie was the first to return fire as she exited the driver side of the Accord. She let loose with her small chrome .25 caliber handgun. She fired at Nitty, striking him in the stomach but not enough for him to retreat. Ty then turned with Ra and they fired on Angie. She was hit several times in the chest before a single slug from Ty's Desert eagle put a quarter-sized hole through Angie's fitted hat. The crimson liquid flowed freely from her wound, staining her pretty yellow face as she fell into the street.

B.O and Bear gathered themselves and returned fire from behind the Accord, forcing Ra to retreat down the block. Ty Nitty was running on the fuel of revenge and adrenalin, and didn't surrender an inch of ground while exchanging rounds hitting the parked car B.O and Bear used for cover. He never saw

Benny emerge from the alley and fire a shot from his .44 bull-dog. He was struck in the back of the skull. The grey matter exploded out the front of Ty Nitty's forehead and he fell face first on the gum-stained sidewalk.

Seeing Nitty's body slam hard to the concrete, Ra took off towards the KFC parking lot, knocking down frightened children in the process. When Ra reached the parking lot, he found that Murder was gone. When Murder first heard the gunshots, he went into a state of panic and sped away. It was too much for him to handle. He thought that somehow he would be the next casualty. He was already on his way to the highway, ready to head back to New York.

Benny, Bear and B.O ran around the opposite corner to Locust Street where Benny's Denali was parked. They safely fled the scene. Ra was stranded with no ride, desperately looking for some place to escape. Within a matter of seconds, the entire Lancaster City police department was scouring the area. Ra began to run west on North Street away from South Duke Street. Parents and bystanders who spotted him fleeing the scene alerted police officers that one of the shooters was fleeing on foot down North Street.

With the police hot on his heels, Ra slipped into a tight alleyway between two row houses. He threw his gun into one of the backyards at the end of the alley, then hid in the opposite yard. Moments later, Ra heard the sounds of dogs barking and police radios coming his way. He pressed his body tightly against the rear of the house. But to no avail. The police had found him. There was nowhere else to run. Ra's options were exhausted. He was slammed face first to the ground and handcuffed. A wait-ing squad car transported Ra to the Lancaster Police Station where he was formally charged with three counts of murder and arraigned before the district magistrate. No bail was issued. He was to be remanded to the custody of the Lancaster County Prison.

Lancaster County Prison was commonly referred to as "The Castle." It was an old prison structure that resembled an old world monolithic building that was constructed of weathered yellow stone with large, looming, pointed towers reminiscent of a castle.

The violent offenders' block, for murders, armed robberies, etc, was unit 3-1. Butter and some of his other homies from the hood were watching the six o'clock newscast on WGAS Newscenter on channel 8. When the anchorman led off with the top story of the evening, a vast silence enveloped the large prison block.

"In the southeast section of the city today, there was a day-time shoot out that left three people dead. The shooting began shortly after 3 p.m. this afternoon when students were released from Martin Luther King Jr. Elementary School on South Duke Street. Fortunately, no children were injured. The motive behind the shooting is unclear, but police say it involved two groups of individuals and it could've possibly been drug-related. What we do know is that nineteen year old Jamil Chambers of Lancaster was fatally wounded, as was a twenty-two year old Lancaster woman, Angela Harris, along with twenty-five year old Tyreek Newsome of Brooklyn, New York. One suspect was apprehended by authorities blocks away from the scene when he was spotted by a pair of third graders hiding in a backyard in the 100 block of North Street. Twenty-six year old Rashawn Coleman, a resident of Brooklyn, New York, has been charged with murder in relation to the shootings." Ra's mug shot photo flashed on the screen. "We'll have more details as the story develops," the anchorman concluded.

Butter was in a state of shock. He couldn't believe what he'd just heard. He rose from his seat at the metal picnic table with a blank stare on his face and returned to his cell. In his cell, he sat on the edge of his bed and tears began to stream down his face. He wrapped his arms around his body and hugged himself. He wished he was hugging his baby brother.

Ra entered the receiving area on the lower level of Lancaster County Prison. He had been transported there by the city police shortly after his arraignment. After he was strip searched, his street clothes and belongings were placed in a property bin that the prison held for you until you were released. Ra was issued a blue prison suit which consisted of a pair of pants, a shirt and a pair of Bob Barker Classic sneakers that resembled Converse Chuck Taylor's.

Ra had never been locked up in his life. But he knew he had to adjust fast and have his game face on. He didn't know what to expect. He figured he was *only* in Pennsylvania. *It can't be all that, it ain't like I'm on Rikers Island or somethin'.* After Ra saw the nurse from the prison's medical staff and given the standard TB shot, he was cleared to go to population.

"Coleman, you'll be going to 3-1," the chubby, short, old white guard with glasses told Ra what housing unit he was assigned to as he handed him his prison-issued identification card and bed roll. He then led Ra to a bank of elevators that would transport them to the third floor.

Once they reached the third floor, Ra exited the elevator and the guard pointed him in the direction of unit 3-1, directly across the corridor. Ra could see into the unit from the hallway through the glass window in the door. Once he entered the unit, he felt the stares from the dudes on the block who mostly were from Lancaster. No face stuck out to him specifically as an enemy, so he felt a little more at ease. *"Fuck them niggas! They can look all they want, but they better not act stupid!"* Ra handed his ID badge to the tall, white C.O. on duty who was sitting at a desk beside the entrance of the unit.

"3065, top bunk," the C.O. said to Ra, pointing to a cell on the upper tier of the housing unit. The unit had metal picnic tables that lined the first floor area of the unit, where inmates were watching television and playing cards. There were cells on the first floor and the second floor. Ra walked through the first floor area and up the staircase to his cell. *"This shit ain't 'bout nuttin',"* Ra thought as he saw a skinny, brown skin old head walk briskly past his cell.

"Butter!" the skinny, brown skin dude in his early forties called him while standing in the doorway to his cell. Butter was in cell 3072, right down the tier from Ra.

"What up, Uncle Ant?" Butter asked his Uncle Anthony as he looked up at him with tears still in his red eyes.

"That niggas here!" Ant said with his poppy-eyes looking larger than normal. Now Ant was an old-school stickup artist from the last generation of the Chambers'. He and his brothers used to terrorize the city of Lancaster in the late seventies and early eighties. Now most of them were dead or fucked up on heroin like Ant was. But don't get it confused — Ant was still a thoroughbred and cold-killer about his work.

"Who?" Butter said rising from his bunk.

"That nigga, who killed Mil!"

"Where he at, Ant?" Butter said with the rage of the fires of hell in his eyes. He looked dead into his Uncle's eyes.

"He right down the tier in 3065," Ant said simply as he removed a ten-inch shank from the waistline of his blue prison pants that he had made from a support that was used on the bunk beds in the cells. Butter took the weapon with the white-taped handle from his uncle and Anthony led them out of the cell and down the tier.

Ra was sitting at the small, metal desk in his cell writing a letter to Moya. The door to his cell was open and he never got the chance to see Ant and Butter slip into his cell and close the door behind them. The next thing he knew, Ant had put him a chokehold dragging his body off the metal stool attached to the desk and slamming him to the cell's cold cement floor. When he saw Butter's face looking down at him, he knew it was over. Butter plunged the sharpened steel instrument deep into Ra's chest cavity. Blood began to gush from the gaping wound as soon as Butter removed the shiv from Ra's torso. He continued to repeatedly stab and fatally wound Ra. He finished him with a vicious poke to the neck region which punctured Ra's jugular vein, ultimately sealing his fate.

Butter and Ant then lifted Ra's tortured body, brought him out on the tier and dropped him over the second floor railing where he crashed onto a metal picnic table below. As Ra laid there, mortally wounded, knowing he was experiencing his last moments of life, he thought to himself *how could his life have come to this? First, Corey was murdered. Then Ty Nitty. Murder's bitch-ass rolled out on me and left me for dead, literally. All that drama and death, and for what? All because we thought shit was too sweet and we could tie it down in a "Quiet Town."*

THE END. 2004.

Block Lingo

Antoine "Inch" Thomas

CHAPTER ONE

"That's exactly my point, son." Lil Frank was sitting on the bench in front of his grandmother's building in the Edenwald Houses chatting with his two homies, *Saheem* and *Ricky*. Leaning back with his arms stretched out and his compadres on either side of him, Lil Frank continued. "Every time *106 and Park* come on, that one broad don't never show us her ass." Lil Frank leaned up and clasped his hands together on his lap.

Ricky, an overweight sixteen-year-old, had his feet up on the bench as he sat on the back part of the wooden seat. He looked down at his good friend and said, "That broad is on some ol' respect type shit, I heard. Niggas said she fuck with somebody in the industry, so I guess she trying be loyal and shit to her man."

Lil Frank peered up at his big boned friend, then glanced over at his other homie who was waiting for him to say something stupid. Frank proceeded to do what Saheem predicted and said something stupid. "You hear this no neck, torso looking like he swallowed a G-5 wagon. I ain't never scared looking ma'fucka, talking 'bout '*niggas said ol girl fuck with somebody in the industry.*'"

Lil Frank turned back to Ricky and said, "Who's niggaz?"

He had his arms stretched out like if he were saying *"Tell me."* Then he immediately continued, "What niggaz, Ricky? What niggas said that?" It was dark outside so no one was around.

"I'm saying," Ricky always began his sentences with, *"I'm saying,"* whenever he was lying. "You know my cousin work at Def Jam, right?"

Saheem and Lil Frank cut in together. "Your cousin don't work at Def Jam, m*aaan.*" The two friends stretched the word '*man*' so that they sounded like "S*mokey*" from the movie *"Friday."*

Ricky continued. "Anyway, my cousin and them be at Def Jam and all that, so you know they be over at B.E.T and they be knowing aye-thing that be popping in the industry, and niggaz hipped me to Shorty's steelo, na mean." He looked at his buddies, and sho nuff, they burst into laughter.

"Ah haa! Ha, ha, ha, ha! Son, son, you hear me?" Lil Frank was looking at Saheem who was still bent over laughing. "Your man *Dame Diddy* over here thinks we're dumb. Do I have *stupid* written on my forehead?" Lil Frank was looking at Ricky again.

"Let's talk about something else, yo." Ricky wasn't looking at any of his friends at this point. His attention was focused on the housing police car that was cruising through their driveway.

When the patrol car was in close proximity of the trio, the driver of the squad car illuminated his side light and aimed it at the teens' faces.

Saheem was blocking his face with his hands and spoke quietly. He hoped the policemen couldn't read lips. "Fucking crackers. I wish I was up on the roof right now. I would've dropped a brick on their fucked up ass car."

The beam shone on Lil Frank. He expressed himself quietly as well. "Your mother is probably at home fucking your brother."

The cop chuckled behind the protection of his window, badge and Glock 9mm.

The light was then diverted to Ricky. Ricky wanted to be smart. He stuck his middle finger up at the police officers with one hand and with the other hand, he grabbed the crotch area of his jeans and yelled, "Fuck you, pig! Suck my dick!"

Saheem and Lil Frank were the skinnier ones of the trio. They had a head start on Ricky once they took off.

"Come on, you fat ma'fucka." Lil Frank was huffing and puffing over his words. He heard the tires of the squad car screech when it jumped the curb, but he kept running.

Saheem was right beside him trying to make it to a nearby building. "Yo, Frank," Saheem gasped, "are you running to 1160 or are you trying to make it to 1170?" He gasped again.

"Fuck you worrying about me for?" Lil Frank heard the vehicle bend a turn right along with them.

Saheem sucked in a little more air. "I just wanna know so I won't run over your ass."

"I'm going in 60, you hit 1170."

"No doubt," Saheem replied.

"Yo," Frank yelled. He put some more pep in his step.

"Yo," said Saheem. His Air Max sneakers were in full gear.

"Where the fuck is Ricky at?" Frank asked, only stealing a glance at his compadre. Before Saheem could answer, 1160 was in reach. Lil Frank grabbed onto the banister and swung a fast right into the lobby of the building. He turned around only momentarily and that's when he noticed the three occupants in the Chevrolet Caprice on Saheem's ass. Ricky was their third passenger. His big ass was handcuffed in the back seat.

Lil Frank jumped on the elevator and pressed six. He was headed to his friend *Meathead's* house to find refuge.

Saheem also got away. 1170 was only about twenty to thirty yards from 1160 so his getaway was a smooth one as well. Saheem ran up the first seven flights of stairs then took the remaining seven on the elevator to the fourteenth floor.

Saheem exited the conveyor at the top floor, then walked the last flight up to the roof. The sixteen-year-old peered off the roof and looked down across the street at the parking lot of the housing precinct. He noticed the lot was empty. *I wonder where they took Ricky*, he thought to himself.

"Hey, nigger," the cops looked at each other as they drove.

Ricky sat back and remained quiet.

"Ever hear of *Abner Louima*?" the senior officer was teasing Ricky.

"Ever hear of *Larry Davis*?" Ricky shot back. Ricky was big for sixteen. He looked to be at least twenty-one or twenty-two. He also looked just like *Grand Puba* from the rap group *Brand Nubians*.

"Yeah, we heard of 'em," the assisting officer replied. He turned around to face Ricky. "We heard Big Bubba is treating him real nice up in Attica too." The racist white cops were taking Ricky to a secluded area so they could beat his ass.

Ricky smiled.

"Fuck are you smiling at, nigger?" the passenger asked annoyed.

Ricky nodded his head upwards telling the cops to pay attention in front of them.

A road block had formed due to a car accident and a police

officer was waving to the cop car that Ricky was in.

"Damn," shouted the senior officer.

His partner reassured him with a pat on the knee. They pulled up. "Hey, officer, what's going on?" the passenger was talking to the cop who was directing traffic.

"A little bang up. An old lady left her glasses at home and apparently didn't see the stop sign. Drove right into this ambulance right here," he pointed behind him. "Luckily, the EMS guys' truck didn't get badly damaged. They were able to help the old gal immediately after the accident. What are you guys up to?" the traffic cop nodded at Ricky.

"Oh, him," the passenger began, "He's lost. We're bringing him home now."

"I ain't lost," Ricky screamed. "These niggaz is trying to kidnap me." He looked at the beat cop who was black, then looked at the driver of the car he was in by catching eye contact through the rearview mirror. "Lemme go, yo!"

"What's the story guys?" the cop asked again.

The passenger shrugged his shoulders and messed up being the rookie, racist cop that he was. "We were gonna teach him a little lesson. You know, rough him up a bit," he smiled devilishly.

"What'd he do?" traffic man looked serious.

"Nothing," the sidekick answered again.

"Uncuff him."

"What?" the assisting officer looked at his partner, then looked out the window at the beat cop.

"Uncuff him before I report you two." They were eying one another.

The crooked cops uncuffed Ricky near the Dyer Avenue

train station. Ricky jogged halfway back to the projects and walked the remainder of the way. All he kept thinking to himself was, *Damn, them ma'fuckas almost had me.*

CHAPTER TWO

Back on the benches in Edenwald...
Lil Frank and Saheem occupied both benches as their long arms stretched across the back support part of the wooden sofa.

"You think they got that nigga for resisting arrest?" asked Lil Frank.

Saheem looked over at his man. "His stupid ass probably caught an ass whooping along with it."

"Why y'all niggas ain't wait for me, yo!" Ricky was approaching his two friends. It took him about thirty minutes to make it back to the projects.

"Fake ass *Warren Sapp, what'd they do to you?*" Saheem asked.

Ricky made his way over to the bench that Saheem had taken over and yanked one of his homie's arms off the backrest. He looked at Saheem first then he looked at Lil Frank and began to explain what took place. "I'm saying," *there he went lying again*, "them ma'fuckas drove me to Orchard Beach. I think they were trying to body my ass."

Lil Frank looked over at Saheem who couldn't wait for Lil Frank to acknowledge him. At the same time, the two youngsters twisted up their mouths as to motion to one another a *"yeah, right"* type of expression. Ricky caught on but since his friends always did that when he was talking, it didn't faze him so he continued with his rhetoric. "As soon as we pulled up, I noticed the Orchard Beach sign and knew I was a goner."

"So what the fuck did you do, *Houdini*, pull a *David Blaine* and disappear?" Lil Frank asked sarcastically. Saheem laughed.

"I flipped the cuffs under my legs, unlocked the door, ran and jumped into the water."

"Yeah, alright, *Jaws*, how'd you get home?" asked Saheem.

"Well first of all, I kept ducking my head under the water so they couldn't see me. Plus, it was hard to find me because it was dark as shit out there in that water."

"You wasn't cold?" Lil Frank was riding his friend. Besides, Ricky wasn't even wet.

"Wasn't cold?" asked Ricky, confused.

Lil Frank closed his hands partially so that his knuckles protruded, then he brought his arms close to his chest, twisted his mouth and pretended to be autistic. "Ayyye, yooo," he dragged his words and moved his arms back and forth, "wass da watter cold?"

They all laughed at Lil Frank's impression of a retard.

Ricky jumped off the bench and tried to grab Lil Frank, but Lil Frank spun on him. Saheem just jumped up and backed up about ten feet.

Ricky was looking to see which one of his friends seemed worth the pursuit but the crazy look Saheem had on his face diverted Ricky's attention.

When Ricky turned around, he noticed two black dudes about 5'10"—5'11", both about 170 pounds walking toward them with hoodies on. The guns they had in their hands were what put the trio on *freeze tag* status.

Lil Frank was about to run until one of the dudes spoke. "Run and I'm a burn your ass up from deep."

Frank looked at Saheem who didn't dare divert his eyes from the chrome 4-4 one of the cats had in his hand.

The other gunman spoke up. "Y'all niggaz out here hustlin'?" He kept his hammer at his side.

Saheem ain't say shit.

Frank didn't either.

But Ricky's stupid ass wanted to play *Dumb and Dumber.* "Them toasts probably ain't even real," he said.

All Lil Frank could do was shake his head.

Bong! One of the cats smacked Ricky in his face with the nose of his gun.

Ricky screamed. "Aaahh, yo!" he grabbed his jaw. "Damn, son, fuck you hit me like that for?"

The gunman answered. "You wanted to know if my gun was real, right?"

"I'm saying, though."

"You're saying what?" Homeboy approached Ricky again.

Ricky shuddered. "My bad. Your heat be the real thing, black."

"Blue steel like a ma'fucka," the gunman sang.

The other gunman stepped up. "Come up off of whatever y'all lil niggaz is pushing out here. I want it all. If a nigga hold out, I'm a bust a cap in one of y'alls' asses." Dude was fanning his gun telling Saheem to give up whatever he had first.

"I ain't got nothing, yo!" Saheem said.

One of the robbers walked up on him. Saheem didn't hesitate. He lifted his arms so the stick up kid could search him. Dude found nothing. He spun Saheem around and kicked him in the middle of his back. Saheem fell to the ground since the kick was unexpected and scraped his knee.

Ricky couldn't help himself. Even though he just got smacked a few seconds ago, he still managed to laugh out loud anyway.

"You think something is funny?" the gunman who kicked Saheem walked over and got in Ricky's face.

Ricky shook his head.

"I ain't think so!" the gunman regained his position. "Fuck you got, you fat, funky ma'fucka?"

Homeboy searched Ricky and for a second time, came up empty handed.

"Fuck is y'all doing out here, smoking?" the thief at work asked.

The other gunman fell back and watched the trio from a distance.

"Yo, Slim!" Ol' boy was talking to Lil Frank now.

"What up?" Frank was scared to blink.

"You got something, lil nigga?" Dude put his gun under Lil Frank's chin and raised his head with a little pressure.

Lil Frank swallowed but didn't answer.

"Oh, we got ourselves a hard rock." The gunman walked away from Frank and approached his partner. As he breezed past him, he mumbled. "Shoot that nigga."

Now, whether it was Allah's work or what have you, but nosy ass Tiarra, a.k.a. *Bruhman, upstairs, fifth floor*, but in this case, *upstairs, second floor*, was hanging out the window with her phone in her hand. As loud as she was without yelling, the assailants heard her every word. "Yup, it's two of 'em. Both black as car oil. It's Endzo and his cousin Chris from Gunhill

Road." She pulled her lollipop from her mouth and smiled.

Endzo and Chris tucked their weapons and took off. The trio happily looked up at light skinned, nosy ass Tiarra, who had just saved their lives. She returned their gaze, winked at Saheem expressing her crush on him, and then closed her window.

The trio sighed simultaneously.

"Let's walk to the store, yo," Lil Frank suggested.

"We ain't got no money, unless you're holding out." Ricky looked at Lil Frank suspiciously when he spoke to him.

"I ain't holding out. I'm broke too. I just wanna walk for a second. That lil attempted stickup them cats pulled on us shook my ass up."

Lil Frank looked up and spotted his uncle approaching. His uncle had just pulled up in a Bentley GT with the words No Regrets printed on the license plates. When his uncle got close enough, the three amigos spoke at the same time. "Oh shit, yo. We're glad to see you." This came from Lil Frank.

"Niggas robbed us, big homie." Saheem gave their visitor the better information of the three.

And as usual, Ricky came sideways with his explanation. "Yo, Inch, some terrorists, Bin Laden, muslim niggas just ran up on us with A.K.s. Fuckin' Habeeb niggaz had C-4 taped to them niggaz and all that, yo!"

Inch was a brown skinned cat with long eyelashes and thick eyebrows. He stood about 5'6"-5'7", about 200 pounds, easy. Son was stocky all day long. But if you didn't know him, you would swear he was a twenty-one year old college cat. Inch liked his ordinary look. That way, the police would look to him as a last resort when niggaz came up missing.

"First of all, Ricky, shut the fuck up!" Ricky knew Inch and he definitely knew about the work Inch had put in. He'd seen Inch check his own two older brothers, one time who were also gangstas, in front of their momma.

About two years earlier, Inch was walking from the store with his momma. He put down the two bags of groceries he was carrying and stepped to his two older siblings who were sitting on the very same bench where Lil Frank, Saheem and Ricky almost got robbed just moments ago. Inch went into his waistband, pulled out a super long 45 automatic and aimed it at his kin. He said, "Why the fuck y'all ain't help Mommy from the store?" Ice was scared of his little brother so he didn't even blink.

Frank was crazy. All he said was, "Get that gun outta my face!"

Inch aimed the gun in between his two brothers' faces, but closer to Frank's, and let off two rounds. Ice got up and jetted. Frank, Lil Frank's father, just sat there. Then Inch's mom chimed in. "Antoine, bring your crazy ass on."

Inch tucked his weapon, winked at Big Frank and said, "Be out here when I come back. I bet you I can make you famous." Then he smiled.

Big Frank got up, waved at his lil brother and said, "Fuck you, you punk! You ain't shit without that gun."

"That's why I always keep it on me. For bitch ass niggaz like you," Inch responded.

"Enough! That's enough!" Inch's mother yelled.

With that, Inch picked up the bags of groceries and entered his building. Ricky and all of his cousins witnessed the altercation and thought Inch was a superhero after that.

Back at the scene, Inch continued. "What the fuck happened, Lil Frank? And you better not lie or I'm a shoot this nigga Saheem just for looking like a nigga that should be named Saheem."

Saheem looked at Inch who pursed his lips back at Saheem and raised his shirt a little bit. Saheem spotted the butt of his gun. Ricky noticed it too and wondered if it was the same gun that he used to scare his two brothers with a couple of years back.

Lil Frank proceeded to tell his uncle what had happened. "Uncle Inch, me, Saheem and Ricky were sitting out here chilling when some niggaz named Chris and Endzo tried to rob us." Frank knew better not to lose eye contact with his uncle.

"Y'all hustling shit out here?" Inch asked.

Ricky shook his head.

Saheem said, "Nah."

Frank said, "Of course not."

"Y'all better not be. I'll fuck y'all lil niggaz up if I find out that y'all out here selling anything. Y'all lil niggaz even look at a box of Newports too long and I'm knocking Ricky's fat ass out first. Then Saheem, I'm a throw you off the short building roof. I know you'll survive but your little ass will be all fucked up." He looked at his nephew. "Frank, if you even play yourself by mentioning any type of drug selling or whatever and I find out, I'm a go and get Lil Momma."

Frank cut in. "Not my moms, yo!"

"You cutting me off?" Inch asked. He was on Lil Frank now.

Frank shook his head.

"I'm a go and snatch up Lil Momma, Big Frank, Saheem and

Ricky's moms and I'm a strip they asses, and y'all niggaz is included," Inch looked at the three youngsters, "then I'm going to make them wear some billboards saying '*We're standing here naked because our children went and did some stupid shit.* Now where the fuck did these Chris and Endzo characters go?"

"They jetted towards the north side," Lil Frank assumed.

"Frank, where's your bike at?" Inch asked.

"In the building," he answered.

"Go get it then."

Lil Frank moved like *Flash* from the comic book.

Inch got on the bike and took off.

"You think he gon' find them, Frank?" Saheem asked.

"I don't know, son. I feel sorry for them if he did though." Lil Frank shook his head and took his seat back on the bench next to his two homies.

CHAPTER THREE

Inch pedaled until he reached the north side of his housing project. Sitting in front of building 1175 were three neighborhood associates. When the trio spotted Inch, they immediately knew something was up.

Two of the guys, Jesse and Jimmy, approached Inch as he pedaled over to them. Jimmy was about 5'10", 165 pounds, brown skinned with corn rolls going to the back. His brother Jesse, three years his senior, was a little darker than Jimmy and about two inches shorter.

Jesse wiped the corners of his mouth simultaneously, using his thumb and index finger as he prepared himself to speak. "Yo, son, what's hood?" Jesse had his hand out but Inch declined with a simple look that said, "Nigga, I ain't here to rap."

Inch stood up, held the BMX between his legs with his thighs, kept his grip on the handle bars, looked at Jesse, smirked, then looked at Jimmy and said, "I'm looking for two brown skinned niggas with hoodies on!" Inch paused and looked into Jimmy's eyes for a sign that he may have seen the perps. He continued when Jimmy didn't answer. "Niggaz tried to rob Lil Frank and them up near the Blue Park."

V.I., a tall, slim, dark complexioned cat with a curly fade and a 40 oz in his hand, hopped off the bench and proceeded toward the trio. As he walked, he spoke. "Who he looking for, Jimmy? 'Cause we just seen two niggaz walk by here."

Inch looked at Jimmy who was looking at V.I. like, *"Mind ya fucking business."* Jimmy knew some drama was about to pop off because when Chris and Endzo walked past them a second ago, the two groups caught eye contact and Endzo flashed his heat on them. Jimmy wanted no parts of the situation just in case it got crazy. So he kept his mouth shut about seeing the duo and was hoping that V.I. could read his mind.

Inch looked back at V.I. but V.I. had received the message. He looked at Inch and said, "Nah, I'm buggin'. That was yesterday when I seen two niggaz walk by here."

Inch wasn't trying to hear that. "First of all, nigga, your ass is ear hustlin'. You're all the way over there. Jumping out there, answering shit I asked *this* man over here. Now if ya crilz hustle was as mean as your eavesdrop game, maybe you'd've cut off that fucked up fade and copped you some new gear."

V.I. tensed up. He wasn't afraid of Inch but he knew that Inch would shoot his ass in a heartbeat so he kept it at that, a stare.

"Yeah, nigga, you better not say shit. I'll have ya peoples dressing you up over the weekend for a closed casket if you jump out there again."

V.I. smiled and walked away. He said to himself, *"I ain't even gonna waste my time on this ma'fucka. He gon get his one day."*

"Yeah, kick rocks, pussy." V.I. continued to walk as Inch taunted him. "You need to chop off that fade. Looking like *Wally* from *Leave it to Beaver*, a black *Wally* from *Leave it to Beaver*."

V.I. kept walking so Inch had to yell, "Niggaz ain't wear

fades since '89. Fuck is you, *Big Daddy Kane* out this mug."
Inch let him walk. Then he turned his attention back to Jimmy.
"Now where'd you say those niggaz went?"

Jimmy looked east towards the diner and nodded upwards.
He said, "They walked towards the 5 train, about ten minutes
ago."

Inch readjusted his heater and rode off.

• • •

Back at the block ...

"So what you think about that bama shit that's taking over
the radio and B.E.T?" Lil Frank was talking to Saheem. The
threesome were still chilling on the benches in front of their
building.

"I fucks with *T.I.* because he's type lyrical, but that other shit
where them niggaz be hollering and screaming and shit is corny
to me." Saheem looked over at Lil Frank.

They both looked at Ricky. Ricky reanimated himself after
being shut down for a minute by Inch. He grabbed, just under
the neck of his white crew neck T-shirt with his thumb and
pointer, hopped from side to side and sang with a southern
accent, "*I bling in my white tee, jewels gleam in my white tee,*"
on the last line, Ricky stood still, shook his T-shirt with the hand
that was still attached to it, shrugged his shoulders to the rhythm
and said, "*Fahget a thow back, I look clean in my white tee.*"

The trio laughed. "Nah, for real though," said Lil Frank,
"Yo, sah, give me like four of the illest rap lines. It ain't gotta be
the illest, but it has to be ill though.

Saheem thought for a moment. "Ahight, I got it," he paused.
Then he sang, "*Viva, Las Vegas see ya/later at the crap tables
meet me at the one that starts a gee up/that way no fraud willies*

present gambling they're re-ups/we can have a pleasant time sipping Margaritas/G-G-geeaahh! Can I live?"

Saheem looked at Lil Frank, and Ricky used his hands to form a diamond sign, raised his hands over his head and said, "The Roc nigga, Hov! Holla!"

"My go, my go," said Lil Frank, "but I'm a give ya'll two bars. Yo, *If Faye have twins, she'll probably have two Pac's/get it? Tu-Pac's."* Frank went on to explain. "Remember when there was a rumor that Pac was hitting Faith?" His compadres looked at him to continue. "Well, *this* song was in reference to that. Meaning if Pac *was* indeed blowing Faith's back out, she could've been really pregnant by him, possibly with twins, and not B.I.G. like she was alleged to have been."

"It was B.I.G.'s, though. Lil C.J. look just like Biggie," Saheem explained.

"Give us something, Ricky," said Lil Frank.

Ricky cleared his throat and sang. *"Mama say mama sah mama koo sa. Mama say mama sah mama koo sah.*

Bang! Bang! Ba Bong! Bong!

Mad shit came flying out from an upstairs window. Ricky and Lil Frank were the lucky ones. Saheems' new *G.Unit* t-shirt had food splattered all over it.

Saheem was wiping himself clean. "Ayo, what the fuck is this?" he said looking down at himself as he stretched his shirt to examine the damage.

Lil Frank walked up on him and touched some of the food particles. He squenched his face up. "Uh, son. Niggaz hit you with some bell peppers."

Saheem squenched his face up too. "What the fuck is a bell pepper?" he asked.

"Nigga, a green pepper," Ricky interjected.

The trio figured it was time to bounce, so they walked over to the lobby of their building and took refuge under the canopy.

• • •

On the corner of Boston Road and Baychester Avenue...

"Yo, Endzo, look at shorty near the bus stop," Chris said, pointing.

"Who, slim with the braids in her hair?" Endzo was looking at the girl that Chris was referring to.

"Yeah," said Chris.

"She ahight. She ain't no dub piece, but she's a working eight because she's type skinny. A fat ass would've made her a twelve piece, son."

"A fat ass is four points?" asked Chris.

"No doubt, son. Two points a cheek. Lemme go holla at shorty and get her number." Endzo went into *mack daddy* mode and approached the young lady. "Excuse me, miss." The ghetto princess was reading a book called Unwilling To Suffer.

She looked up at Endzo, noticed that he was kinda cute and smiled. "May I help you?" she asked flirtingly.

"Ma, you look mad familiar. What's your name?" Endzo asked.

"That line was corny, mister, but since you tried, you get an 'E' for effort." The girl offered her hand and said, "Melsoultree, what's yours?"

Before Endzo could answer, everyone heard two quick 'boom, booms' then the entire glass shattered at the bus stop.

Inch was firing from across the street near the diner. The Desert Eagle he had was screaming at its target.

Melsoultree screamed and took off running.

Endzo ducked, jogged behind a nearby car and started firing back. *"Bock, bock, bock, bock!"*

He let off four shots at Inch. His shots missed their target but exploded into the diner behind Inch where two policemen were on break eating jelly doughnuts.

• • •

Back at the block...

Lil Frank, Saheem and Ricky were in the building when Monica, the block freak, entered.

"Yo, Monica, what's up?" Lil Frank asked. He was holding on to his nuts.

"Y'all got some weed?" she asked looking at all of them. Monica was sixteen with a fat ass and big titties. As far as her face was concerned, if ugliness were bricks, she'd have her own projects.

"Nah, but we can get some," said Saheem anxiously.

Ricky just kept smiling.

Fifteen minutes later, Lil Frank had Monica leaned back on the steps with one of her pant legs off, running up in her with no condom.

Saheem and Ricky were the lookouts. And had it been up to Ricky alone, who couldn't keep his eyes off of Lil Frank's ass humping on Monica, to watch out for whoever, they would've messed around and gotten knocked by someone walking in on them.

Saheem was next, and he couldn't wait.

• • •

Back on B-Road...

"Calling all cars. This is Echo, Alpha, Eleven. Shots fired at the corner of Boston Road and Baychester Avenue. I need all available units in the vicinity to approach with caution," said one of the officers at the diner.

"Roger that," stated the female dispatcher at police headquarters. She switched to a channel where everyone could hear her. "This is 'R'-one, Radio-One, over! I have multiple gunshots fired at the intersection of Boston Road and Baychester. I repeat, multiple shots fired at Boston Road and Baychester Avenue! All units approach with caution. The suspects are heavily armed and considered very dangerous. Over."

Squad cars from all of the surrounding precincts were on their way to the scene.

When the screams from the sirens got louder, Chris and Endzo ran toward the number 5, Baychester Avenue train station, which was like a hundred and fifty yards away.

Inch looked up and said, "Damn!" That's when one of the jelly doughnut policemen took a shot at him. *Bong*! The shot barely missed his head as he could hear the slug zip by him.

Inch crouched low on the bike and aimed the cannon at the white officer. He took a shot, "*Bloom!*" Mr. Policeman got hit in the chest. The vest he was wearing saved his life, but he still came up off of his feet and was knocked unconscious by the impact of the bullet.

Robo Cop number two witnessed his partner go down and did some movie shit. He charged Inch and was screaming. Aarrrgghh!"

Inch raised his cannon at Super Cop and put a baby missile in the cop's forehead. The officer's head opened up like if a watermelon was hit by a sledgehammer, and his body snapped backwards like if he had gotten clothes lined.

Sleepyhead number one recovered, but didn't realize that his partner's funeral would be televised in a few days. He also didn't realize that he'd be buried on the same day as his partner, that is until he heard someone behind him.

"Mmgg mmgg." Inch cleared his throat.

Popo turned around and was face to face with the barrel of Inch's Desert. The fat cop was sitting on the ground in the parking lot of the diner and Inch was sitting right behind him, mocking him.

Inch cocked the hammer back and said, "Bet you I could make you famous!" When the cop locked eyes with Inch, Inch looked up in the sky where a news chopper had zoomed in on them. The cop looked up too. His face was strewn across the television screens of damn near all of America with their *"Special New Bulletins."* News anchors were describing the scene to their viewers.

The cop looked back down at Inch and when he tried to scream, "No!" the bullet from the large handgun entered the officer's mouth without touching his lips or teeth and disintegrated the back of the cop's head.

Everyone at home cringed at the sight of what had just happened. Inch looked back up at the camera on the helicopter, which had zoomed in even closer on him and mouthed the words, "That's how you push a niggaz wig back." Then he got up and ran.

By now, Lil Frank, Saheem and Ricky were up at Lil Frank's house watching everything unfold on the news.

Surrounded in the middle of the street on Boston Road near the *Orient* Restaurant and Take Out, Inch said, "Fuck it," to himself.

Trapped by like six precincts, which was equivalent to damn

near a thousand police, Inch raised his Desert Eagle and rang like three of the police's alarms. That brought the police death toll to five.

Inch got shot one hundred and fourteen times. But they were all rubber bullets. Sure, the police would have loved to kill him, but the news camera from up above saved his life. He had too many people rooting for him. If Inch would've died, there would have been rioting all throughout New York City. That would've meant more deaths and an enormous amount of financial damage to the city.

Inch got a pass that evening and as soon as he hit *Riker's Island*, he popped off again on a captain this time. *"The drama must continue,"* he thought and uncheeked the two *Gem Star* razors he kept in his ass for times like that.

One week later...

"Yo, Saheem, what's popping?" Lil Frank asked. They were parked at their second home, the bench in front of their building.

"Shit, what up?" Saheem looked over at his homie.

"That shit was crazy, the shit that went down with my uncle, yo."

"Word, son. That shit was ill." They looked at Ricky.

"Lil Frank, ya uncle is a beast, yo. Straight up. As far as I'm concerned, and this is on the real, but that was *'That Gangsta Shit'*. Bttaatt, Bttaatt, Bttaatt!"

THE END

Attention

Attention
Aspiring Author:

Amiaya Entertainment LLC. Is looking for participants who are willing to contribute a short story to our "Gangsta Shit" series.

"That Gangsta Shit Vol. II" is gonna be the most anticipated Anthology to hit the streets since Vol. One. If you want to make history with us and become a part of the Amiaya Entertainment LLC. Legacy, climb aboard. But first, we need to see if you can get it cracking.

That Gangsta Shit Vol. One was the real deal but our goal is to make Vol.II twice as serious. Do you think you have what it takes to get it popping? Is your stuff original? Can you create drama? Can you show me what beef is, or what gulliness is about? What about that thug ish, can you scribble Amiaya Entertainment LLC. up some chaotic madness full of confusion and mayhem?

The bottom line is this I've produced a track like if I was Dr. Dre (That Gangsta Shit Vol. One), and now it's time to drop the remix with seven selected authors.

If you can't leave the reader's smelling gunsmoke, don't participate. If the shoe is too big to fill, kick rocks. But if you know without a doubt that you have what it takes, holla at us over here at Amiaya Entertainment LLC also log on www.amiayaentertainment .com.

To see if you qualify, send us the first two chapters of your short story. Your story must be about 10,000 words no more than 13,000 and no less than 9,000.

The stories that are accepted will be owned and published by Amiaya Entertainment LLC exclusively. The authors will be credited for their work and given a fee. The first portion of the fee will be provided to you once your story is submitted, accepted and edited, and the final portion will be sent to you with a copy of the book once it's complete.

Your stories must be typed, double space. The deadline is August 1, 2005 and the book will drop shortly afterward.

Authors, writers, essayists, journalists and wordsmith's look at it for what it is. It's a promotional tool for some and for others, it's a dream come true. I'm the Dr. Dre of this thing; all y'all have to do is spit. Holla at us if you think you can handle it. Oh yeah, it better be Gangsta and it has to be hood.

Also on a more softer note, for those of you writes who'd rather read and express yourselves in a more laid back manner, Amiaya Entertainment LLC is also looking for participants who are willing to contribute a short story to our "Ghetto Love" series.

Ghetto Love Vol. One will feature 7 short stories based on love. The same rules apply, however, no bodies have to drop and no drugs need to be sold. To qualify, it has to be "ghetto" and it must be "hood".

So writer's, get all y'all "Shaniqua" characters together that still leaves her hot iron on the stove to press her hair for her date with "Black" to the local movie theater. Taking a cab to your favorite Cineplex is "hood", jumping out without paying is "ghetto".

Think you can handle it? Holla at Amiaya Entertainment.

Like Our "Gangsta Shit" series, the payout is the same, the format must be the same and the deadline is the same. August 1st, 2005. Don't miss out on your opportunity to become a part of the fastest growing independent publishing company of 2005.

I thought I told you that we won't stop!

One!

Amiaya Entertainment LLC.

Fan Mail Page

If you have any further questions, comments or concerns,
kindly address your inquires in care of:

Antoine "Inch" Thomas
&
Travis "Unique" Stevens
&
Ralph "Polo" Taylor
&
Vincent "V.I." Warren
&
T. Benson Glover

At

AMIAYA ENTERTAINMENT LLC
P.O.BOX 1275
NEW YORK, NY 10159

tanianunez79@hotmail.com

COMING SOON
2005

FROM AMIAYA ENTERTAINMENT LLC

A Diamond in the Rough

by

James Morris

www.amiayaentertainment.com

Flower's Bed

The Most Controversial Book Of This Era

Written By

Antoine "Inch" Thomas

uspenseful...Fastpaced...Richly Textured

PUBLISHED BY AMIAYA ENTERTAINMENT

From the Underground Bestseller "Flower's Bed"
Author Antoine "Inch" Thomas delivers you

NO REGRETS

It's Time To Get It Popping

"Gritty....Realistic Conflicts....Intensely Eerie"
Published by Amiaya Entertainment

ORDER FORM

Number of Copies

That Gangsta Sh!t	ISBN# 0-9745075-3-9	$15.00/Copy _____
Unwilling To Suffer	ISBN# 0-9745075-2-0	$15.00/Copy _____
No Regrets	ISBN# 0-9745075-1-2	$14.95/Copy _____
Flower's Bed	ISBN# 0-9745075-0-4	$14.95/Copy _____

Mailing Options

PRIORITY POSTAGE (4-6 DAYS US MAIL): Add $4.95

Accepted form of Payments: Institutional Checks or Money Orders

(All Postal rates are subject to change.)

Please check with your local Post Office for change of rate and schedules.

Please Provide Us With Your Mailing Information:

SHIPPING ADDRESS

Name:_____

Address:_____

Suite/Apartment#:_____

City:_____

Zip Code:_____

(Federal & State Prisoners, Please include your Inmate Registration #)

SEND CHECKS OR MONEY ORDERS TO:

AMIAYA ENTERTAINMENT

P.O.BOX 1275

NEW YORK, NY 10159

212-946-6565

www.amiayaentertainment.com

MelSoulTree

Some say she's an R& B Soul singer with a Gospel twist. Others say she is an R&B Soul Singer with a Jazzy twist. Yet, everyone agrees she is **MelSoulTree...Melissa ROOTED in SOUL!!!** **MelSoulTree's** melodious voice and vocal range has been compared to the likes of Minnie Riperton, Phyllis Hyman, Chaka Kahn, Alicia Keys and Mariah Carey. In order to capture the true essence of her voice you have to experience her "live" or listen to one of her recordings.

This talented vivacious beauty hails from NYC's borough of the Bronx. Born Melissa Antoinette Thomas she began to develop her love for music at the tender age of 4. She was exposed to different styles of music via the radio, her father (a poet & musician), her mother (a singer) and a musical family rooted in R&B Soul, Gospel, Jazz and Hip Hop music styles. **MelSoulTree** has been blanketed with music all her life. Despite all her influences she began studying to become an attorney. However, the call of music was so strong it dismissed that idea right away! By pursuing her love of music, her singing talents have taken her to places that one could only dream of. She has established herself as a gifted singer and songwriter. As an international artist she has toured extensively throughout Germany, France, Switzerland, Argentina, Uruguay, Chile, Canada and many areas of the U.S. as a featured soloist singing R&B, Jazz and Gospel music.

Some of **MelSoulTree's** many accomplishments include:
Graduating at the top of her Music class in the area of Jazz Vocal Music from the City College of New York under the direction of vocalist **Sheila Jordan** and bassist **Ron Carter.**
Working with the legendary **D.J. Grand Master Flash** and being featured on the chart topping **"New Jack City"** movie soundtrack song **"Lyrics 2 the Rhythm"** produced by the **Giant/Warner** label.
Recording for the **Wild Pitch**, **Audio Quest** and **Select** Record labels.
Honored to work with **William "Smokey" Robinson** and **William "Mickey" Stevenson** in their Musical Stage play **"Raisin' Hell"**.
Former lead vocalist for the underground New York City based band **Special Request.**
Former lead singer and songwriter for the **Lo-Key Records** female group **Legal Tender.**
One of the youngest members to sing with the **Duke Ellington Orchestra** under the direction of **Paul Ellington**.
A frequent featured soloist for the **Princeton Jazz Orchestra.**
Although born long after the 60's era, she is currently one of the youngest singers touring with the world renowned Phil Spector's group **"The Crystals"**. She is known affectionately as "The Kid" by many of the veterans of the music business.

Can you believe most of these accomplishments where achieved as an unsigned artist? She is now establishing herself as one of the most sought after independent solo artists. Experience her for yourself during one of her live performances or again and again on CD. Don't miss the opportunity of witnessing the unique sound and vocal range of **MelSoulTree... Melissa ROOTED in SOUL!!!**

For CD, ticket and booking information use one of the following contact methods:

On the WEB...*visit one of the secure <u>MelSoulTree Websites</u>:*
www.soundclick.com/MelSoulTree
www.MelSoulTree.com

**FOR MAIL ORDER FORMS &
FAN CLUB INFORMATION...**

MelSoulTree
P.O. Box 46
New York, NY 10475

**The MelSoulTree/Granted Entertainment Hotline...
(212) 560-7117**
Coming in 2005...the long awaited album introducing...
MelSoulTree...Melissa ROOTED in SOUL!!!